Still dressed in **[the]**
silk robe from t...
Tess opened the...

She blinked once, the impact of a blue Air Force uniform registering slowly on her unconsciousness. Raising her eyes, she gasped in stunned surprise. Automatically, her fingers went to her slender throat in reaction. "No…" she whispered hoarsely, trying to shut the door.

"Tess! Let me in." Shep effectively blocked the door. Her strength was no match for his. Fear mixed with anguish as he hurriedly scanned her ashen features. Her eyes were great pools of blue agony. His heart squeezed as he slipped inside, quickly taking off his flight cap.

"I had to come, Tess," he said huskily, shutting the door behind him. "I got word three hours ago." He scowled, watching an incredible array of emotions move across her face. He reached out in an effort to comfort her.

Tess shrunk away from his hand, gasping, "No!" Tears trickled down her drawn face as she backed away from him. "Go away! Oh, God, just leave me alone! Cy died because of me. Because of you! It's my fault. I should never have let you kiss me! Someone told him I was having an affair with you!"

Dear Reader:

Romance readers have been enthusiastic about the Silhouette Special Editions for years. And that's not by accident: Special Editions were the first of their kind and continue to feature realistic stories with heightened romantic tension.

The longer stories, sophisticated style, greater sensual detail and variety that made Special Editions popular are the same elements that will make you want to read book after book.

We hope that you enjoy this Special Edition today, and will enjoy many more.

Please write to us:

Jane Nicholls
Silhouette Books
PO Box 236
Thornton Road
Croydon
Surrey
CR9 3RU

LINDSAY McKENNA
Love Me Before Dawn

Silhouette Special Edition

Originally Published by Silhouette Books
a division of
Harlequin Enterprises Ltd.

*First published in Great Britain in 1994
by Silhouette Books, Eton House, 18-24 Paradise Road,
Richmond, Surrey TW9 1SR*

© Eileen Nauman 1984

*Silhouette, Silhouette Special Edition and Colophon are
Trade Marks of Harlequin Enterprises B.V.*

ISBN 0 373 59131 4

23-9403

Made and printed in Great Britain

LINDSAY McKENNA

spent three years serving her country as a meteorologist in the U.S. Navy, so much of her knowledge about the military people and practices in her novels comes from direct experience. In addition, she spends a great deal of time researching each book, whether it be at the Pentagon or at military bases, extensively interviewing key personnel. She views the military as her second family and hopes that her novels will help to dispel the "unfeeling machine" image that haunts it, allowing readers glimpses of the flesh-and-blood people who comprise the services.

Lindsay is also a pilot. She and her husband of fifteen years, both avid "rock hounds" and hikers, live in Arizona.

Other Silhouette Books by Lindsay McKenna

Chapter 1

I DON'T WANT TO GO, TESS THOUGHT. SHE STOPPED arranging the mass of dark auburn hair at the nape of her neck and studied her strained features in the antique mirror. Why can't I be enthusiastic? Cy is excited about this party. She avoided her blue-eyed reflection, studying the ivory, high-necked gown instead. Reflexively her slender fingers tucked in the last strands, fashioning a chignon. With the hair pulled back from her square, high-cheekboned face, she looked older than her twenty-four years. As she raised her eyes she saw the anguish clearly written in them. Would he notice it? She sighed to herself. Not likely. As one of the chief design engineers at Rockwell International, Cy Hamilton had eyes only for the B-1 bomber blueprints.

"Darling? Are you about ready?" Cy sauntered into the large, tastefully decorated bedroom. He ran a hand through his graying hair, a paternal smile fixed on his mouth. He came over, giving her a perfunctory kiss upon her cheek. "You look lovely, as usual."

Tess forced a smile for his benefit. "Thank you, Cy. I'm almost done."

He stood behind her, his arms crossed against his

chest, watching her critically in the mirror. "God couldn't have created a more provocative creature. I swear, I fell in love with you the first time I saw you at Rockwell." He smiled wryly. "You were quite a sight, you know. Your blue eyes sparkling with life and your lips," he leaned over, lightly touching his lips to hers, "sweet temptation."

Tess felt the heat of a blush rushing upward along her slender neck and into her face. She chided herself for still blushing at age twenty-four. Would she ever outgrow that embarrassing trait? "Really, Cy!"

He chuckled indulgently, retrieving her delicately wrought shawl of old Irish lace from the bed. Her grandmother had given it to her. It was a family tradition to pass the shawl to a deserving member of the clan. At first Cy had tried to discourage her from wearing it to social functions. He wanted her in modern, sophisticated clothes that befitted her position in the company. He smiled to himself: she was such a child yet. Perhaps being pushed three grades ahead in the first years of schooling had affected her emotionally. He arranged the ivory and pale pink shawl around her proud shoulders, giving her a pat on the arm. Looking at Tess with pride, he wondered if others besides himself saw the incredible intelligence behind that delicate Irish face.

Cy remained silent as they drove to the party. Tonight marked another important step in the B-1 bomber project. Right now, the tail section, wings and fuselage lay on the hangar floor. His brow furrowed in thought. "I think," he began slowly, glancing over at Tess's clean, delicate profile, "this party is going to be a political shakedown of sorts."

"How well I know!" It was common knowledge that Senator Stockwell was going to publicly confront his nemesis, Senator Browning, at the party. Tess shook her head. "Cy, you never told me that being your administrative assistant was going to get me involved in so much political intrigue." Tess had come to Rockwell International as part of the management team on the B-1 project. Although she lacked a degree in aeronautical engineering, her MBA gave her the necessary background to handle all accounting and finances for the drafting section that Cy supervised. Without her keen, creative input, his department would not have run so smoothly. Yes, she and Cy made an unbeatable team. They each thrived on challenges of different sorts. Cy had gathered together the top draftsmen and design engineers in the country to build the long-range bomber. She looked after all the details ranging from accounting to lab tests, making sure Cy was never burdened with minor but often important problems. She placed her hand against her breast. "I wish I was more sophisticated . . . more—"

"Tess, you're learning beautifully. I'm very proud of your progress to date. Remember, you only received your MBA from Harvard two years ago. You can't help it if you've been sequestered in school until recently. Education has honed your fine mind, and it's only natural that your social expertise is less well developed." He patted her hand, seeing her distress. "You'll do fine," he soothed.

"I worry about not saying the right thing the right way," Tess protested softly. Already her throat was closing up from tension. Oh, God, why couldn't it just be another chatty, boring cocktail party? Why did it have to be a sit-down dinner for one hundred and fifty of the most influential people involved with the innovative bomber? Not only would top Rockwell officials be there, but key political figures, lobbyists and aggressive, shrewd staffers. And then there was the Air Force. Actually, Tess felt the safest with them. The military and civilian test pilots were harmless in comparison to the politicos.

"Well," she murmured throatily, "if you find that I've disappeared, you'll know I've discovered a secluded balcony away from all the intrigue, Cy. I much prefer the landscape to the lobbying that's going to go on."

Cy chuckled indulgently at his young wife. At forty-nine he couldn't have stumbled into a better living situation. He had been in search for an administrative assistant to help him juggle his load as chief engineer on the aeronautical design project. So impressed was he with Tess, he soon made her his wife as well as his team member. And the arrangement was working well. Tess was growing into her job and performing admirably despite the fact that she was one of the few women in top management within Rockwell. By the time he retired, Tess would be a perceptive, capable diplomat capable of standing on her own within the company.

"I do have matters to discuss with Senator Diane Browning from California," he said in a by-the-way tone.

"At least it will be a friendly conversation."

Cy chuckled. "Yes, she's on our side. Thank God for hawk senators."

Tess wrinkled her nose. "Going to speak to Senator Stockwell?"

"Of course. The cardinal rules of politics—smile, be polite, and be inoffensive."

"I can smile, I can work at being polite. But inoffensive?" Tess groaned, throwing her head back and closing her eyes momentarily. "St. Patrick deliver me from this den of wolves I'm dining with tonight. Just don't let me become their meal."

"You won't," Cy said, laughing. One moment Tess could be so serious and adult. The next she would lapse into the naive candor he was trying to curb. "You're much too small a fish in the political pond, so to speak. I think it would be a good idea if you acquainted yourself with the military tonight while I make the rounds. You're familiar with the B-1 blueprints, but you haven't made the effort to see the actual building of the plane or to acquaint yourself with the pilots who will test it."

"I know, part of my education," she mimicked gently. How like Cy to guide her into the next lesson in his plan. "Test pilots are far safer than politicians. I'll welcome the change," she returned fervently.

"They are 'safe,' as you say," Cy nodded. "Most of them are fairly taciturn. They're taught to test and observe. Chances are you'll have to carry the conversation with them unless you get them talking on the B-1."

"That's fine with me."

The California night was warm for October. Cy proudly escorted his tall, lissome wife into the lobby of the elegant hotel in downtown Los Angeles. Guiding her with a sureness born of his status and position in the company, he motioned Tess into the brass elevator.

Tess nervously hid her damp hands by burying them in the shawl against her breast. Inwardly she steeled herself, fighting back the panic that would fill her the instant the doors opened. Life had been so simple back on campus. The moment she married Cy, she had stepped into an unfamiliar, changing landscape. A landscape that she feared she would never be at home in.

Captain Shepherd Ramsey rested his lean, wiry body against the wall. With his back protected, he idly scanned the milling crowd of people. This was a black-tie dinner. A slight deprecating smile pulled at his well-chiseled lips. The blue of his Air Force uniform stood out against the black tuxedos of the civilians present. Black and blue, he thought wryly. A lot of bruises. Plenty of in-fighting between the Hill and us. He inhaled deeply and released his breath slowly, continuing to scan the crowd. It looked like a gathering of beautifully colored birds with the women present. He spotted gowns by Halston, Yves St. Laurent, Geoffrey Beene and others whose names he was sure his wife was memorizing. Raising one dark brown brow, he lifted his strong chin, searching the crowd for Allyson.

He caught sight of his wife carrying on an animated conversation with a staffer from Senator Diane Browning's office. The staffer had probably been sent ahead to check out the atmosphere of the dinner since Browning was due to drop in unexpectedly on a courtesy visit sometime during the evening. Shep lifted his Scotch to his lips, sipping the smooth golden liquid. He didn't know which he disliked more: staffers or the politicians themselves. But, they were a fact of life.

Major Tom Cunningham, another test pilot, ambled over. He matched Shep's six-foot height, looking almost like a brother to the captain. The major's light brown eyes darkened with silent laughter. He stood easily at Shep's right arm. "Well, what do you think of this shindig?" he asked in his Arkansas drawl.

Shep shrugged his broad shoulders. "Boring as hell but necessary."

"Kinda reminds me of the good ole days when chickens were pick'n'dough out of a bread pan. See how the less important ones are orbiting the staffers? God, the intrigue is so damn thick in here I could cut it with a knife."

"Yes, and Allyson is in all her glory."

Tom raised his head. "Don't knock it, buddy. She probably helped get you into test pilot school with her manuevering. It doesn't hurt to have a politically savvy Air Force wife."

Shep frowned, not liking the thought that Allyson might have been responsible for his acceptance to the test pilot school at Edwards Air Force Base. He also

heard the wistful note in Tom's voice and turned to his
friend. Tom had lost his wife to cancer two years
before. It had been hell on all of them. Shep had stood
by his Air Force Academy brother through it all. Had
that been the beginning of the end of his marriage with
Allyson? She had complained mightily of his absence at
parties when he stayed with Tom at the hospital.

He moved the ice cubes around in his scotch, lapsing
into thought. Allyson. Beautiful, poised, cosmopolitan
Allyson. At twenty-eight he found it difficult to explain
why he had married her. Why couldn't he have had a
relationship like Tom and Marie's? They had been
devoted to each other. And he'd enjoyed being with
them because of the warmth that flowed between them
and out to all those around them. But Allyson always
chafed at the bit when he wanted to go over to their
home for dinner. It was all right to spend a certain
amount of time with Tom, she informed him, because
he was a major. And after all, Shep should be seen with
higher ranking men, but there was no need to spend *so*
much of their time with the other couple.

It was in the closing days of Marie's illness that Shep
realized he didn't love Allyson. At least not in the way
he had wanted to love his wife. Tom had remained at
Marie's side constantly, holding her hand, talking
soothingly to her. It was Tom's ability to reach out and
touch, that same holding, touching, and sharing Shep
valued and missed, but Allyson deemed it inconsequen-
tial.

After Marie's death both he and Tom had gotten
orders to test pilot school. Shep had breathed a deep
sigh of relief, glad that Tom's grief would be consumed
in the demanding rigors of the schooling. It was their
shared grief over Marie's death and then the help
they'd given each other during the grueling training
course that welded them into an inseparable team.

Shep glanced over at his friend, an undisguised smile

on his mouth. "They do look like a bunch of chickens don't they? All scrambling around, clucking and squawking."

Cunningham grinned wickedly. "For a city boy, you're learnin', son. We got a couple of big dawgs coming tonight. I'm kinda wait'n' to see if Browning and Stockwell show up at the same time. Wouldn't that be something? Prodefense woman senator meets antidefense male chauvinist. Some feathers ought to fly over that confrontation."

"Conflagration is more like it," Shep growled. "Stockwell has his head up his—"

"Easy, son. Remember, we're just measly ole test pilots. We don't get asked our politics or party preferences." He rubbed his hands together. "And frankly, I can hardly wait to get my hands on the stick of that B-1. Pure sex, son. Yes, sir, pure sex to fly that bomber."

Shep laughed deeply. "You damn Arkansas hillbilly."

"And you stand there with that bland look on your face and tell me you ain't excited about gett'n' in that bomber too? You might fool most people, Ramsey. But you don't fool me. Beneath that cool Maine facade of yours beats a red-blooded heart and soul. Hell, it's a good thing you have me around to knock down some of those walls you like to hide behind. Get you loosened up a little."

"Look, people from Maine are supposed to be unreadable," he argued in good-natured defense. "I can't help it if you always seem to be able to read me anyway."

Tom nodded his head sagely. "All I gotta do, boy, is look in them gray eyes of yours and I got you by the throat. Funny, Allyson can't read you the way I can."

That was true, Shep thought. Allyson spent all her time scheming over the future. She never wasted time on small but important moments in the present. How many times had he wanted to share the beauty of a pale apricot sunset or a silvered mass of clouds struck by the sun? Too many times, a voice admitted deep within him.

"Hey . . ." Tom exclaimed, nudging Shep's elbow. "Who is that delicious-look'n' lady that just stepped through the doors? My God, I think I'm in love."

Shep looked up toward the entrance. And for a frozen instant in time he felt as if someone had stolen the breath from his body. She was dressed in a long ivory gown delicately touched with lace. The high Victorian collar only accentuated the old-fashioned aura surrounding her. She was a complete contrast to the chic modern women here and the contrast struck him deeply. His eyes traveled from the slender lines of her gown, across her small, firm breasts, to her face.

"Damn," Tom breathed. "Isn't she—"

"Beautiful," Shep finished, straightening up. Trained to observe, he noticed that every male in the place had turned and looked at the woman. Shep's eyes narrowed as he detected a certain tenseness in her porcelain features. Her eyes, the incredible azure blue of the sky, were wide, almost child-like as she nervously glanced around. His body tightened with desire as he watched her mouth. Her lips were full, slightly parted, and incredibly expressive. Dark auburn tendrils curled at her temples, softening the severity of her simple hair-do. Why did she wear her hair like that? Shep had no trouble imagining that dark mass flowing freely across her shapely shoulders. He noticed she was gripping her husband's arm tightly. Didn't the man realize how frightened and uncomfortable she was? Shep frowned, squaring his shoulders. Compared to the sleekly dressed women here at the party she seemed to be out of place, part of another time.

"Darling . . ."

Shep tore his gaze from the woman and reluctantly

turned toward his wife. Allyson smiled brightly. Her green eyes were narrowed and intent as she breathlessly glided up to Shep. She curled her lacquer-tipped fingers around his hand. "Look who's here. Now that's someone you need to know." Allyson cast a brief, plastic smile at the major. "Hello, Tom."

"Allyson. How are you tonight?"

She laughed gaily. "Fine. Just fine. Now Shep, you have to go over with me and I'll introduce you. That's Cyril Hamilton and his wife, Tess. He's the chief engineer for the aeronautical portion of the B-1 and she's his administrative assistant. Although," Allyson drawled in her best whiskey voice for added dramatic effect, "everyone knows he's grooming her to replace him someday in the Rockwell hierarchy."

Shep glanced down at his black-haired wife. "Oh really? And how do you know that?"

Allyson shrugged her shoulders in a very eloquent fashion. Her emerald green gown fit her petite figure beautifully, bringing each luscious curve to full ripeness. Shep looked again at Tess Hamilton. The difference was frightening. Alluring.

"Darling, I make it my business to know who's in and who's out on this project. I've been dying to meet Cy! You'll be working directly under him so you might as well come and let me introduce you."

"Correction, Aly, he's working for us, remember? This is an Air Force project and Rockwell is the contractor."

She pouted. "But that doesn't really matter. He's a VIP and you want him on your side. You have to work together; that's the bottom line."

Shep slipped his hand beneath his wife's elbow. She loved to irritate him by dodging certain facts. He turned to Tom. "See you a little later, buddy."

Cunningham smiled politely, resuming his Air Force officer demeanor. "Later," he agreed.

A staffer from the Hill came up, grabbing Cy's large, fleshy hand and pumping it expertly. Tess remained at her husband's side, keeping her eyes lowered most of the time, terribly unsure of herself. Sensing the approach of more strangers, Tess raised her head. Her heart pulsed erratically as her eyes met and locked with the smoky gray gaze of the man who stood before her. Bits and pieces of information whirled through her mind—the Air Force blue of his uniform, his gentle gray eyes assessing her with keen curiosity, his intense masculinity.

Her lips parted as she saw him smile down at her. It was a reassuring smile, telling her silently that she was safe with him. Tess was unable to tear her gaze from his face; she felt mesmerized by the gentle strength she saw there. His hair was a dark umber brown, neatly trimmed, with a few rebellious strands that refused to stay in place dipping down on his brow. He was a lone eagle, her imagination whispered. Indeed, he did look like an eagle with his gray eyes and black, penetrating pupils. His face was lean, like the rest of him, and oval, with a strong chin. His eyes were wide-set and alertly intelligent. His nose was aquiline, adding to his hawk-like appearance. If it weren't for the fact that his well-chiseled lips turned up at the corners, she would have been frightened of him initially. There was a calculating coolness in him that was softened by his smile.

She barely heard the introductions. The woman at the captain's side had deftly maneuvered between her and Cy. Tess raised her hand automatically to greet the strangers. She was aware of the officer's long, spare fingers wrapping around the damp coolness of her own. He murmured something, inclining his head forward, his eyes never leaving her flushed features.

"Tess, why don't you spend some time with Captain Ramsey?"

Tess blinked once, tearing her gaze from the officer. "What?" she barely whispered, her throat constricted. Cy offered her a paternal smile as Allyson draped herself over his arm. "Why don't you and Captain Ramsey talk about the B-1? I'm sure he'd like to know the progress on the defensive avionics system. That contract was just awarded and I'm sure he'd be interested in some of the details." Her heart was pounding as Captain Ramsey placed her arm under his own. Immediately she sensed his controlled strength. Tess was intensely aware of his maleness. Why was he affecting her so strongly? Her mind gyrated out of control as she compared him to Cy. The love she and Cy shared was quiet, uneventful, and devoted. This officer was creating a firestorm within her suddenly aroused senses. And more than anything, Tess knew he was aware of the effect that he had upon her. She felt terribly unsure of herself as he led her adroitly through the milling crowd. Tess regretted her lack of experience with men. Why had she stuck her head in books all those years? Why hadn't she developed outside relationships? Because you were scared, too afraid, she told herself. And now . . . now this officer was affecting her like some lost and forgotten aphrodisiac. Her body knew. But her mind refused to admit it.

Oddly, Tess felt safe with him. She didn't know why. He seemed to intuitively know how to make her feel more secure in these surroundings. More secure around him.

He leaned down, his features mobile and readable. It surprised Tess because he had seemed distant an instant before. "Would you like a drink? Looks like you could use one."

She responded immediately to the intimate, quiet quality of his husky voice. She managed a nervous smile. "I—yes. I'm sorry, I don't mean to appear so flighty. It's just that . . ." Tess saw him nod, his fingers briefly squeezing her arm.

"You don't belong here," was all he said. "Wait by the balcony doors. What do you drink?"

Her heart was skipping beats. Tess groaned inwardly as she blushed a second time. "Just wine."

Shep stood there, drinking in the sight of her upturned, flushed face. She couldn't be any more beautiful in that moment. Her blue eyes were wide and trusting, her lips were like rare, dark pink flower petals. She was looking to him for protection and that was something he wanted to give her. It would be easy to bestow it on her. He heard the uncertainty of her soft wispy voice. It sent an unnamed quiver through his taut body. "Red or white? What about champagne?"

Tess laughed softly. "Not champagne or I'm afraid you'll find me under some table."

He smiled. "Okay. We don't need you under a table. I'll be back in a moment."

Tess watched him turn and walk away, her knees feeling weak. Was it the aura of power at this gathering or simply the presence of Captain Shepherd Ramsey that was making her feel like this? She had to get hold of herself, regardless. Gripping her small evening bag until her knuckles whitened, Tess tried to calm her nerves.

He was never out of sight, even though he had left her side. She was amazed at his calmness. He walked like a panther prowling disinterestedly through the clusters of people, head held high, aloof, unique. Were all test pilots like that? Such men had charisma, she knew. It was the glamor job of the Air Force, but Ramsey's appeal went deeper than that.

She took a deep, steadying breath, realizing that she was glad to be in his care. With him, she could relax.

Chapter 2

"YOU KNOW, FOR A PARTY THIS SIZE, YOU'D THINK THEY'D have wine at the bar." Shep apologetically handed her the glass of champagne and gave her a wry smile. "Guess we'll have to make sure you don't go under the table."

Tess reached for the glass, her fingers making contact with his own. A pleasurable tingle went up her arm. Had he hesitated before pulling away? So much was happening that she was unable to be certain of anything where he was concerned. "That's all right, Captain Ramsey," she heard herself say, "I'll just hold it. That way everyone will think I'm imbibing."

"I see. Play the game, is that it?" He pushed open the balcony door, guiding her out onto the tile patio.

"I find game playing very taxing, Captain."

He pulled her gently to a stop at the waist-high stone balustrade. As much as he wanted to keep holding her arm, he allowed his hand to drop to his side. He had read fear in her eyes upon first meeting her. Was she unsure of herself with men? Looking down at her youthful features, he knew the answer to that. "Call me Shep," he urged. He turned and leaned against the still sun-warmed stone which overlooked the glittering valley of Los Angeles. "You couldn't play a game if you tried," he said, amusement tinging his voice. "Your eyes give you away."

She took a gulp of the champagne, resting against the balcony, facing him. He was so close . . . "Cy has told me again and again to maintain a poker face." She chewed on her lower lip, completely crushed by the fact that Shep could read her so easily.

Shep turned his head toward her. "Why?" he asked, perplexed. Why take away her natural spontaneity? He watched a variety of emotions flit across her features. Her skin was a flawless peach color, her nose and cheeks lightly sprinkled with freckles. He noted with pleasure that she wore little makeup; she made no attempt to hide those telltale freckles. He smiled to himself. Despite her uncertainty in these surroundings, she was not afraid to show her individuality.

Nervously, Tess took another gulp of champagne. "Administrative assistants are supposed to know how to deal effectively with every management situation. And with aplomb. Part of it is controlling your body language and facial expressions."

Shep grinned. "Whoa . . . if I don't hear an MBA talking, I'll eat my wings."

Tess laughed liltingly. She liked his smile. It was devastating. "Are all test pilots as perceptive as you are, Shep?"

"You aren't going to fall into the trap of stereotyping test pilots, are you? How long have you been with Rockwell and the B-1 program?"

She shrugged. "Two years. I joined the company after coming out of Harvard with my MBA." She gave him a mischievous look. "See, you were right. I do have an MBA. And if it isn't your perceptiveness that told you that, then you're reading my mind."

"I'm reading your mind," he returned. "You're easy to read." God was she easy to read! He had to keep himself from becoming too familiar with her. It was too easy to let down all his shields and simply be himself. He found himself wanting to tease her playfully, to make her eyes glint with the laughter he had seen dancing in their depths moments earlier. "Can I get personal for a moment?" he asked.

She regarded him solemnly for a long second. Finally, she inclined her head forward. "Yes."

"I was just wondering if your family was Irish."

Tess gave a sigh of relief. He could have asked her anything, and she would have found herself giving the answer. Shep was someone whom she could easily confide in. "One hundred percent. My great-grandparents came from a small seacoast village in southern Ireland."

"The land of fishermen and potato farmers?" he teased gently.

"And don't forget, Ireland raises some of the finest Thoroughbreds in the world too. It's a country with many faces." Tess finished the champagne, placing the glass on the rail in front of her. The momentary silence lengthened between them as they both gazed out over the dark valley. "L.A. is so huge," she murmured finally, almost to herself. "I wish we lived out in the country."

"You're a woman who would rather stick her toes into the warm earth instead of dressing elegantly for parties like this."

She grimaced. "Tell me about it! Cy cringes everytime I put my hair into braids."

Shep turned, studying her. "Oh? Somehow I picture you being very comfortable in a pair of well-worn jeans instead of designer clothes."

"That's true." She gave him a searching look. "How could you know that?"

He raised the glass of Scotch to his mouth and took a

sip. "How old are you, Tess? Do you mind if I call you by your first name?"

She shivered in response to the sound of her name on his tongue. "No, I'd love it. I hate standing on formality. And to answer your question, I'm twenty-four."

"I thought so," he murmured.

That secretive grin of his got to her and she laughed. "What does that mean?"

"Hmm, just that you've probably spent all your adult life in the ivory towers of higher education. You haven't had much of a chance to mingle with people on a purely social level. And the fact that you got your MBA when you were twenty-two implies that you jumped a couple of grades somewhere along the line" —he shook his head in a rueful gesture—"which means you probably didn't get much time to grow up."

Tess nodded. "Ever since I can remember, my parents had me in some sort of school. I guess they discovered I was bright when I was around two years old." She shrugged her shoulders. "From then on, it was a matter of bringing out my gifts."

"Don't sound unhappy about it," Shep soothed. "And certainly don't apologize for your intelligence." He grinned suddenly. "Even if you are a woman," he taunted without rancor.

Tess placed a hand on her hip, lifting her chin in defiance. "You're a chauvinist after all, Captain!"

Shep held up his hand. "No way, lady. We've got women in all phases of the Air Force, even flying planes. There's talk that someday we'll have women test pilots. No, I'm a believer in what women can do. Peace?"

Tess tried to stare him down and then burst out into laughter. "Fair enough."

Shep warmed to her bell-like laughter. He took a deep breath, captivated by her unstudied loveliness.

What was she doing here? She was like a flower on the desert, natural, unpretentious. Was her powerful, influential husband trying to mold her into someone like Allyson? The thought chilled him.

He observed her dispassionately for a moment, trying to be objective and finding it difficult.

He could not fault her on beauty or personality, and certainly she was very intelligent. Her only flaw was that she did not belong. But was it right to curb her naturalness? To rob her of that effortless laughter, the sparkle in the depths of her blue eyes, just so she would fit in? No, he told himself. No. A sense of despair settled over him. He looked at her again. There was nothing he could do. She was married. And so was he. He felt a knife twisting in his heart. Tess was the kind of woman he had hungered for all his life. The thought jolted him.

"Shep?"

He frowned. "Sorry," he muttered, "I was thinking."

"About what?"

He took a good stiff drink of the scotch, looking back over the scintillating night lights of L.A. When he didn't answer, she moved closer, until mere inches separated them. Groaning inwardly, he wondered if she knew what she was doing to him. One look at her worried face, and he knew it was a guiless gesture on her part. There was a genuine concern registering in her eyes. She had seen his agony. Damn! He forced himself to adopt a mask of cool, calm composure.

Tess reached out, touching his arm momentarily. "I know, you're thinking about the B-1! Are you worried about the flight date? That we won't make the June 1974 commitment? I'll bet you can hardly wait to fly the bomber."

He gave her a tight smile, forcing himself not to react to her touch. It was as if a butterfly had briefly grazed his arm. His mind was running rampant, unchecked. What would it be like to kiss those full lips? To feel her response to him? She might be married, but he guessed that her husband had never fully brought out her ability to love. Angrily Shep cut off all thoughts of wanting her . . . needing her. It took every fiber of his being to do so. "I understand that the avionics contract was just awarded," he answered, his voice carefully neutral, slightly strained.

"Yes, it was. But I would think you'd be more interested in the Preliminary Flight Rating Test which will take place in March."

Shep put a tight leash on his emotions as he turned to drink in the sight of her upturned features. Her eyes . . . oh, God, he could lose himself in the depths of her warm blue eyes. "I am interested," he agreed. "The PFRT is the last test before we actually place the engines in the bomber." Did his voice sound like a monotone to her too? It sounded flat, uninterested. Hell, he wanted to discuss anything with her other than business. He wanted to know about her, her background, her likes and dislikes. His mind leaped from one question to another.

But before he could formulate any of them, they were interrupted by the waiter calling them to dinner. Shep slipped his arm around her small waist and led her slowly back to the opened doors. "Thanks for coming out here with me," he said, meaning it.

She looked up at him. He was incredibly handsome in the dim light. The silver bars of his rank glimmered on his broad shoulders. The feel of his hand against her waist seemed so right. It had been natural to turn toward his body and fall in step beside him while they walked. His touch was firm, knowing. Her flesh tingled where his fingers rested, and Tess was incapable of stilling her singing heart. "I have a feeling we're both the same," she said. "You don't like these parties any more than I do. You certainly appear to be more at ease here than I, but you strike me as a man who prefers the company of a few close friends and family."

Shep ushered her into the large, brightly lit room. Reluctantly he dropped his hand from her waist, keeping it on her elbow instead. "Are you sure you aren't mind reading now?" he teased gently, meeting her gaze.

The intimate huskiness in his voice caused her to blush. She felt as if he had caressed her. What was happening? Again, that same sensation of confusion and heady excitement deluged her.

Shep was suddenly aware of an excitement that rippled through the gathering. He pulled Tess to a halt at the edge of the milling crowd, spotting Senator Diane Browning of California. She entered with a group of staffers, camera people and several other hangers-on. He leaned over and whispered intimately, "Here's the gal who's fighting for us in the Senate. Have you ever met Senator Browning?"

Tess stood on tiptoe to catch sight of the woman. She smiled up at Shep. "Cy talks about her all the time. I've never met her personally, just some of her staffers from time to time. She's terribly attractive, isn't she?"

He smiled to himself. Tess didn't see the ramrod way Browning carried herself or the way the senator jutted out that strong chin of hers. She saw only the tasteful business suit the older woman wore and the golden hair knotted severely in a chignon. "She looks a little like you," he confided to Tess.

"Now I know you're flirting, captain." Her blue eyes sparkled with merriment.

He grinned. "And I just paid you a compliment. A sincere one, I might add. Although you're far more beautiful than she could ever be."

Tess blushed fiercely, unable to hold his gray gaze. Intuitively she knew that Shep Ramsey didn't go

around flirting haphazardly. No, there was a quietness
to him, a central core that many people did not reach.
He was more introvert than extrovert although he had
extended himself to make her comfortable. "I suppose
the senator and I wear our hair in a chignon because it
looks more businesslike. That way the men we have to
work with deal with us on a professional level."

"Did Harvard teach you that?" he drawled, a smile
lifting one corner of his mouth.

It was her turn to give an impish grin. "No. I learned
that the hard way."

Shep looked at the reddish-gold highlights of her
hair. The desire to loosen the carefully hidden pins and
allow that fiery mass to tumble free was tempting. "A
pity. Frankly I think you would look devastating with
your hair down. There isn't a man here who wouldn't
succumb to your beauty."

She felt her heart soar. Something in his voice—the
husky inference in it—made her deliciously aware of
being a woman. Tess was confused. Cy had never made
her feel so desirable, so. . . . She frowned. Shep Ramsey made her feel the power of her own femininity.
That discovery frightened her badly. Taking a step
away from him she murmured, "I think it's time I found
Cy. It looks as though they're going to begin seating all
of us."

Shep maintained his distance, realizing he had made
her uncomfortable. "I think I see your husband and my
wife. Come on, I'll escort you over to them."

As they approached, Allyson gave him a dazzling
smile, her hand still draped casually on Cy Hamilton's
arm. "Darling! Cy and I have been having the most
wonderful discussion."

"I'm sure you have." Shep nodded gravely in Hamilton's direction. He watched through hooded eyes as
Tess attached herself to her husband. The difference
between them was a chasm. Hamilton looked fifty-five,

not the forty-nine Shep knew him to be. His hair was prematurely gray, his face heavily lined with the responsibility he carried. And Tess was so young! Even younger emotionally than physically. She was just beginning to explore life. He found himself wanting to share those discoveries with her and quickly shoved the thought into a closed, secret compartment of his heart. Tess's features had been glowing and alive when she had talked to him earlier. Shep watched as the natural spark in her subsided and she became once again a silent shadow of her aging husband.

"It appears you get the honors, Captain," Hamilton said. "You'll be seated next to Senator Stockwell."

Shep pursed his mouth, glancing down at Allyson. "I didn't want to eat very much anyway," he answered dryly, not allowing the true extent of his feelings to be known. That was all he needed. Chad Stockwell had fought against the B-1 program since its inception. The congressman was obligated to attend the dinner because it was taking place in his home state. But that didn't mean he would be gracious about it, especially when his opponent, Senator Browning, was in attendance as well.

"Are you sure there isn't a seating mistake?" Tess asked.

Shep looked up at her, grateful for her concern. Allyson simply looked bored and disappointed. And Hamilton was obviously just glad that he didn't have to sit next to Stockwell. But Tess was sensitive enough to realize the implications of putting a military officer beside a dove congressman. To make matters worse, it was an insult to Stockwell to place him next to a mere captain. He should have been seated beside one of the generals who were attending this affair. Shep didn't like being used to snub the congressman. Who the hell was running this show? he wondered angrily. But he controlled his anger and smiled coolly. "I doubt if it was a mistake, Tess. Thanks for being concerned though."

Hamilton eyed him appraisingly. "Apparently, Captain Ramsey, someone must think you have the 'right stuff' to take this kind of encounter."

"Frankly, sir, I'd rather be behind the stick of an F-15 out of control in a graveyard spin."

Hamilton smiled slightly. "Yes, I think I would too. Good luck, Captain. And by the way, I'm very impressed with your credentials. Your lovely wife has been filling me in on your career. I'm sure our test pilots from Rockwell are looking forward to working with you and your colleagues."

For Shep, dinner was a long, drawn out affair during which he tried valiantly to converse with Senator Stockwell. Afterward everyone got up and drifted into small clusters to continue talking. Allyson started making her customary rounds of the different Air Force officers, making sure none were overlooked. He hid his surprise when Cy Hamilton headed in his direction with Tess at his side.

"Captain Ramsey?"

Shep gravely inclined his head. "Yes, sir?"

"Tess hasn't seen the B-1 prototype yet over at our Palmdale plant. And as my administrative assistant, she needs to get out and start nosing around." Cy glanced down at her warmly, patting her hand. "I wonder if you might have a few hours free next week to show Tess around? She's seen blueprints until she can draw them in her sleep. Now she needs to see the actual bomber. How about it?"

"I'd consider it an honor and a pleasure, Mr. Hamilton."

Cy smiled genially up at the officer. "Good, good. May I leave my lovely wife in your capable hands, Captain, for a few minutes? I must chat a moment with

Senator Browning before she leaves. Tess, I'll drop by after a while with your wrap and then we'll leave."

Tess opened her mouth to speak and then closed it. She felt vaguely disturbed by Shep's presence. Even so, a smile touched her lips as Cy left.

"You look like the cat that ate the canary," she noted drily.

"I am. I was just trying to figure out a way to see you one more time before you left this evening." He slid his fingers beneath her elbow, guiding her toward the balcony. "Ready for some fresh air?"

Tess hesitated. "I—"

"What's this? My Irish lass is frightened?" he teased. "Relax, I enjoy your company. I intend to remain in control of myself." He smiled, watching her visibly relax. She moved forward at his coaxing.

"Not all women of Gaelic ancestry are fearless. Some of us get frightened. Cy says I get scared too easily."

Shep opened the door, ushering her through it. "You're lacking in confidence. But I don't see you chickening out in an emergency situation."

Tess tilted her head, trying to understand him. "Why do you say that?" she demanded, halting near him at the balustrade.

"The way you carry yourself. You have a proud, natural carriage. You walk with your shoulders back and chin up. A woman that's afraid tends to round her shoulders, take a much smaller step, and is inclined to keep her eyes fixed on the ground or only a few feet ahead of her. You," he murmured, losing himself in her widening blue eyes, "look ahead. Far ahead. I can see why your husband chose you to occupy such a powerful position in the company you work for. You have moxie, lady. Something very few women possess."

She colored. "I don't understand how so many

people can see all that in me when I don't feel it in myself." She laughed. "Are you sure test pilots aren't dyed-in-the-wool romantics, Shep?"

Grinning, he murmured, "In a sense, I think we are. We see ourselves as unique. We are able to take something new and untried and coax, cajole, or force it to meet its potential. There is something idealistic or romantic in being able to accomplish that. Or," he said, becoming more serious, "in dying if you don't succeed."

Tess sobered considerably at that. What possessed men to risk their lives that way? Was it a death wish? A heroic, subconscious passion to leave the earth as someone who had shoved back the limits of the unknown? A sudden, inexplicable dread washed over Tess. Looking up into Shep's confident, stalwart face, she could never imagine him dying in a fiery crash. There was something too special, too vibrant about him. She couldn't bear the thought that he might die, like a good percentage of test pilots, behind the stick of an unmanageable aircraft.

She chided herself sternly for dropping into the mire of depression. Rallying herself, she forced a smile. "From what little I know or understand about your career, Shep, I gather that test pilots seem to enjoy the surprise of the unknown. I think you like to pit yourself against it. No matter how much time you spend with our engineers, planners, and mechanics there is still that missing piece from the puzzle. You don't know how the B-1 will handle until she's airborne. You can only calculate the fly-ability of the plane by the computer printouts on the models in the wind tunnel tests."

He looked at her with surprise. She was talking his language now. And very easily. "I'm having a hard time reconciling your image with what's coming out of your lovely mouth. On the one hand you sound like an

engineer. On the other I see a very romantic-looking
woman right out of old Ireland.''

She bowed her head, overwhelmed by the sincerity in
his voice. "Please . . ." she whispered achingly.

Shep moved within inches of her, a troubled expression in his eyes. "You don't even know how to take a
compliment," he whispered. "Hey . . ." he coaxed,
placing his finger beneath her chin, forcing her to meet
his eyes, "You can't tell me other men haven't complimented you, Tess. My God, you're too lovely. Too . . .
fresh and alive." Her skin was velvety to his touch. He
knew he ought to remove his hand but the feel of her
skin sent waves of arousal through his body. Very
gently Shep caressed her cheek.

Tess drew in a breath, acutely aware of time melting
into nothingness as he slid his hand beneath her jaw,
tilting her head up. Up to meet his descending mouth.
A mixture of confusion mingled violently with molten
desire inside her. He hesitated, a bare inch separating
his mouth from her full, glistening lips. Her eyes had
darkened to cobalt, flecked with bits of gold. Shep felt
her tremble, caught the fleeting fear in her gaze.
Cupping her face, he gently pulled her close to his
body, wanting to erase the fear he saw.

His breath was warm against her face as she stared up
into his eyes. Her heart beat heavily in her breast, her
breath catching as he brought her against him. His
mouth, so strong-looking, lightly brushed her lips,
parting them gently. A quiver coursed through her at
even that slight touch. A small cry lodged in her throat.
This shouldn't be happening, her mind screamed. Her
heart thrilled to his masterful caress. Before she could
pull away, his mouth fitted perfectly against her own,
claiming her completely. Forever.

A shadowy figure remained frozen by the balcony
doors, watching. Quietly, he reclosed the doors. A look
of crafty pleasure registered on his features as he

turned, moving back toward the knot of departing guests. This was exactly what he had been hunting for. He would use what he had stumbled upon at the right time and place. Yes, Cy Hamilton was practically in his pocket now. All that remained to be accomplished was the timing of his disclosure.

Chapter 3

"TESS, AREN'T YOU GOING TO MEET CAPTAIN RAMSEY today?" Cy inquired, looking at his watch. "You'd better get going if you're going to make that luncheon date with him, you know."

Tess stood in front of the large picture window, staring out over the smog-ridden form of Los Angeles in the midmorning light. It was Monday and the gears of the engineering department were turning in earnest at Rockwell. Cy had worked all Sunday at the office as usual, overseeing details on the B-1. She had remained at their posh Beverly Hills home thinking about the dinner party the night before. She had allowed Shep Ramsey to kiss her . . . to steal the very breath from her starving, hungry soul. Her eyes clouded with pain and remorse. It shouldn't have happened. She should never have allowed him to touch her. The war continued within her and her stomach felt as if it were twisted in knots.

"Tess?"

"What? Oh, I'm sorry, Cy. I was thinking."

He raised his head momentarily from the blueprints spread out on his large drafting board. "You seem nervous. Is everything all right? Last night you tossed and turned a great deal."

Her heart contracted in anguish. Touching her forehead in a nervous gesture, Tess turned, forcing a smile for his benefit. "I haven't been feeling well. Really Cy, I ought to cancel that engagement with Captain Ramsey. I—"

"You need some good desert sun. That's what I get for taking you out of your natural environment of woods and meadows. I've worried what city living might do to you. I know you're an outdoors girl. I think some fresh air, a walk in the sun will put the color back into your cheeks again." He studied her. "You do look quite pale. Please, go. Besides, I'm booked with one meeting after another this afternoon and I won't have time to discuss that contract you're handling. Perhaps tonight we can go over it after dinner."

Tess pursed her lips, walking back to his desk. "Cy, you're working far too hard! You're putting in eighty hours a week on this. It's not necessary. Four or five hours of sleep a night just isn't enough!" She reached out, gently massaging his stooped shoulders as he leaned over the blueprint. "Please, darling. Come with me. You show me the B-1. We'll let Captain Ramsey be our guide." Her voice grew desperate with pleading. "Darling, please . . . for me?"

Cy chuckled softly. "I love you so much, Tess." He slid his arm around her waist, giving her a quick hug. "The offer is very tempting, but these meetings won't run without me being there. Now you'd better hurry. It's a two-hour drive up to Palmdale, and I very much want you to see that beautiful bomber. I'll see you tonight when you get back."

Her mouth was dry and her throat constricted as she walked into the restaurant at the Palmdale facility.

Clutching her leather shoulder bag, Tess caught sight of him and froze. Shep came out of the shadows, the light playing across his face. He was a lone eagle, his gray eyes narrowed and intent as he closed the distance between them. Today he was in his regular Air Force uniform, looking masculine and lean. Her lips parted slightly as he halted a few feet from where she stood. Tess tried to decipher the unreadable quality of his facial features. What was he thinking? Feeling? Would he try to kiss her again? Her heart began to race in panic at that last thought. No, it mustn't happen. Not ever again!

"Tess?" he murmured huskily.

She melted inwardly at the sound of his voice. She blinked back a sudden flood of tears that made her eyes look even more lustrous. "I didn't want to come," she blurted out unsteadily. "I was afraid. And guilty. I'm afraid of myself and what I'm feeling. It shouldn't have happened, Shep . . . I can't live with myself knowing that I've cheated on Cy. I—"

He reached out, taking her elbow, guiding her into an adjoining room. "We have to talk," he agreed. "Come on, let's get you a chair and a drink to calm your nerves. You're white as a sheet."

She held the drink with both hands, seated away from most of the other luncheon guests. After taking two healthy gulps of the vodka gimlet, she felt a little calmer. Shep made no move to touch her or talk while she drank. Finally she raised her head, meeting those incredibly warm gray eyes. He was relaxed, the expressionless mask having dropped from his features. He offered her a slight smile.

"Better?"

Tess gave a nod of her head. "Better," she agreed hoarsely.

"I owe you an apology, Tess," he began. "I took advantage of the situation. I'm a gentleman, and it was

my responsibility to control myself." He shook his
head, looking mystified. "There are things I want to say
to you, but I can't because you're married."

Her dark lashes framed widening eyes. "I am married. And I love my husband very much, Shep," she
said in a trembling voice. "I know I don't have very
much experience. And I can't explain why I let you kiss
me." She dragged in a deep breath, hands pressed
against her hot, flushed cheeks. "But please, for God's
sake, don't do it again. I—I can barely live with myself
now. If Cy knew—"

"No one saw us, Tess." He leaned forward, a new
urgency in his voice. "Look, one kiss doesn't mean
you're having a full-blown affair. It's not the end of the
world. Put it into perspective." His mouth thinned as
he assessed her worriedly. "I'm sorry. Truly sorry for
evoking this kind of pain in you. I never intended to do
that, Tess, believe me. You didn't do anything to
deserve this kind of hurt."

Tears slid down her cheeks and she brushed them
away. Drawing a handkerchief from his back pocket, he
placed it in her cool, damp fingers. Shakily she wiped
the tears away. "All I want to do is see the B-1 and then
leave, Shep." How could she explain that her heart
craved what Shep Ramsey had offered her? But her
head was telling her that she was married to Cy.

"It's not as simple as that," he corrected gently.
"You know we'll be seeing each other in the future
because of the bomber. You can't run away and hide
from this, Tess. Neither of us can," he concluded with
more authority. "I promise not to make it any more
awkward than it's already become. But you're going to
have to put any guilt you feel over this into proper
perspective and then lay it to rest. Otherwise you'll
only tear yourself apart." He frowned, watching pain
cross her mobile features. How could he have forgotten
for one instant that emotionally she was a naive

eighteen-year-old and not a mature woman of twenty-four? Agony slashed at his heart because he had selfishly inflicted this pain on her because of his own desire.

Shep idly sloshed the Scotch around in his glass, staring moodily at the ice cubes. He had done a great deal of thinking since kissing Tess. Most of his thoughts were centered on his disintegrating marriage. Allyson was a social climber. She lived for it. It hurt him to think that all she had seen in him when they married was a way to reach the top. But he knew she'd always dreamed of becoming a general's wife. And God knew, he had the proper background to make him eligible in another twelve years. He took a sip of the Scotch, glancing over at Tess.

Her cheeks were tear-wet and flushed, her lashes thick and dark with tears. Instinctively, Shep knew Tess wasn't concerned with the trappings of the material world. Hers was a world of emotional sensitivity. A world he had been craving to be a part of since he had been old enough to recognize it. And emotional sensitivity was something entirely foreign to Allyson.

"Come on, Tess. Finish your drink and I'll take you to look at that bomber you're building," he said.

Tess raised her head, meeting his gray gaze. A new kind of warmth invaded her heart, soothing the ragged edges of the guilt. A tremulous smile touched her lips.

Shep escorted her inside a large, rectangular hangar. Inside sat the first two prototypes of the B-1 bomber. Workmen on tall, skeleton-like ladders swarmed over the two planes. Shep showed his security badge to the guard. Tess brought out her badge, too, and attached it to her camel hair coat.

"Compared to the B-52, the B-1 looks like a glamor girl," Shep said, gesturing to the lean-looking bomber.

Tess nodded as her gaze traveled from the needlelike

nose over the swept-back canopy of the cockpit to the sleek, aerodynamic shape of the main fuselage. "The B-1 looks more like the French Concorde," she agreed, and then smiled. "Although, I think we have a better design."

"The Concorde is designed for speeds of Mach 2. This bomber will hit subsonic speeds at low·level."

"Do you like the design, Shep?"

He turned, looking down at her. "As my friend Major Tom Cunningham put it, the plane is pure sex."

She laughed with him. The B-1 was a Thoroughbred. It was a beautifully crafted plane and much smaller than the aging, eight-engined B-52. The B-1 could carry twice as many weapons, and once tested, it was hoped its overall performance would far surpass any existing bomber. "When you stop to think that there are over three thousand contractors and subcontractors working to put the B-1 together, it boggles your mind."

Shep nodded, leading her around to the tricyclelike landing gear that raised the bomber twelve feet off the ground. A huge nacelle placed beneath each wing would hold two engines each.

"Speaking of contractors, I'd rather fly this thing than have to deal with them." His slate-colored eyes sparkled with mirth. "Trying to handle the three thousand companies involved would be enough to give me gray hair long before my time."

Tess sobered. "I know," she answered, worry tinging her voice. "Cy deals directly with both the Air Force and the contractors. He works far too hard."

Shep leaned against one of the thick white steel landing gear struts, studying her. "Your husband is in a very powerful and influential position at Rockwell. I'm sure he has to work hard to keep the whole thing moving. What's the matter, don't you like the prestige that goes with that position?" Shep was thinking that Allyson would revel in it.

Tess gave a vague shrug. "Money isn't everything, Captain. Sure, it's nice to have it but"—she smiled, her eyes crinkling with silent laughter—"sometimes, quite frankly, I'd rather be back in my jeans and pigtails."

"And out walking in the woods. Right?"

She tilted her head, perplexed. "Now, how did you know that?"

"Anyone who has freckles is an outdoors girl," Shep baited, grinning.

Tess blushed, avoiding his caressing gaze. Even with their truce, she still felt inexorably drawn to him, like a moth to a flame. Noticing his bronzed skin, Tess countered, "You're a country boy yourself."

"Oh? Does my Maine heritage show through that strongly?" he asked, continuing to wander beneath the carriage of the bomber.

Tess turned, smiling up at him. "So! That's where you get your poker face. You're so hard to read when you don't want to be read!"

He pursed his mouth, giving her a sidelong glance. "Hmm. Tom teases me a lot about my stone face sometimes. He tells a lot of jokes to get me to loosen up."

"Always too serious?" she ventured.

"Yes."

"The New England sense of responsibility?"

"Right again. Sure you aren't a mind reader?" Tess shared his smile.

"No. Just putting two and two together. I met a few young men back at Harvard who had that same serious look. Most of them came from poor families. They were used to working their way up through the ranks." She glanced up at him. "Did you?"

"What?"

Tess sensed his hesitancy to talk about his past. "I'm sorry, I'm prying," she said.

Shep halted near the large tail and stabilizer section, which rose loftily above them. "No, you're not prying." He studied her upturned face. She was the exact opposite of Allyson. In Tess's eyes there was only curiosity and genuine concern. But in Allyson's he could always detect signs of an ulterior motive. He stuffed his hands into his pockets. "I did come from a poor family, Tess. I was the oldest of six. My father was a potato farmer up in central Maine." His brow wrinkled with memories. "Dad suffered a back injury when I was seven and I ended up doing most of the farm work. On top of that, Mom was never in good health. She was frail." He smiled fondly. "I never could figure out how she had all six of us."

"So you ended up not only with extra farm chores but helping to raise your other brothers and sisters?"

Shep nodded. "Yes. When Dad wasn't around I ended up being like a second father to the younger ones. Mom expected me to keep them in line."

"No wonder you don't smile much," Tess whispered, understanding the responsibility that had fallen on his shoulders as a youngster. "That must have been very tough on you."

"It was, but it taught me discipline at an early age. I discovered I could do things I never thought I could."

"Is that why you joined the Air Force?"

He halted, looking up at the hangar ceiling. "Let's put it this way, Tess. I didn't want to spend the rest of my life fighting poor soil conditions and severe weather trying to plant potatoes. I saw what it did to my parents, I guess I wanted something better."

In that instant, Tess saw Shep in a new light. He was a proud man. But his pride came from the knowledge that he had survived and gone on to be successful on his own terms. "I admire you, Shep. I really do," she murmured, awed.

"Don't be too impressed," he answered gravely. "I really had no choice. I either worked or everybody starved."

He slipped his hand beneath her elbow and led her out of the hangar. The Mojave winds were whipping tumbleweeds along the desert surface to their right. Opening the car door, he helped her in. Taking off his flight cap, he shut the door. Several strands of dark hair had dipped to his brow and he pushed them back with his long, tapered fingers. The interior of the car was warm from the sun and Tess leaned back.

"Why the Air Force? Why not industry? You certainly have the drive and motivation to do whatever you want."

He rested his hands on the steering wheel, considering the question. "In the woods when I was waiting for a deer to come by, I'd sit quietly in a tree and watch the birds. There were several Bald Eagles that nested near my home and I used to watch them. I saw the freedom they had as they rose above everything, Tess." He was quiet for nearly a minute. His voice grew softer as he continued. "I wanted to feel the wind tearing at me, to experience that sensation of soaring. I wanted their freedom to turn, wheel, dive, or glide thousands of feet on invisible air currents." His voice became inaudible as he remembered his boyhood dream. Even now the thrill of flying was with him. He wanted to slip the grasp of the earth's gravity and fling himself skyward, just as those magnificent eagles had done with such effortless grace. He glanced over at Tess, suddenly feeling shy. He had never shared his wishful childhood dream with anyone. Not even Allyson.

Shep turned from Tess to clear his throat and then continued in a more even voice, "I didn't have the money to take private flying lessons. So, I put myself through college in five years and then joined the Air Force. I did very well in flight school and was assigned to fighters. Later on, I transferred to FB-111's, a medium-range bomber and then to B-52's just in time for the war over in Nam. I stayed with the Buff's until test pilot school came through for me. Next month I pin on my major's leaf."

She gazed at him admiringly. "And you have no-where to go but up. You're an inspiration to everyone, Shep."

He shrugged, starting the car engine. "I wouldn't know about that, lady. Don't be so quick to put me up on a pedestal."

"Why not? You certainly deserve to be there."

"Every idol has feet of clay, just remember that, Tess," he warned. He met her eyes. "And I've already shown you just how fallible I am with you. Come on, it's almost four o'clock. Let's get you back to the restaurant so you can pick up your car. I'm sure your husband will be wondering where you are."

Derek Barton entered Cy Hamilton's spacious, well-appointed office with a look of serious intent on his narrow face. The dark brown corduroy suit he wore seemed to accentuate the planes of his lean face and the darkness of his restless gaze. Hamilton looked up from his drafting table, a scowl already developing on his brow.

"I thought I told my secretary I wasn't seeing anyone else today," he growled, returning to the plans and ignoring Barton.

Barton halted at the desk, crossing his arms comfortably. "Everyone is gone for the day, Mr. Hamilton." He gave Cy a plastic smile. "It's nearly six o'clock. How about taking a break and I'll buy us some dinner over at—"

"No, thanks, Barton. What's on your mind? Is it that subcontract of yours? I told you before, if you've got any problems with it, don't bring them to me. It's a

performance contract. Your bearings meet our specifications or we don't accept them. It's as simple as that."
He glanced up at the contractor. "Now why don't you
leave?"

"Mmm, I don't think you'll want me to leave without
talking to you first," Barton hinted, a wolfish smile
hovering around his almost lipless mouth. "No, this
time it involves something I think you'll be very
interested in."

Cy ignored him. Barton was one of the few subcontractors who could get under his skin. His bids were
always late and incomplete. Then he whined until the
Air Force accepted them even after the deadline. He
was a wheedler, a conniver, and a weasel and Cy didn't
trust him or his company's work. How many times had
Tess gone to Rockwell's lab to check the quality of the
steel alloy that was used to make the bearings? Cy
doubted that Barton's work met the specs, but what
was he going to do when low bid always got the job? He
glared up at Barton. "I suggest you say your little spiel
and then go."

Barton shrugged. "Okay, Mr. Hamilton. Your wife
has been over at our company offices a great deal
lately—"

"I send her over there," Hamilton growled. "As the
specifying agent, Rockwell has the right to inspect your
work, Barton. She's done nothing wrong by going over
there and picking up the lab reports on the bearings!"

"No—no, I agree," Barton said slowly, barely able
to hide the excitement he was feeling. "What I'm trying
to say is that I recognize your wife when I see her."

Cy raised his craggy head, staring at the contractor.
"Meaning what?"

Barton hesitated, using the interim silence to build
Cy's curiosity. "Your wife's very young and very attractive, Mr. Hamilton." He didn't want to come out

and say, half your age. "It's hard for a man not to take a long, appreciative glance at her. I've noticed that when she walks through our company's various divisions. Every man stops work and looks up when she walks through the area."

"What the hell are you getting at?"

Barton turned on his heel, ambling a few feet away before turning and facing Hamilton. He was enjoying Cy's discomfort too much to rush. This was one way to get back at Hamilton for harassing him about the parts his company turned out for the bomber. The Rockwell engineer had interceded once and rejected a shipment of bearings after testing them. Barton remembered that day well. The general from Wright-Patterson Air Force Base had called, informing him that the bearings hadn't met the specifications and his company would have to supply replacements. It had been a costly rejection. If it hadn't been for Hamilton's wife, he could have gotten away with the delivery. He'd almost saved sixty thousand dollars. And in the end, she had cost him half a million. That was what it had cost to replace the order with bearings satisfying Rockwell specifications.

"There's been plenty of talk about your wife's position in the industry."

"She's qualified in every way," Cy snapped. "And I don't give a damn if you good ole boys want to deal with a woman or not. As long as she knows what she's doing, you're just going to have to roll with the punches, Barton."

"Looks like you'll have to roll with a few punches yourself, Mr. Hamilton. I happen to know for a fact that your pretty little wife is having an affair."

Hamilton's eyes narrowed dangerously. He placed his pen on the desk, giving Barton his full, undivided attention. "You lying—"

The contractor's face hardened. "Use your head,

Hamilton. Why should I come in here with that kind of an accusation if it wasn't true? I would have everything to lose and nothing to gain by such an accusation."

There was some logic to that, Cy realized. Why would Barton come in stirring up unnecessary trouble when he'd been in hot water already? A pain began throbbing in his chest and he raised his hand, massaging the area absently. "All right. What do you know?"

"She's seeing an Air Force officer. A test pilot."

A coldness washed over Cy. Every fiber of his body experienced one sensation: fear. His voice sounded strangled. "Who?"

"Captain Shepherd Ramsey."

"Where? When?"

Barton remained serious, delighting in the grayness now coming to Hamilton's suddenly pale-looking features. "Saw 'em just the other night at that fancy party we all attended. They met out on the balcony. I'm surprised more people didn't see them kissing each other. I just happened to walk out to grab a breath of fresh air when I stumbled on them."

The dull, heavy feeling was spreading in Cy's chest and he pressed his fist harder against his body. "Is that all?" he demanded hoarsely.

"I understand she went up to Palmdale today," Barton continued slowly. He looked at his watch, making the gesture significant. "It's six-thirty. Where is she? I called earlier today and her secretary said she was having lunch with the captain. Long lunch, ain't it, Hamilton?"

It was almost nine-thirty when Cy heard the front door of their home open. He raised his head, remaining on the couch with the newspaper thrown nervously across his lap. He had been too upset to read it. Tess hurried into the living room, her eyes dark with apprehension.

"Oh, Cy! I'm sorry I'm late. I had a flat tire on the way back, and there was no phone nearby so that I could call you." She shrugged off her coat, allowing it to hang over the back of the couch as she walked over to him. Pushing back several tendrils that had escaped from behind her ear, she sat down. As she looked at him, she realized something was dreadfully wrong. His face was ashen. Reaching out she gripped his hand. "Darling, what's wrong? You look awful!"

"I haven't been feeling well since about six tonight," he admitted heavily. It was true, the heavy pressure in his chest had continued after Barton told him about the affair. He looked up into her beautiful flushed features. She appeared so damned innocent looking. So untouched . . .

Tess leaned over, caressing his cheek. "My poor darling. Have you eaten yet? Probably not. You get so busy you forget. I'm starved, Cy." She started to rise but he gripped her hand.

"Stay a moment, Tess. There's something we have to talk about."

Her brows knitted worriedly. He sounded like a man who was lost, without hope. Chewing on her lower lip, she sat back down. "What's wrong, Cy? Has something happened at work? You aren't well."

He took a deep, unsteady breath, gripping her hand tightly. "Derek Barton came in today with some very disturbing news."

"Him!" Her voice took on a scathing tone. "Why doesn't he leave you alone? The man is unbearable."

"He didn't come today with any problems concerning the contract."

Tess tilted her head, puzzlement written in her face. "What then?"

Cy swallowed hard, finding it hard to breathe. He took two half breaths, forcing the words out. "You were seen in the arms of Captain Ramsey at the party,

Tess. And I can't help but wonder if you were late this evening because of him . . ."

Horror coursed through her, and Tess pulled her hand free, covering her lips. Her mouth went dry, her heart plummeting. Cy gasped, falling back against the couch, clutching at his chest. A small cry escaped her and she leaned forward, gripping his shoulder. "Cy! What's wrong? Oh, my God. No!"

Chapter 4

MAY 24, 1974

CHAD STOCKWELL LOOKED UP AT HIS STAFFER, GARY Owens, who was following the B-1 program. The Senator tapped his short, square finger on the top of a pile of papers in front of him. "According to this, Rockwell is behind schedule in getting that bomber assembled and ready for flight, Gary. What's the economic impact of such a lag?"

Owens, a Yale graduate, adjusted his conservatively colored tie. "Senator, I think I'd better give you a bit of background before answering that. The Air Force targeted the first engine test of the B-1 in March. It didn't go down. They're still hoping to make the first flight in June. Apparently more time is being spent on piecing the air frame together than had been anticipated. There's a great deal of pressure being put on Rockwell by the Air Force to get the entire project back on schedule. If they keep going like this, it will probably be the end of 1974 before they test fly that monstrosity."

Stockwell frowned, moving quickly through the figures. "What I'm really concerned about is if they're going over the fiscal year budget allotted to them by Congress."

Owens allowed himself a brief, pleased smile. He had done a great deal of digging, involving phone calls to the Pentagon, Wright-Patterson Air Force Base, and Rockwell to piece that answer together. "Yes, sir, they are. And any delay in the program tends to add to the price. What it comes down to, Senator, is this: one B-1 used to cost the American public forty-four million dollars. Now, with Rockwell lagging behind, the unit program cost has risen to fifty-four million."

Stockwell pursed his fleshy lips, feeling anger and indignation over the entire situation. "Damn them. They were planning to order 241 B-1's. Do you realize what the price tag on that will be?" He hit his intercom button, signaling his secretary.

"Yes, sir?"

"Betty, get me the engineer who's running the show from Rockwell on the B-1."

"That would be Mr. Daniel Williams, sir. I'll ring his office right away."

"Thank you." Stockwell looked pleased. "Nothing like getting the full story from the source, Gary. Sit down. I want you in on this conversation with Williams." He frowned, searching his memory. "I thought Cy Hamilton was the top dog at Rockwell?"

"Cy Hamilton was, sir, until he died of a sudden heart attack a few days after the B-1 party, Senator. Dan Williams was pushed into the slot to keep things on an even keel."

"Didn't work, did it?" he murmured, grinning.

"No, sir, I don't think so."

"Mrs. Hamilton?" Her secretary Ruth Caldwell poked her head around the opened office door.

Tess sat with her hand propped up against her wrinkled forehead. She looked up. "Yes, Ruth?"

"It's Senator Stockwell's secretary on the phone."

Ruth gave a grimace. "I told her Dan was out on business for the day. So he wants to talk to you."

Tiredly Tess rubbed her face. Would she ever sleep soundly? She doubted it. Depression seemed to color her whole world black. "All right," she answered softly, the exhaustion evident in her tone. "I'll take the call."

This was all she needed. Since Cy's unexpected death, Tess had been asked to help Dan Williams take over the job as chief engineer. In a way, she was grateful for the twelve-to-fourteen-hour days. At least when she was working, she didn't have to think. She didn't have to feel that knife-twisting pain in her heart. Cy had died in her arms thinking that she had had an affair with Shep Ramsey. Her lips pursed into a familiar line of pain and guilt. Thank God for Dan Williams. He drove her mercilessly, not realizing he was doing her a favor. If her mind was occupied, she could ignore the anguish she carried in her heart. Expelling a long sigh, Tess picked up the white phone.

"Good morning, Senator Stockwell. This is Tess Hamilton. May I help you?"

"Mrs. Hamilton, I'm sorry to hear about your husband. Cy Hamilton and I go way back."

A little warning signal went off immediately in Tess's head. In the last seven months she had found out about the games politicians played. They would use anything they could to throw one off guard, so they could get some straight answers. Well, with Stockwell, she was going to be very cautious."

"Thank you for your condolences, Senator."

"A terrible loss, Tess. You don't mind if I call you Tess, do you?"

Tess groaned inwardly. She didn't want him to use her first name. She did not want to be familiar with Stockwell in any way. She hadn't liked what she'd seen of him at the party, and his damaging press releases about Rockwell and the Air Force reinforced that dislike. "Yes, well, what can I do for you?"

"Just a few small, unimportant questions, Tess."

I'll bet, she thought, keeping her pen poised over a pad of paper to jot down his questions and then her answers. Her palms grew damp; she sensed Stockwell was after a great deal more than his lighthearted conversation indicated. "Go on," she urged.

"I was just curious as to why the engine test of the first B-1 didn't take place in March as originally scheduled."

"We've been installing several systems, Senator. Delivery of some of the subassemblies such as valves, pumps and wiring has taken longer than originally anticipated. The engineers have tried to estimate the completion date of each task. Each of these individual activities, no matter how large or small, are then run through our scheduling computer. Some of the plumbing must be put in first before the wiring can be placed. Everything has to go in a prearranged order."

"But Rockwell has people there who have scheduled large projects on complex aircraft before. They know the time involved on something of this size and complexity."

Tess's mouth thinned. "Senator, if you recall, the B-1 was originally designed in 1967, which means the plans are seven years old. As you well know, technology has rapidly advanced in those years. To be able to accurately project cash flows and time schedules on something that's going to be built seven years in the future is nearly impossible. Extra time has been needed for design changes to continually update and modernize the B-1 changes that were not anticipated seven years ago. We've done the best we can under the circumstances."

"And the cost estimate?" Stockwell asked.

"The rates are higher than anticipated. No one seven years ago could have predicted today's skyrocketing costs."

"Indeed. Each B-1 unit was supposed to cost forty-four million. Now, according to what my staff can figure out, it will be something like fifty-four million. That is extremely distressing, Mrs. Hamilton."

Her stomach knotted as she heard the threat in his voice. Instinct told her he was going to take that information and run with it. She groaned inwardly: Stockwell knew how to manipulate the press to his full advantage. She could already see the glaring headlines now. Maintaining a neutral tone she murmured, "Senator, I've given you the reasons for the delays. We're working our crews to maximum efficiency to adjust for the schedule changes. I realize that time means money. And with the present inflation rate, it means at least a six percent price hike."

"My staff tells me it's going to be a lot higher than that, Mrs. Hamilton."

Tess gripped the phone receiver tightly. "I'll talk to Mr. Williams when he comes in, Senator. I intend to document our conversation on paper. I think that when you take into account the seven-year delay between designing the plane and actually building it, you'll understand why Rockwell is a few months behind schedule at this point."

Tess sat immobile for a few moments after the Senator hung up. It was a lovely June day outside the windows of her large, airy office. Slowly getting to her feet, she shakily touched her brow, wandering over to the filmy blue curtains. Moving them aside, she gazed at the smog-ridden Los Angeles landscape. The main Rockwell office was located in El Segundo, a small suburb near the Pacific Ocean.

Her mind clicked with possibilities over Stockwell's phone call. He would use the information. She could picture him gleefully calling a press conference and expounding on the cost estimate rise while conveniently omitting the reasons behind it. Damn inflation, she groused mentally. Damn everything. Closing her eyes, Tess shook her head.

Since Cy's death, everything seemed to have gone wrong. The actual assembly of the B-1 had been slower than forecast. There were problems joining the tail structure which had in turn delayed installation of the fuselage, the center wing box and the pivotal fittings for the wing. Now the cockpit capsule was finally in place, the wiring complete for the most part. Dan had urged her to accompany him up to the Palmdale plant on several occasions, but she had found excuses not to go. Shep Ramsey might be there, and she didn't want to risk running into him.

A new stab of pain went through her. Oh, God, Shep, she cried to herself. Tess wrapped her arms about her body. She experienced the agony of Cy's death all over again, and the guilt she had felt when Shep Ramsey came to visit her the next day. No—no, she didn't want to have to go through it again! She compressed her lips, closing her eyes, trying to shake loose the image of Cy's death. How many times had she relived that night, and the events of the following morning? In the midst of all her anguish, it had been Shep Ramsey who had given her stability. . . .

Tess had heard the doorbell ringing that morning. Dully, she had looked up, finally realizing that someone was at the front door and she had to answer it. Her mind was sluggish, numbed with shock as she rose and mechanically moved one foot in front of the other. After the ambulance had taken Cy's body away the doctor gave her tranquilizers and sleeping pills to help her rest that first night. It was somewhere around eleven A.M. when she finally awoke from the drugged sleep and heard the doorbell ring. Still dressed in her dark burgundy silk robe from the night before, her long auburn hair unbound, she finally opened the door.

Tess blinked once, the impact of a blue Air Force uniform registering slowly on her consciousness. Raising her eyes, she gasped in stunned surprise. Automatically, her fingers went to her slender throat in reaction. "No . . ." she whispered hoarsely, trying to shut the door.

"Tess! Let me in." Shep effectively blocked the door. Her strength was no match for his. Fear mixed with anguish as he hurriedly scanned her ashen features. Her eyes were great pools of blue agony. Dark shadows lingered beneath them, the aftermath of too many tears. Her flawless peach-colored skin was pale, almost translucent. She looked dead. Her beautiful hair spilled across her slumping shoulders, framing her pain-ridden face, making her look even more pale, if that were possible. His heart squeezed as he slipped inside, quickly taking off his flight cap.

"I had to come, Tess," he said huskily, shutting the door behind him. "I got word three hours ago." He scowled, watching an incredible array of emotions move across her face. He groaned inwardly, realizing more than ever how much he cared about her. He reached out in an effort to comfort her. It had been an automatic reflex.

Tess shrunk away from his hand, gasping, "No!" Tears trickled down her drawn face as she backed away from him. "Go away! Oh, God, just leave me alone! Cy died because of me. Because of you! It's my fault. I should never have let you kiss me!" She sobbed, fleeing to the safety of the living room.

Shep caught up with her, gripping her arm, spinning her around. "What are you talking about?" he breathed, forcing her to a stop. "Tess! Get hold of yourself! Tell me what happened."

She sobbed, burying her face in her hands. "Someone saw us kissing on the balcony!" she wailed. Lifting her tear-stained face she choked out, "He told Cy! He told him I was having an affair with you!" She began to sob in earnest, trying to pull away from him. Guilt surged over her as she remained helplessly entrapped by his restraining hand.

Shep's mind raced. One part of him wanted to take her into his arms, to hold her and keep her safe. More than anything, Shep wanted to protect her and take away the pain that seemed to radiate from every part of her being. But who had seen them? And why would he tell Cy? What kind of vindictive game was being played? Had the story caused Cy's heart attack? Worriedly he studied Tess. She stood before him, trembling with fear and pain. "Dammit, Tess, come here," he growled, and pulled her into his arms.

An anguished cry escaped from her as he crushed her against his body. He buried his head against the silken folds of her hair, holding her tightly. "Ssshh," he crooned softly, "it'll be all right, honey. Ssshh, that's it, go ahead, cry. Get it out. I'm sorry. So sorry this has happened. You don't deserve this. None of it."

Huge, tearing sobs broke from her as she gave in, collapsing against the strength of his body. Tess buried her head on his chest, the backlog of fear, shock, and horror rushing out in strangled, gulping sounds. Just having Shep's arms around her made her feel cared for, protected. She was barely cognizant of his soft, unintelligible words in her ear. His fingers gently stroked her head to soothe her, to take away the agony.

They were standing in the hall. Shep slipped his arms beneath her quivering body and picked her up. He carried her into the living room, halting near the couch, acutely aware of the warmth and pliancy of her body. She was in his arms, her hair like raw silk, the scent and touch of her skin a mingling of sandalwood with velvet.

Shep didn't want to let her go. She was alive. So incredibly alive. She was everything he had imagined. And more. Much, much more. He wanted to carry her into the bedroom and lay her down beside him. Shep knew he could assuage her pain, give her a momentary sanctuary of peace and strength through the act of loving her.

The night they first kissed, their union had completed each of them, and Shep instinctively realized that he could create the same harmony now. The same incredible sense of loving communion that had given both of them those precious, fleeting moments of wonder and peace.

He was torn between laying her down on the couch and carrying her into the bedroom despite her protests. Some indefinable emotion rose in him, nearly over-whelming his senses as he held Tess in his arms. He was aware of the arousal of his body, of his emotions as he felt the pliancy of her flesh against his hands. Reluc-tantly, Shep lowered Tess to the couch, then brought her back into the protective circle of his arms.

Shep had expected her to pull away, but to his surprise, she fell back into his embrace. His heart sang with silent joy at the simple gesture. Despite Tess's words, there was still trust and an intangible bond of unnamed emotion between them, an emotion that allowed her to come to him for comfort.

Finally, after nearly half an hour, she quieted. Shep absently stroked her hair, feeling the rapid beat of her heart against his chest. He closed his eyes, resting his head against her hair. Her breasts were soft against the wall of his chest, her body fitting perfectly against the planes of his own. The urge to deepen the intimacy of his slow, stroking motions on her beautifully curved back was a continuing agony. She was so warm, her scent intoxicating his heightened senses. Leaning over, he placed a kiss on her temple, aware of the silken hair beneath his mouth and the yielding softness of her flesh. It would be so easy . . . so easy to cup his hand beneath her chin, lift it upward, placing her tear-stained lips against his mouth. Desire pulsated through his tightly controlled body. Each beat of her heart was like a throbbing invitation, fanning the flames of hungry desire to roaring life within him. No woman had ever affected him on such a primal level.

Putting a rein on his needs, Shep closed his eyes, resting his head against her hair. It couldn't be, he thought morosely. Not now . . . not like this. . . . If I did make love to her, she would never forgive herself or me. I can't risk that. He briefly opened his gray eyes, pain clearly written in their depths as he stared emptily off into space. Tess would hate herself and hate him. And Shep cared too deeply to let her be hurt any more. He thought too much of Tess to compound her problems. Gently, Shep ran his fingers through her hair, glorying in the sensation. Despite everything, he was determined to see Tess through this and try to reestablish a relationship with her at some point later on. A feeling of contentment washed over him, a warmth that he'd never experienced before. "Better?" he inquired, his voice barely above a whisper.

Tess nodded once. She pulled her hand from around his waist and tried to dry her thick, tear-wet lashes. He dug out his handkerchief, placing it into her fingers. "Seems like you're always crying when we're together," he noted wryly, gazing down at her and recalling her tears at Palmdale.

Tess mutely agreed, pulling free of him. She stared at him gravely, aware that his left arm remained around her waist. There was a naturalness to their relationship. Why did she feel safe and stable when Shep was with her? She shouldn't. Where had the horror of guilt gone? Right now she felt calm. As if she were in the eye of a hurricane. His gray eyes were dark and searching upon her face. There was worry coupled with anxiety in their depths. She swallowed against the lump that was forming in her throat, realizing how deeply he cared.

"Can you tell me what happened, Tess?" he coaxed gently.

She dropped her gaze to his handkerchief, twisting it between her fingers. "I—I was late getting home because my car had a flat tire."

"A flat tire? Why didn't you call me, Tess? I would have driven out and helped you."

She shook her head. "I know you would have, Shep. I—I was afraid to."

He watched her closely and understood what she wasn't able to say—any time spent with him was a special, unfulfilled agony. He squeezed her arm. "It's all right," he soothed. "Go on."

Tess gave him a helpless look. "When I finally got home, Cy was sitting here." Her voice wobbled and she held her hand across her mouth. "He—he said someone had seen us on the balcony. And then"—she sobbed harder, fighting back the deluge of fresh tears— "he wondered why I was late coming back from Palmdale. He knew I was with you. . . ."

Shep clenched his teeth, drawing in a deep breath while she cried. He gripped her arm. "Tess, who told him all this?" he demanded tightly. "Who?"

"Derek Barton! He's a horrible little man! A subcontractor to Rockwell on the B-1 project." She drew in a shaky breath, trying to get a hold on her rampant emotions.

Anger, more chilling than a glacier in the Arctic, flowed through him. "He lied," he breathed softly. "The bastard lied."

"And—and Cy's dead because of that rotten, horrible lie! Oh, Shep—" she whispered painfully, "I can't stand living with the pain of knowing I killed him."

He gripped her by the arms, giving her a small shake.

"Stop it," he growled. "That's not true. Cy was a dedicated man. You said yourself he was a workaholic. He'd been putting in too many long hours. A man of his age who's working like that is prone to a heart attack, Tess. What have the doctors said?"

Shakily she wiped the tears away, looking up at him morosely. "They're supposed to call this afternoon."

His face softened. "And the funeral?"

Tess winced. "Two days from now."

His grip tightened momentarily until he realized he was hurting her. Relaxing it he said, "Do you have anyone to help you with the details?"

She made a weak gesture with her hand. "Rockwell people. They've been very supportive."

"I mean a friend? Someone close who can help pull you through all of this."

Her mind fled over a list of the women she knew. The Rockwell secretaries hated her because of her position in the company. She had few outside friends. There was no other woman at her level, or even above her, whom she could confide in. She shook her head. "I—no, I don't. It's hard to explain. I spent my time either at the office with Cy or here at home with him."

He pursed his lips, watching her closely. "Tess, let me be here for you. It's the least I can do under the circumstances."

Her eyes widened, broadcasting her anguish. "I can't, Shep—Barton will be spreading rumors. I—" She halted, her voice growing hoarse. "No, you can't. By now he's probably spread it all over the aeronautics industry. If you're around, there will be more ugly talk. I can't bear it. I couldn't take it," she whispered, burying her face in her hands.

Frustration curled in his stomach, tightening it. His gray eyes flashed with checked anger. "I'll get him if it's the last thing I do," he snarled softly.

She jerked her chin up, staring at him. The sudden change in his face frightened her. "Shep!"

He smiled coldly, gripping her cool hand. "Don't worry. I'm not going to kill him. He deserves that, but I won't do it. Someday we'll meet and then. . . ." He stopped, realizing he was upsetting Tess. "Sorry," he murmured. "Forget it. I won't do anything, Tess. Look," he coaxed gently, "call me if you need me. I'll come, no matter what time of day or night it is. Promise me that, Tess."

She was aware of the strength of his hand around her own. Just his touch soothed the ragged edges of her composure and gave her stability. "But—your wife. What will she think? God, I don't want to be responsible for any more problems, Shep. You're going up for major. I don't want to cause you any trouble. This gossip will spread to the Air Force community. It could jeopardize your chances for the rank."

He gave her a self-deprecating smile, one corner of his mouth barely curving upward. "This can't hurt my chances for major, Tess."

"I don't understand."

"It must have been one hell of a party we attended last weekend. Yesterday Allyson told me she wanted a divorce. Seems she's found herself a full colonel who's going up for general in another year." He looked away, suddenly bitter. "I should have expected it. Aly was always a social climber."

Tess rubbed her forehead, trying to banish his words from her mind. That had all happened over seven months ago. She had barely reacted to the news of Shep's pending divorce from Allyson. She had been in shock at the time, unable to feel anything as she murmured the proper words of sympathy. Her azure eyes grew dark now with remembrance of the gossip surrounding Cy's death. It had started at the funeral and gathered tidal wave force during the months afterward. Even now, seven months after his death, the guilt and grief continued to shadow her waking hours and haunt her restless sleep.

Fortunately, Dan Williams made brooding almost impossible. To escape the guilt and pain that haunted her, Tess lived her entire life at the office, much as Cy had done. Was she really like him? she wondered dully. Tess watched the fleecy white cumulus clouds drifting over the valley toward the San Gabriel Mountains.

Because of the guilt she carried, Tess had decided to cut all communications with Shep Ramsey. She recalled the pain and disillusionment in his voice when he'd told her that Allyson was leaving him. She wondered how Shep was faring. Had the gossip cost him his promotion to major?

From time to time a memo would cross her desk with his name in it. He was currently undergoing further training in the flying simulator with the rest of the men who would eventually pilot the B-1. And every time she saw his name, her heart would wrench with newfound pain and longing.

Miserably, Tess turned away from the window, walking back to her desk. She had to quit thinking about Shep. About what might have been. . . .

Chapter 5

"WE'VE GOT TROUBLE. I CAN SMELL IT," DAN MUTTERED, reading the follow-up memo covering Tess's conversation with Senator Stockwell. He put the copy down on his desk, looking across the room at Tess. "Stockwell will call a little impromptu chalk-talk with those antidefense lobbying groups," he said tiredly. "The news will spread like wildfire. I can see it now—all the newspaper and television reporters jumping on the figures without ever giving the reason for the rise in cost. Damn." He got to his feet, thrusting his fingers through his thinning gray hair.

Tess shrugged wearily. It was Thursday morning and clouds covered L.A. like a suffocating white blanket. She didn't know which was worse—the fog or the smog. "I'm alerting our public relations people to start scanning some of the nationally known newspapers for stories on it," she said.

Dan came around the desk and halted. He looked dapper in his brown corduroy suit, white shirt, and burnt sienna tie. "So typical of the media. I've never grown used to the fact they're looking for a sensational story, not the truth." He glanced at his watch. "Well, you about ready?"

Tess looked up at him, surprise registering on her features. "Ready? For what?"

"Don't you remember? Our meeting with the Air Force up at Edwards. We're to attend a luncheon and then we're off to an engineering update with the test pilots and simulator people. What's wrong? You look like you've seen a ghost."

Tess's heart beat wildly in her chest. Shep Ramsey would be there! Oh, God! No. She had avoided him thus far. She couldn't face him. Not after all the horrible gossip. The innuendos . . . Swallowing convulsively she murmured in desperation, "I have a schedule conflict, Dan. I can't make it."

One gray eyebrow rose. "Oh? Come on, it'll do you good to get out of the main office. Besides, I do need your help on this thing today. And remember, two weeks from now I'll be out of the country. You're going to have to fill in on my behalf. Now cancel that other appointment and let's get going."

It was a two-hour drive from the bowels of L.A. up through the San Gabriel Mountains and into the high desert. Edwards Air Force Base was surrounded by two dry lake beds, Rosamond and Rogers. Both could be utilized as landing sites for test aircraft during an emergency. Edwards also sported one of the longest runways in the world. The yellow ochre of the flat desert melded with the bone-whiteness of the lake beds, making the landscape seem endless to Tess. The hard-packed sand surface was dotted with sagebrush, mesquite, Joshua trees, and aimlessly wandering tumbleweeds.

She kept her hands tightly clasped together in her lap during the trip. Her mind dwelt on Shep Ramsey. What would he do when he saw her? She broke out in a light perspiration, unsure of her own reaction. Everyone on base must know the sordid details of their supposed affair. Every set of eyes would focus on her and Shep. She chewed on her lower lip, wishing to save him the embarrassment that was sure to result from her going there today.

Her stomach was so knotted by the time they arrived at the officers' club at Edwards, Tess felt stabs of pain. I'm going to get an ulcer, she thought. She had worn a plum-colored dress of Qiana. The easy folds of the cloth were gathered at the waist to emphasize the cleanness of the design. Nervously she tugged at the sash and followed Dan into the club. The darkness temporarily blinded her after being out in the bright sunlight. Tess heard several male voices and blinked, stopping at Dan's shoulder.

"Major Cunningham," Dan said, holding out his hand. "How are you?"

"Just fine, sir. We boys from Arkansas are always fine."

Tess looked up into Cunningham's handsome face. He nodded toward her, offering his hand. "Mrs. Hamilton, it's a pleasure to meet you. Shep will be along shortly. He's finishing up a session in the flight simulator."

She smiled weakly, gripping his hand. It was warm and hers was ice cold. "Thank you, Major." Her eyes adjusted to the semi-gloom. Dan proudly introduced her as his assistant, and Tess shook the hands of the five Air Force test pilots, acutely conscious of their collective stare. She wanted to melt into the ground. They knew. They all knew. Luckily, Tom Cunningham seemed to sense her discomfort and directed his conversation toward her while Williams conversed with the other pilots.

"I wanted to extend my condolences on your husband's death, Mrs. Hamilton. I meant to write you a note." He managed a shrug. "You know how men are about writing. So maybe you'll accept my apologies now."

"Thank you, Major."

"Call me Tom. Better yet, since you're going to be getting more involved with all of us as time goes on, call me Cowboy. Shep always teases me about riding those razorbacks down in my neck of the woods."

She couldn't help but relax beneath his soft Southern drawl. He was truly an officer and a gentleman. "How about if I call you Tom when we're in groups like this, and when we don't have to be so professional or aware of social decorum, I'll call you Cowboy?"

He grinned broadly. "Good enough, Mrs. Hamilton."

"Call me Tess, please. I'm afraid I don't have any nicknames like you do."

Tom smiled genially down at her. "I know one guy that has some pretty sweet names for you," he said, confidentially lowering his voice. He became serious. "Look, Shep Ramsey is my best friend, Tess. He's like a brother to me. I know the hell both of you have gone through these last few months, and I'd sure like to see you two get together."

Tess glanced up at his open, readable face. His tone was concerned, his expression genuine. She swallowed painfully. "I didn't want to come up here, Tom," she said in a rush of words. "I couldn't get out of it. I didn't mean to make it embarrassing for Shep. God, I feel like crawling into a hole!"

"What for? You didn't do anything wrong!" Tom lowered his voice, glancing around before he spoke. "I don't know which one of you is more upset over this situation. Yet when I mention Shep's name to you, I see a light in your eyes. Why don't you two quit reacting to the gossip and begin seeing each other?"

Tess stiffened. "Because he's not officially divorced yet, Tom. That's why."

"Yes, he is. Aly took off in February. The divorce was quick and clean."

She stared up at him. "I—I didn't know," she began lamely.

Tom grimaced. "How could you? You two have been avoiding each other like the damn plague."

A trace of anger came through in her voice. "I'm sure you've heard all the juicy gossip about our affair that never happened?"

He waved his hand. "You gonna let other people tell you how to live your life, or are you gonna make the decisions?"

Tess reacted sharply. "No one runs my life!"

"No? Then how come you never answered Shep's phone calls and returned his letters unopened?" He moved a step closer, his eyes hardening. "Listen, you're playing around with my best friend. He was just as torn up over this as you were. Shep's taken it on the jaw here at Edwards from everybody. But he's taken it in stride and hasn't run away from it like you did."

Her nostrils flared in fury. "This is none of your business!" she whispered tautly. Tess turned to leave, but there was nowhere to go. The lobby was filling up with uniformed officers. She turned back toward the major, trembling. "Why are you doing this?"

His face lost some of its hardness. "Because in a few moments Shep is gonna come through those doors. He deserves your courage, Tess. He doesn't need a woman who will hide and run on him. Stay here and stick it out with him." He gave her a quick pat on the arm. "Come on, I know you're made out of strong stuff. *You* just don't know it yet," he coaxed gently.

Shep was the last to arrive. Dressed in olive green flight suit and black boots, he stood out from the rest. Her heart skyrocketed, and suddenly she felt an incredible surge of joy lifting her depression. He stood taller than most of the officers as he looked around. Looking for her? She was opening her mouth to call his name when their eyes met and locked. His gray eyes dark-

ened, and he stared across the room. He looked older.
Tired. Tess feverishly scanned his face. There was
darkness beneath his eyes and a grimmer set to his
mouth. The corners were pulled in as if he were in pain.
He had lost the golden tan, his skin now appearing to
be sallow. Had he been sick? It was summer. Shep
should have been out in the sun. Her mind spun with
bits and pieces of things she wanted to say.

Tom gripped her arm and leaned over. "Speak to
him, Tess. He's been through hell. I'll sit with you two
when it comes time to eat lunch."

Suddenly it was as if nothing else mattered. As Shep
slowly walked toward her, she wondered why she
hadn't returned his phone calls or letters. He offered
her a slight smile, taking off his flight cap, letting it
dangle from the long fingers of his left hand. After
shaking Dan's hand and trading small talk, Shep made
his way to her side.

"So, Dan finally got you up here," he said, halting
inches from where she stood.

"Drag would probably be a better word," she offered, her voice barely above a whisper. The heat of a
blush swept across her face as she saw him smile.

Shep relaxed a little. "You look pretty good for being
dragged, lady."

Tess warmed to his teasing and took a steadying
breath. "I—"

Shep shook his head. "Not here, not now, Tess," he
warned huskily. His gray eyes narrowed intently, hungrily appraising her upturned face. "I want to see you.
Alone."

She trembled inwardly at the fervor in his hushed
voice. "Yes," she agreed. "We need to talk. I need to
apologize to you for so much."

Relief washed over Shep's face. "Tell Dan I'm
driving you back to L.A. after the meeting. We can talk
in the car. Anywhere. Just as long as I can see you,

Tess. We'll meet in the bar after the meeting and then go to my car, okay?"

Sitting next to Shep at the luncheon was sweet agony. Tom sat to her left, keeping them both entertained with the latest stories and jokes. Tess maintained a professional air despite the feeling of excitement bubbling up within her. Tom had wisely chosen a table at the back of the room, out of the way of prying eyes. Occasionally, Tess would look up and catch Shep staring at her. His gray eyes were warm, searching and—she couldn't put a name on the emotion she saw in his look. Whatever it was, it sent her pulse pounding unevenly. He affected her so strongly that she never tasted the food she forced herself to eat.

The meeting took place around an oval mahogany table. Dan Williams went over technical changes and reiterated the current project schedule. The test pilots scribbled notes and asked pertinent questions concerning the modifications. They then discussed the changes with the two Rockwell engineers who had come up expressly for the meeting.

After the last questions were covered, the test pilots were dismissed. Tess immediately felt a new air of tension when General Roman and his top aides, a full colonel and a lieutenant-colonel, remained. The general stared at them from beneath his bushy brows, his thin mouth set in a grim line. A major closed the door quietly, and the four Air Force personnel stared across the table at the four Rockwell officials. Roman shot a glance at the major. The major promptly drew out a copy of *The New York Times,* placing it in front of Williams.

"What the hell is this?" Roman grated, stabbing a finger at the newspaper.

Dan picked up the paper, reading the headlines: B-1 MISMANAGEMENT TO COST BILLIONS MORE.

"Everything's breaking loose on the Hill because of

this," Roman continued stormily. "The Department of
Defense is up in arms. The B-1 office at the Pentagon is
deluged by calls from every minor and major newspaper around the country wanting to know more details
on these allegations." His green eyes hardened. "And
to top it off, Stockwell held a chalk-talk conference
with the antidefense lobbyists yesterday afternoon.
Now just what is the story on this, Williams?"

The colonel picked up where the general left off.
"Mr. Williams, we're getting a lot of heat on this issue.
We've got to effectively band together so that the
American public doesn't think their money is being
frivolously wasted by the defense industry because of
your poor management."

Williams lifted his head, his eyes flashing with anger.
"I agree we have to meet this question as a team,
General. And I also agree that there have been some
management problems at Rockwell." He jabbed his
finger down at the table, indicating the modifications to
the B-1 that they had been discussing earlier. "These
changes were not anticipated seven years ago. General
Roman, you hired us to build you the most modern,
up-to-date bomber in the world." He turned, glaring at
the general. "We're going to deliver that plane. But in
the meantime, we've updated it with seven years worth
of technology. That means electronics research, new
computer programming, changes in wiring and minor
alterations within the fuselage to accommodate these
modifications. The inflation rate is shooting straight
through the roof. Believe me, no one is more aware of
that than Rockwell."

Roman got to his feet, some of his initial anger
dissipating. He put his hands behind his back, slowly
pacing the length of the room. "The American public is
being led to think that you're being inefficient, Williams. Stockwell is making us look like fools. The

newspapers are emphasizing the higher cost of the B-1 and ignoring the reasons for the price hike."

"Typical news reporting," Williams responded tiredly. He got up, rubbing his forehead. "Look, we need to get our public relations department in touch with your public affairs people. I asked Fred Berger to make those very contacts this morning. We're going to have to launch our own campaign to combat this one-sided news reporting."

"Otherwise," the colonel broke in, "the Congress is going to be hit hard by lobby groups screaming for a scapegoat in this. And it will be the Air Force that takes the brunt of it. As usual. There are plenty of people out there who still harbor post-Vietnam antiwar feeling. They don't want to see their tax dollars going for another combat aircraft."

Roman snorted. "And what any of them fail to realize is that without a strong Strategic Air Command, the Soviets will run over us. Literally and figuratively speaking." He shook his head, suddenly looking much older. "I expect you to act on this immediately, Williams."

"We will."

The general looked down the long table at Tess. "You'd better read that paper, honey, because you're being quoted in detail."

Tess tensed, holding the general's gaze. "Sir, my name isn't honey. It's Tess Hamilton," she reminded him. This wasn't the first time Air Force men had treated her like some secretary who didn't have a brain in her head.

Roman halted, holding her angry gaze. "It's going to be mud if you don't get this problem squared away," he warned. And then he looked up at Williams. "Since when do you allow assistants to speak to senators?"

Dan glanced over at Tess. "General Roman, Tess

knows the job better than I do at this point. She's been with the program for some time. I've just stepped into it. She has full authority to speak to anyone who calls the Rockwell office." He opened his briefcase, jerking out a copy of a memo. "Here," he said tightly, throwing it at the surprised colonel. "This is a backup letter regarding Stockwell's call to our office and Mrs. Hamilton's answer. I think if you read it, you'll see that her responses were accurate and well thought out. Unfortunately, like the news media, Stockwell took what he wanted to take and left the rest of the story out."

They emerged from the animated discussion an hour later. Tess pulled Dan aside for a moment. "I'll meet you at the car in fifteen minutes, Dan."

He smiled wearily, some of his defensive armor slipping away. "Fine. But hurry, we've got a lot of dike-plugging to do when we get back to the office. We have to stop Stockwell before he ruffles any more feathers on the Hill."

She nodded, gripping his arm. "Thanks. I'll hurry." She walked quickly out of the room to the darkened area of the bar. Only a few off-duty pilots were there, and Shep was easy to spot in his green flight suit. The moment she appeared at the door, he rose, coming to meet her. Taking her arm, he escorted her outside. The wind was hot and dry, but far preferable to the icy chill of the meeting room.

Tess turned, looking up at him. "Everything's hit the fan, Shep. I've got to go back to the office with Dan."

He scowled. "What happened?"

"Stockwell took half of what I said about the cost rise on the B-1 and smeared it all over the newspapers. I've been misquoted, and now the lobby groups are pressuring the Air Force." She reached out instinctively, touching his arm. "It's going to be a long night."

He managed a cryptic smile. "Look, it's Thursday.

I've got this Sunday off. I'm not letting you go, lady, without a promise to see me then. Any plans for that day?"

Tess felt her heart begin to race unevenly as he reached over, gently capturing several strands of her hair and tucking them behind her ear. A shiver coursed through her as his fingers brushed against her skin. She had forgotten how wonderful his touch was and found herself craving more of him. "I—no."

"Good. Because I'm going to steal you away to my mountain retreat. I'll call you Friday afternoon at the office and we'll discuss the details. Fair enough?"

She nodded. Despite the emergency situation Tess felt buoyed up with hope. Shep made her feel as if she could tackle any problem successfully. A soft smile touched her lips as she gazed up into his light gray eyes. "Fair enough."

His call came at three P.M. Friday afternoon. Tess answered her phone for the fiftieth time that day. "Tess Hamilton speaking."

"You don't say? Are you ready to be stolen away on Sunday?" Shep asked, his voice husky.

Tess leaned her forehead against her hand, releasing a sigh. "It's so good to hear a friendly voice!"

"That bad?"

"Horrible. Stockwell really stuck it to us this time. He's got every major antidefense lobby group screaming for an accounting of what's going on."

"Your weekend still open?"

Tess closed her eyes. "Saturday isn't. And Sunday is iffy. Dan and I stayed up until two this morning, and then it started again at eight. We're both beat."

"Do you like the mountains?" he asked, his tone melting away her tension.

"Love them. Why?"

"We'll spend a day at a rustic cabin up in the Sierras.

I know a beautiful spot among the sequoias above Bakersfield. Sound good?"

She laughed softly. "It sounds like heaven!"

"No, lady, you're heaven. How about if I pick you up at nine o'clock Sunday morning? We'll have breakfast on the road and reach the cabin about noon."

A clean feeling rushed over her tense body. "It sounds wonderful, Shep," she agreed. "I'll see you at nine, then."

"Be sure to bring along jeans, climbing shoes, and socks. This is strictly civilian attire. No uniforms to remind us of our jobs or responsibilities."

"I wish it were nine A.M. right now," she confided fervently.

Chapter 6

THE DOORBELL RANG. OR DID IT SING? TESS HURRIEDLY dashed burgundy lipstick across her mouth and walked quickly from the bedroom. Taking the stairs two at a time, she reached the bottom, hurried to the foyer, and opened the door. Shep stood there, hands resting on his hips, looking boyish in well-worn jeans and a western shirt with the sleeves rolled upon his forearms. Gone was the veneer of the career Air Force officer. He looked years younger, standing before her with the dark shadows gone from beneath his mirthful gray eyes. He shared a warm smile with her. "Are you the same Tess Hamilton that works at Rockwell?" he teased.

She stepped aside, allowing him to enter. "Does a pair of jeans and a pink tank top change me that much?"

Shep raised an eyebrow, a wicked glint in his gaze. "You have no idea how great you look, lady," he said, his gaze sweeping her from head to toe.

Tess blushed fiercely. "Womanizer," she accused, "you test pilots are all alike! I'll be right back. I packed a small bag." She hurried down the hall, feeling the heat prickling in her cheeks. Her heart sang with

newfound happiness. She had lain awake half the night
wondering if she should go with Shep or not. It had
only been seven months since Cy's death. One part of
her cried out for some harmless form of male compan-
ionship. A larger part of her shied away from any
contact with a man. Worriedly she picked up the canvas
bag and her denim jacket and tried to push those
depressing thoughts out of her anxious mind. Marshal-
ing her courage, Tess decided that she *would* enjoy the
day.

At nine o'clock in the morning, the L.A. freeways
were fairly clear of traffic going south. But going north,
traffic was heavy. It seemed as if half the city wanted to
escape to the mountains. Shep maneuvered skillfully
around the hulking campers of other vacationers. Soon
they were up and over the Grapevine, a long, winding
section of the freeway going over the mountains near
Bakersfield. The sun was warm through the car's tinted
windshield, the sky a cleaner blue as they left the smog
behind them. Tess rested her head against the seat,
simply enjoying Shep's closeness.

"Tired?" he inquired sometime later.

She moved her head to the left, opening her eyes. "A
little."

"A lot, I think. Did you get that news problem
straightened out?"

"Somewhat. Newspapers are funny—if it's a shocking headline, they'll print it instantly. But if it's ho-hum
facts and figures, they either won't print it, or they print
it and stick it in some itty-bitty corner where no one will
see it."

Shep shook his head. "It must be incredibly frustrat-
ing."

Tess waved her hand and muttered. "Let's quit
talking shop. I need a little R and R."

"Okay, you've got a deal. Let's talk about you,
instead."

She shook her head. "No way. Let's get on a safer subject: you."

He grinned. "That's a pretty boring subject. I'd rather talk about you. Your past. Where you grew up. What kind of parents you have. Things like that." He met her gaze warmly. "That's not talking shop."

She pursed her lips. "No," she admitted hesitantly, "it isn't."

"What's the matter, are you classified top secret?" he teased.

Tess grinned. "No. But I am off limits in certain ways," she warned seriously.

He shrugged. "Is that what has you worried?" he asked softly.

"Well—"

"Relax, my Irish lass. Today is a day for friendship. Feel better now?"

Tess gave him a cautious look. "Quit looking like the cat that swallowed the canary, Shep Ramsey. You could have told me that earlier and I wouldn't have lost half a night's sleep worrying about it!"

It was his turn to smile. Reaching out, he captured her hand, and gave it a firm squeeze. "Look, we both need the time, Tess. Time to relax and get to know each other. We've been through a hell of a lot. And I think the mountains are a good place to relax, talk, and do some walking together. That's all I want from you, lady."

Her heart blossomed with the unspoken love she felt toward him. His voice was deep and filled with undisguised emotion. Tess reluctantly pulled her fingers from his hand, guilt reestablishing itself within her heart. "It sounds wonderful," she whispered, meaning it. Oh, God, why couldn't she quit feeling miserable? Her heart sang with joy at being with Shep once again. Why couldn't her damned head forget the past? Forget her transgressions? She chewed on her lower lip, aware of the warring emotions clashing within her. Tess didn't want to share her anguish with Shep. He had suffered enough. Desperately, she forced her mind to concentrate only on the beauty around them.

They followed a winding road high into the Sierras. Everywhere Tess looked, giant sequoias towered above them. The white pine, blue spruce, and tamarack were dwarfed in comparison to this race of giants that ruled the western side of the mountain range. They stopped at Giant Lodge and a new thrill of excitement raced through her. Getting out of the car Shep shrugged on a knapsack, and led her near the edge of a huge granite escarpment where they stood and overlooked the V-shaped valley below them.

Tess felt as if years of responsibility were slipping from her shoulders as she stood there next to him. The sun was high above them on that June afternoon. Bluejays squawked raucously from a nearby spruce tree. Shep's face revealed his eagerness to begin the hike. Tess had never seen him so animated. It was as if all the military veneer and seriousness had disappeared beneath the magic of the pure mountain air. His happiness infected her with joy and she smiled brilliantly at him.

"I come up here every chance I get," Shep murmured. He lifted his head toward the sun, drinking in the warmth it offered. "This is a healing place. As a matter of fact, the Indians consider this whole area sacred ground."

Tess smiled. "Now you sound like my grandmother."

"I always love throwing off the trappings of civilization and getting back into the wilderness where we belong. Did your grandmother have a love of the forest?

Tess gave him a fond smile. "I'll tell you about her sometime, Shep. I think you'd both get along very well because of your love of the woods."

He reached out and gripped her hand, pulling her along. "Come on, this is our time," he coaxed softly.

She was caught up in the magic of the cathedrallike surroundings. Breathing deeply, Tess allowed him to guide her to a small trail which led down into the quiet valley below them.

The silence was comforting as they walked down the steep trail that wound between huge boulders and small trees that would someday grow into enormous sequoias. Here and there chipmunks scampered across their path. Civilization was left behind. They were as alone as if they were the only two people who existed in the whole world. At one point Shep halted, leading her to a rock outcropping. A fine film of perspiration covered his face. He sat beneath a small pine, inviting her to sit next to him.

His hard body was warm as she rested her back against his shoulder. Digging into the knapsack, he produced a small box of raisins, handing them to her. "This will keep your energy up," he explained, looking over at her intently.

Tess felt her breath stop, her heart hammering in her breast. His eyes were a light gray and eaglelike in intensity as he hungrily gazed at her upturned face. She reached for the raisins, their hands making contact. An electric impulse surged up her arm, sending a dizzy feeling through her.

"God, you're beautiful," he breathed. Her hair, which had been pulled back into a chignon, had been loosened by the wind. Tendrils curled damply around her forehead and cheeks, softening the natural angularity of her features. Her eyes, once lifeless, now glowed with new hope. There was color once again in her flushed cheeks, making her radiant. He turned around, facing her. "Just one thing is missing," he murmured. He reached out, gently loosening the pins which kept her glorious mane of auburn hair captive. The strands

were like clean silk through his fingers as the knot
uncurled, the cascade overflowing into his hands. A
look of satisfaction came to his gray eyes as he coaxed
the strands across her shoulders so that they curved
below her breasts.

Tess's heart ached with new awareness of him as a
man. His gesture had been simple, yet so eloquent. It
touched Tess deeply and she managed a smile. "I'm
having a tough time remembering that you're a test
pilot who thinks in unromantic terms of mathematics,
electrical engineering, maps, and graphs," she murmured.

Shep reluctantly removed his fingers from the silken
gold and red tresses. The sunlight filtering through the
boughs of the pine struck her head, creating a halo-like
effect around her beautiful auburn hair. He sat back,
satisfied, resting his arms against his knees as he studied
her. "Doesn't everyone have a more vulnerable, sensitive side to themselves that they tend to hide from the
world at large?" he asked.

Tess nodded, studying him silently. His face was
open and readable. His gray eyes alive, a burning flame
deep in their recesses that sent an ache through her
body. No longer were the lines of responsibility etched
around his mouth and across his forehead. She picked
up a few brown pine needles, running her slender
fingers across the dried exterior, feeling for the life
within.

"Yes," she answered slowly, her voice barely audible
above the sighing of the wind through the boughs of the
tree. "I like this part of Shep Ramsey. Why do you hide
it? I don't understand."

He cocked his head to one side, silent laughter in his
gray gaze. "And you don't hide the real you? Do you
know what I see before me now? A girl-woman who is a
part of this natural environment. And who did I see at
that party where we met? A beautifully dressed woman

making polite conversation with her business associ-
ates. And how about Thursday? Your hair was drawn
back to make you look older. The dress you wore spoke
of your good taste. But it was business. Everything
about you has been business up until today." He smiled
gently. "You're a farm girl at heart, Tess. Look at
you—you pick up the pine needles in your hands to feel
their texture, to smell their scent. Earlier I saw you stop
and run your hand down the trunk of a fir just to feel
the roughness of the bark. And you should see your
face . . ." He ruefully shook his head. "You and I both
hide our real selves from the world."

Tess colored, but for once she wasn't embarassed by
the blush that swept across her freckled cheeks. "Typical test pilot," she muttered, getting to her feet and
dusting off her pants. "Always observing everything.
Even little, minute things."

Shep slowly got to his feet, shrugging on the knapsack. He reached over, capturing her hand. "I have
other observations to make, too, but I'll save them for a
more appropriate time," he murmured, watching her
eyes widen in surprise. As they continued down a
narrow deer path, Shep lapsed into silence with Tess at
his side, her hand in his. Everything seems so natural,
he thought, finally feeling at peace for the first time
since Cy's death.

The urge to stop and simply take her into his arms
and kiss her was overpowering. But they had time now
and Shep didn't want to rush her. He gave an imperceptible shake of his head, realizing that they had
literally crashed into one another at the party. It had
been instant attraction so powerful that neither could
think coherently. He remembered that night. Tess was
no longer that unsure young woman. She seemed to
have matured overnight. But in the process she had lost
the spontaneity, the naturalness he had once admired.

Shep squeezed her hand momentarily. I'll help you

regain that part of yourself, he said in his mind. I'll give you the love and support to be all that you can be, Tess. One day . . .

At the bottom of the narrow valley they came upon a small stream that rushed over multicolored rocks of all shapes and sizes. Shep urged her to drink from it. Tess knelt down, cupping the water in her hands, sipping it cautiously. As she raised her head up, her face registered a mixture of surprise and delight. The water was icy cold and sweet. He smiled, pulling out a small woven tablecloth of bright red and spreading it beneath the large arms of a sequoia. The tree seemed to be king of the entire valley, proudly surveying all in its realm. She got to her feet and joined Shep. Even now her heart pounded with awareness of him. Tess found herself wanting to be close to him, to be touched by him.

"What's for lunch? I'm starved," she said, smiling.

"Would you believe chicken salad sandwiches, apples and M & M's for dessert?"

Tess giggled. "M & M's? Are you expecting to lure leprechauns from the depths of the forest by leaving them a few morsels under a tree?"

"No, they're for us. Not leprechauns!"

She pouted momentarily, her blue eyes alive with mirth. "Spoilsport. Killing all my wild imaginings."

Shep handed her a sandwich. "Sorry, lass. I guess the practical side of my nature wins out. The chocolate is a good source of energy."

"It's a good thing yours does because mine doesn't. Not on a day like this." She inhaled deeply, feeling giddy and childlike once again.

He smiled. "We're a natural balance for one another," he said softly. He winked at her. "You go on imagining that there are fairies or leprechauns."

She sighed comfortably. "How did you know that as a child I was always dreaming?"

"I see the daydreamer in you. It's in your lovely blue eyes." He grinned wickedly. "Just how the hell did you get an MBA, lady? Why didn't you end up an artist? Or a writer?"

Tess returned the grin, hungrily biting into one of the delicious-tasting sandwiches. "I was hot on math as a two-year-old. Does that explain it?"

"And when did you do all this dreaming?" he prodded.

"Oh, I'd be up in my room hurrying to get my homework done. Then I'd sit by the window, watching the sunset. I'd watch the colors change, imagining that there was an invisible artist up there in the sky with a brush rearranging colors right before my eyes. Sometimes there would be broad, bold strokes and other times, soft watercolor tints from his magic palette of paints." She gave him a sheepish look. "Does that sound crazy?"

Shep shook his head. "No," he answered seriously. "Because when I'm flying up there at the limits of the sky I always feel like I'm a part of something greater."

She tilted her head. "Oh? In what way? Describe it to me."

"Promise you won't laugh?" he asked.

"Scout's honor," she returned solemnly.

He finished his sandwich and rested his head against the tree, looking up through the thick, powerful limbs that held scraggly fan-shaped leaves. "Sometimes, Tess, in a quiet moment when we aren't running tests, I'll go up in a T-38 just to escape the confines of the earth. I like to get away from the people, the noises, the crowded space. I can be tense and have a splitting headache when I strap into the cockpit. But climbing into that blue sky with nothing but vivid color surrounding me, the quiet vibration of the plane slips away, and I feel like I'm one with the sky." He lifted his head, staring into her wide azure eyes. Eyes that he could drown himself in. "It's an indescribable feeling. As if I've become a part of something larger, more spiritual, if you will, in that moment of time. When I fly back and land, I feel at peace within. My tension is gone, the headache has disappeared and I'm happy again." He shook his head ruefully. "Maybe I'm just running away for an hour or so to recapture my sanity. I don't know."

Tess reached over, placing her hand on his arm, feeling the tautness of his skin, the wiry texture of the dark hair on it. "No," she whispered, "it's a healing place for you." Her lips parted, full and inviting. "My grandmother, Caitlin O'Gentry, gave me my link with nature. She taught me that everything is alive. This tree, that plant. Even the rocks hold a living spirit. And yes, she taught me to believe in fairies, gnomes, elves and leprechauns. She used to steal me away to her home on weekends." Tess laughed softly in remembrance. "Gram used to tell my Mom and Dad that they should let me grow up like a normal child." Her eyes grew misty. "She used to tell me she was rescuing me from all the schoolwork. Gram felt I devoted too much time to study and not enough time to play. She made up for what I was missing. I'd go walking with her on early mornings just as the sun was peeking over the horizon and the dew was still on the plants. Gram would stop at certain places and ask me to close my eyes and tell her what I felt. Or heard."

Shep gently entwined his fingers through her own. "And what did you feel or hear?"

She closed her eyes, caught up in the fond memories of days that had meant so much to her. "I thought I heard laughter sometimes. At first I told Gram it was the wind in the trees. And she'd laugh in her kindly fashion and tell me to open my eyes. There would be not a breeze moving through the trees. And then she would ask me to close my eyes and feel." Tess turned, taking in his understanding face. "At different spots where we walked, I could feel a warmth or love surrounding us. In some areas, there would be an incredible sense of peace or protection. In others, disharmony." She blushed, averting her gaze. "I'm sure this sounds crazy!"

Shep shook his head. "No, honey. Because I get that same feeling of peace and contentment when I'm up in the sky." He stared at her intently. She was so close . . . so incredibly alive, pulsing with the heartbeat of the world around them. He reached out, sliding his fingers across her shoulder, pulling her toward him. Bringing her chin up, he captured her face, lowering his head to meet her parting lips.

His mouth brushed across her lips. Tess shivered outwardly, wildly aware of his roughened fingers against the curve of her jaw, holding her captive to his searching, hungry mouth. The second time he kissed her, it took her breath away. His mouth pressed firmly against her lips, questing, branding. The natural scent of his body was a heady aphrodisiac, sending her senses spinning, out-of-control. A soft moan rose in her throat as his tongue stroked the inner recesses of her mouth, tasting, tantalizing her to join him. She turned, pressing herself against his chest, her arm curving naturally around his neck in response. The warmth of his breath fanned across her face. His mouth grew gentle with her lips once again, inviting her participation. Wanting, needing her to return his ardor.

Shep groaned as he felt the tentative pressure of her lips against his mouth. He sensed her building desire, her hesitancy, her lips soft and tremulous beneath his own. Gently he eased the pressure, allowing her to explore him at her own pace. He fought for control of his raging hunger. It would be so easy to lower her to the scented carpet of pine needles and make love to her. So easy. . . . The tentative touch of her lips against his own was devastating to his crumbling defenses. She was a butterfly barely touching his mouth. She smelled of pine, fresh air, and the musky scent of her own body.

Tess felt bereft as he gently pulled away from her. Her eyes were dazed looking as she searched his face. She trembled beneath the hands he placed on her shoulders. Heart pounding, she felt molten fire throbbing and pulsing within her. Just a kiss? she thought. No, it had been much more than that. She stared at Shep in childlike wonder.

He took a deep breath, gripping her shoulders and giving her a small shake. "God, you're so much a woman," he breathed solidly. "And if I kiss you one more time, I won't be responsible," he continued thickly. "You need time. I've got to give it to you, honey. You can't be rushed." He expelled a long breath, allowing his hands to drop away. Leaning back against the tree he muttered, "God, I want you so much."

Tess closed her eyes, getting to her knees, hands clasped in her lap. What was happening? Her body seemed to have a life of its own. She had never experienced such huge draughts of pleasure through the simple act of kissing. Cy had never provoked such violent desire in her. She gravely met Shep's dark eyes. The fierce intensity of passion in them sent a shiver of expectancy through her. The realization that she wanted him just as much as he wanted her shook her completely.

"Shep, I—"

He reached out, sliding his fingers down her arm. "Ssshh, words aren't necessary. Just feel, Tess. Just feel. . . ."

Chapter 7

TESS GROANED AS SHE TOOK OFF HER SHOES, TENDERLY rubbing her sore feet. She sat at a table on the small porch of the cabin. The two-room structure was made from rough-cut whole logs which had been painted a rust brown color. Shep glanced up after depositing an armload of cut wood beside the iron cooking stove.

"Blisters?"

"No. They're just a little achy. I'm not used to traveling on foot more than one floor at a time, you know."

He grinned, rising to his full height. As the day had unfolded, Tess had seen a miraculous change in Shep. She marveled at his knowledge of the forest and its inhabitants. They must have hiked at least ten miles that afternoon before returning in the early evening to the cabin. She had had such a delightful time that the miles and hours had slipped away without notice. And that one unforgettable kiss. . . . Tess raised her head, staring at Shep's mouth, which was now fixed in a wicked smile. She returned it, enjoying the sparkle of silver deep in his eyes as he came around and sat down with her at the small wood table.

"Here," he murmured, "the least I can do is rub the lady's feet for her. Sit back and enjoy it."

She laughed, allowing him to place her leg across his thigh. Very gently, he began to stroke away the miles. Tess closed her eyes. "This is ecstasy!" she moaned, delighting in his skillful manipulation of her aching feet.

"You're not getting off scot-free, you know," he growled.

Tess opened one eye, giving him a wary look. "Oh?"

"Up here in the mountains we all pitch in and help. I'll let you off easy tonight. If you'll peel the potatoes, I'll get the fire started."

"Who's cooking?" she asked.

"Me. Why? Don't you think pilots can do the menial, earthbound things performed by the rest of the populace?"

She grinned. "Who knows? I've heard that you test pilots with the golden arms are so highly trained that you aren't like the rest of us common folk!"

Shep gave her an intent look. "It's a good thing I've rescued you from that narrow line of thinking, lady." He released one leg and brought up the other, beginning to massage the foot. "Golden arm or no golden arm, we're human. Very human," he added huskily.

Tess avoided his eyes, knowing instinctively what he meant. Ever since the kiss, there had been a pulsing, subtle excitement between them. New ties had been established in those fragile, beautiful moments. Her body responded to his searching gray gaze, and she warmed beneath his stare. "So human that you can burn a meal?" she retorted genially. "Really, I'll do the cooking if you want," she offered.

Shep glanced at the black stove. "You ever cooked on one of these things?"

"Well . . . no . . . ."

"It's a wood fire and it heats unevenly depending

upon the type of wood being used. If the wood is too dry, it burns hot and fast—which means your meal can get done too quickly or get burned. And if it's green wood, it's a low-heat fire, and then nothing gets done very fast."

"Doesn't sound too promising," she decided. "You act as if you know what you're doing. I'll be the helper tonight."

He smiled wryly, giving the bottom of her foot a pat. "I always knew you were practical when it counted," he said, rising. "Tonight we'll have steak, fried potatoes and a salad. How does that sound?"

Tess laughed. "Wonderful! Who would think you would know so much about so many things?"

He moved around the small porch, beginning to build a fire in the old iron stove. "Stick around, lady," he murmured, "there's more that I want to share and show you," he promised, glancing over at her in the twilight.

The meal had been succulent. They sat at the table, their elbows propped up on the surface, slowly sipping rosé wine from plastic cups. The last vestige of dusk had long since been swallowed up by the encroaching night. Tess heard the laughter and voices of other campers at cabins to the right of them. "Up here," she mused softly, "it seems like everyone laughs a lot."

Shep stirred, gazing across the table at her. "Up here, there's an air of relaxation. Of peace. You can feel it." He set his cup down. "Feel like a walk?" he offered.

She pursed her lips. "You'd better define walk, Shep Ramsey. The last time it ended up being ten miles."

He got up, ambled around the table and held out his hand to her. "Just to Beetle Rock," he promised.

She tilted her head. "Where's that?"

"You don't trust me?"

Grinning, she got up. "No."

He clasped her hand, pulling her beside him, slipping his arm around her waist. An unnamed happiness coursed through him as she slid her arm around his waist. "Beetle Rock is that granite escarpment we first walked across this morning." He led her down the three wooden steps and guided her from the pine-needled carpet to the rock. "There. We're on Beetle Rock now. Think you can walk a few feet further?"

Tess laughed fully, pressing her head momentarily against his shoulder. "Okay, I owe you an apology!"

"Are all Irishwomen so distrustful, I wonder?" he mused.

Tess barely heard his teasing retort. Her lips parted as her gaze swept upward. "Oh, Shep . . ." she breathed.

He stopped, holding her close, enjoying her response to the newly fallen night. Above them a ceiling of stars appeared so close that all one had to do was reach out and touch them. The Milky Way lay slightly to the north, like a sandy shore with thousands of stars posing as grains of sand. To the south was an area of darkness that appeared to be a cosmic ocean in the heavens crashing toward that star-laden shore. He leaned over, inhaling her natural sweet scent, placing a kiss on her hair. "Beautiful, isn't it?" he murmured.

Tess trembled within his embrace as she stared skyward in awe. "They're so bright!" she exclaimed.

"No smog up here, thank God," he growled. "Also, we're at seven thousand feet, and that makes us closer to the heavens."

She turned, facing him. "Do you realize how long it's been since I saw stars shining like this? Why, it must be at least ten years!"

He smiled down at her. "You mean the lady with the MBA living in her ivory tower at Rockwell misses all this?"

"What are you trying to say?"

Slipping his other arm around her waist, he drew her gently against him. Her thighs fitted snugly against his legs, sending an aching awareness through every fiber of his body. He tilted his head, gazing down at her questioning features. A curious smile played on his mouth as he studied her in the intervening silence. "Do you really want to know, Irish princess?" he murmured.

Tess barely nodded, resting her hands against the wall of his chest. "Yes," she answered, her voice barely audible, "I want to know what you think."

He lifted his head, staring out into the darkness of the valley they had walked in earlier. "When I first saw you, I thought you looked conspicuously out of place. I was struck by the fact that you looked so fresh and vibrantly alive compared to everyone else at that party. While they were wearing the latest designer outfits, you came dressed in a very old-fashioned, beautiful gown of ivory and lace." A tender smile pulled at the corners of his mouth. "In your own way, Tess, I think you were making a statement about yourself. Maybe you didn't even realize it consciously yourself. You are different from the people who inhabit the business world you live in."

"Survive in would be more like it," she said, frowning. Shep was too close and too alluring. Gently she stepped away, silently asking to be released. Reluctantly, he allowed his arms to drop. She turned away, chewing on her lower lip. "I'm coming to realize that I really don't know myself," she admitted. Wrapping her arms against her breast she walked a few more feet and stopped. "Every day I go to work, Shep, it's an uphill battle. It seems as though all the men in management below me are jealous of my position. I know they'd like to get rid of me, but so far I've managed to stay one step ahead of them."

She turned, her face filled with pain. "I don't know what a test pilot's world is like, but I can tell you it's hell in my world. There are so few women in management in Rockwell." She gave a shrug. "Of course, it's part of the defense industry, so it's no wonder chauvinism exists. It's a male bastion, so to speak." She walked back to where he was standing. "When Cy brought me in as his assistant, I took the heat from the women below me. The men figured that I was little more than a bed warmer to keep Cy company." Her eyes darkened. "That hurt, Shep. It hurt me deeply. You tease me about my MBA. Some of the men say I slept with my professors to get that too."

He reached out, gently stroking her cheek. "If it helps any, Tess, I know you earned every bit of that degree. And further more, princess, you're holding your own now even without Cy being there. Aren't you?"

She hung her head, compressing her lips. "Yes. And that's causing another ripple in the company. Now that they know I can do my job, some of them are plotting to get rid of me in other ways." Tears welled up in her eyes as she looked up at him. "Damn it, Shep, why are they doing this? I used to be so idealistic. I came to Rockwell with a burning team spirit. All for one and one for all." She wiped a lone tear away in a cutting motion. "I'm too trusting, I've found out. Do I have to take on masculine characteristics in order to survive? To keep my job?"

He frowned. "Come on, let's walk a little," he suggested, bringing her beside him. The night was cool but sun-warmed granite still provided some warmth. Shep guided her down an incline and brought her to a stop at a rocky outcropping. After pulling her down beside him, he kept his arm around her shoulder. "You are living in a different world from me, Tess," he began. "Although in some ways, Air Force politics are just as fierce." He turned, resting his head against her hair. "You're going to have to toughen up in order to survive. You'll have to learn their games and play it their way if you want to stay."

"Does that mean distrusting these men and not believing anything they say until I can learn the truth myself?" she asked bitterly.

"Yes, you must learn to correctly judge people and protect yourself from the backbiters."

"Whatever happened to the Golden Rule?" she complained miserably.

Shep smiled, loving her closeness. "Didn't they teach you business politics when you got your MBA?"

She shrugged, sniffing. "They hinted at it. I guess they figure if you're going after an MBA, you've got the heart of a shark, the mind of a weasel, and the soul of a barracuda going for you," she returned, anger in her voice.

"And you're not like that."

"No, not by nature. I get pleasure from the challenge of my job. I don't get a thrill stepping on someone's head to make a point."

"You're a guppy, not a barracuda," he soothed, smiling down into her blue eyes.

A smile fled across her lips. "Do all test pilots have that die-hard sense of humor?"

He laughed softly, giving her a reassuring hug. "Yeah, I suppose we do. Look," he murmured, getting serious once again, "keep your eyes and ears open, Tess. Don't get caught in the crossfire of politics if you can help it. If things get nasty, you and I can discuss it. I don't want to brag, but I'm pretty aware of politics and maybe I can give you some pointers. Just know that I'm here. A shoulder to cry on."

She sniffed, wiping the tears from her cheeks with

the back of her hand. "That's all I do around you. Don't you get tired of it?"

Shep slowly got to his feet, pulling her up. She leaned tiredly against him, head on his shoulder, for a long, heart-stopping moment. He pressed a kiss to her hair. "I'll never get tired of you, lady. Come on," he coaxed, "let's get you back to L.A. You're exhausted."

Tess nodded. "But it's a good kind of exhaustion, Shep. For once I wore myself out physically." She cast a grim look in his direction. "At least I didn't flay myself emotionally today." The answering pressure of his arms was comforting. How many times each day had she felt guilt and remorse over Cy's death? Every time she thought about the possibility of meeting Derek Barton either by chance or in a business meeting, her stomach knotted. What would she do? How would she handle it?

Monday was going to come too soon, Tess realized. Precious, quiet moments like this were only an instant's reprieve from the harshness of the real world. Taking a deep breath, she bowed her head, doggedly walking beside Shep in silence.

Tess walked into the office at seven thirty A.M. and knew it was going to be a bad day. Dan's secretary was already hard at work, and all three buttons on the telephone were blinking, indicating waiting calls. Grimly, Tess pressed on toward her office, trying to internally fortify herself. Where had the weekend gone? Was it only a lovely dream? She didn't ever want to push Sunday out of her mind or her heart. A warm feeling uncoiled from the center of her body as Tess remembered Shep's kiss. It would have been so easy to allow him to make love to her. But she wasn't emotionally cleansed of her own guilt. Shep had accepted that unspoken rule without pressuring her. And by doing that, he had allowed her to be herself. Something that she desperately needed in the present chaos that surrounded her.

"Tess!" Dan called, waving her into his office.

She stopped, turning into the brightly sunlit area. "All hell has broken loose with this Stockwell allegation," he informed her. "Public relations has scheduled a news briefing for the press at nine this morning. I want you to attend."

She nodded. "Okay, I'll get together with PR and see what they need in the way of information." She hurried to her office and picked up the phone. Fred Berger, the head of Rockwell PR, answered, his voice suave and cool as ever.

"Fred, this is Tess. Dan just told me—"

"This is it, Tess. We've got every antidefense reporter in L.A. coming to this briefing. And they're armed to the teeth with Stockwell's allegations. You got the facts and figures on the B-1 scheduling with you?"

"Yes. I'll bring all pertinent information to your office right away and maybe we can parry their misguided attack."

"Rabid is more like it," Fred returned drolly. "Look, I'm going to need you or Dan at that press briefing. I know they're going to hit us with some hair-raising technical questions."

"You've got it," she promised grimly, cursing Stockwell in the back of her mind.

Tess tried to appear relaxed in the midst of the flashing cameras and television lights. The large press room was filled to capacity, and there was an explosive feeling in it, a restlessness that made her want to fidget. She admired Fred's coolness in the face of the relentless press. They were after blood on this one. Once again she mentally reviewed her conversation with Stockwell. Had she been diplomatic enough? Had she not expressed herself properly? Stop it, she reprimanded herself. You did the best you could with the facts. Facts.

That was laughable. The press was here this morning
with half facts. Half truths. Grimly she pursed her lips,
waiting.

Fred took control of the press briefing, pointing to
the scheduled timetable and explaining why certain
portions of the B-1 production had fallen behind. His
explanation was exactly what she had told Stockwell.
Scanning the faces of the reporters, Tess knew they
weren't satisfied with the answer. They didn't want to
hear the truth. They wanted to blow it completely out
of proportion for the sake of sensationalism.

Immediately after Fred had finished, there was a
deluge of questions.

"You keep saying that Rockwell is behind because of
production problems. If you have blueprints, engineers, and schedules, how could you be so many
months behind? Aren't these delays going to cost the
taxpayers even more money?"

Fred glanced over at Tess. He introduced her to the
press. She got up, walked to the podium, and adjusted
the microphone. The flash of bulbs unsettled her but
she remained outwardly calm. She handled the first few
questions smoothly, but felt a surge of anger when one
of the reporters began harassing her.

"Did you fall behind simply because you're getting
into unknown areas or are you mismanaging the problems that have come up?" he asked.

"When you have an engineering development program where you are working on the very frontiers of
technology, you must deal with unknown factors," Tess
explained patiently. "The schedule I've laid out for you
represents our master plan. It is composed of twenty-
two thousand interrelated activities. I'm afraid you
can't merely put on more workers to solve some of
these complex technological problems. Rest assured
that we are doing everything possible to get back on
schedule."

But the reporter was not satisfied. "That might solve your funding problem in fiscal year 1974, but it doesn't solve the problem in '75 or '76. I mean, we all know the facts of life on a major development program. Any delay costs money because of our present six to eight percent inflation."

"If you'll go to the third paragraph on page three of the document we handed out to you, you'll see that we've addressed that question. We're counting on Congress to avoid complicating matters any further. They provide the funding. If it's on time, we will be too."

"But you're behind because of mismanagement?" he repeated doggedly.

Tess gripped the podium. "No, sir, we are not. I'll try to put this in simpler terms. We're behind because this is an advanced technology prototype. We're dealing with human beings who, with all their years of experience at scheduling, have done the best that they could under the circumstances. If we were building a second, third, or fourth B-1, the time would be cut down a great deal. On this prototype no one wants to hurry and make mistakes at the cost of men's lives."

Afterward, Tess went back to her office and collapsed in the chair. She rubbed her head, grimacing as the pain shot sporadically through her temples. Fred ambled in a few minutes later, smiling broadly.

"Hey, sure you don't want to transfer over to public relations and work with us?"

She gave him a half smile. "No, thanks! I felt like you threw me to the vultures."

"Actually, you kept them at bay. You did a real good job, Tess," he complimented.

Looking up at him she asked, "Why can't they understand the simplicity of our problem? A new airplane takes a longer time to build than one that's already in production. Plus," she growled, "we've had seven years' worth of catch-up to do. Don't they realize what seven years of technology means? It's like going from the cave era to the computer, in some respects. Especially in avionics."

He pursed his lips, agreeing. "Listen, the press never wants to be educated on the details. All they salivate for is the one statement that will make a story. Regardless of whether it's only half the truth." He smiled. "Great job, Tess. Hope the rest of your day is a little less hectic."

Chapter 8

SENATOR DIANE BROWNING LOOKED UP WHEN SHE HEARD her assistant, Greg Saint, groan. "Here he comes, Senator," was all he said. She wondered to herself how Chad Stockwell could have had the luck of stumbling into her at an out-of-the-way restaurant. Rarely did she frequent the posh establishments and eateries of the Hill. Today she had gone to her favorite haunt, the Golden Parasol Club in Alexandria, for a quiet lunch. The interior of the restaurant had a 1920's atmosphere and was decorated with old bicycles on the walls, their tires and chains interspersed with pastel-colored umbrellas here and there. The columns were encased by mirrors, giving the spacious rooms an even airier feeling. The judicious use of hanging plants made the restaurant a pleasant, peaceful escape from the pressured workaday world. Senator Browning's wing-shaped golden brows knitted together momentarily. She glanced to her left. "He's by himself," she murmured. "I wonder if he's meeting someone or . . ."

Greg grimaced. "Knowing him, he's hunted you down for a reason."

Diane grinned slightly, nodding in Stockwell's direction as he spotted her. "God knows, he must feel out of place here, where only working people come to eat. He must feel like a fish out of water." Indeed, Stockwell always made sure he was seen at the most glamorous powerbroker settings in the District. "Do me a favor, Greg," she murmured, affixing a smile on her thin lips. "Take the car back. I'll get a cab or a ride back with him. He looks like he wants to twist arms a little. No sense in your getting in the middle of it."

Greg rose unhappily. "I'll grab a roast beef sandwich on my way back. You want a bulletproof vest?"

Diane's green eyes sparkled with challenge. "No, but our good friend the senator might wish for one when it's all over."

"The turkey deserves it. See you later, Senator."

Chad Stockwell smiled equitably as he approached. "You're a hard lady to track down, Senator. Mind if I join you for an impromptu lunch?"

Diane gestured for him to sit opposite her at the table.

"Not at all, Senator."

Stockwell gave her his best political smile. "Wanted to chat about the lack of progress on the B-1. Has the Rockwell lobby been keeping you up to date on the plane's problems?"

Diane fingered the menu, keeping her eyes trained on it and not him. "I've been in touch with the Air Force people over at the Pentagon. I'm looking into your allegations about appropriations money being wasted, if that's what you're referring to," she answered slowly.

The waitress came by and they ordered lunch and drinks. Diane ordered a Kahlua and coffee. Stockwell ordered Scotch. She wanted to keep her mind sharp for the confrontation. If his satisfied expression was anything to go by, he must feel the conversation was already in the bag. His bag.

Stockwell toyed with the plastic stir stick in the drink. "You probably realize that the unit cost of one B-1 bomber used to be forty-four million dollars." He released a painful sigh, wrinkling his brow. "Add to that the cost of research, development, testing, and evaluation, and the total unit price shoots to fifty-four million dollars per aircraft. Let's see, if you multiply that figure times the 244 aircraft that are supposed to be ordered, we come up with an eleven-billion-dollar price tag."

He smiled wolfishly at Browning. "Do you realize that averages out to around fifty-five dollars from every man, woman and child in the U.S. to pay for this fiasco?"

Diane took a sip of her drink, watching him over the rim. Setting the glass down with careful deliberation, she folded her hands in front of her, leaning forward on her elbows. "First, the forty-four million also includes ground support equipment and spares, and it applies only to the prototype unit. Second, you're confusing 'then' dollars with 'now' dollars. It's inflation that is responsible for escalating the original price per unit to new highs, not mismanagement of the program. I'm sure the Air Force and Rockwell are not out to take money indiscriminately from the public. I hope you understand that I'm just as concerned about this problem as you."

The waitress brought their lunches, providing a lull in the conversation. When she had left, Diane launched into her reasons for supporting the B-1. It was all material they had been over before, but she felt obligated to set the facts before him once again.

When she had concluded, Stockwell became pensive, thinking about the potential of the defense program she had outlined. "Look, the B-1 is not a worldwide panacea."

"Of course it isn't. I admit it won't stop a political crisis in the Middle East, Cyprus, Ireland or wherever. It won't stop natural disasters from occurring. But what it can do is ease the pressure of armed confrontation. In turn, it will eventually reduce money spent in national defense programs and defuse crises affecting our interests. I think it's worth that price tag and so do my constituents."

He shook his head. "Well, I've got equally as many who don't see it in your way, Senator. You know, if our friends the Democrats take power in the next election, they'll kill the B-1 program," he murmured.

Diane shrugged. "This is more than a political concern. The defense of our country is at stake."

Stockwell leaned back in his chair, a thoughtful look on his square face. "I'll tell you what, Senator. If you'll take a neutral position on the B-1 program, I'll get Reilly to throw his support behind your efforts on equal rights for women. What do you say?"

Diane toyed absently with her spoon. He hadn't heard a word she had said. The damned defense of the country was at stake and all he was doing was politicking. The B-1 was essential. But Stockwell was so well fed on rhetoric that he couldn't tell honesty from political yammering. She clamped down on her anger, giving him a tight, no-nonsense smile.

Stockwell brightened, as if sensing a victory. "Tell you what, I'll sweeten the pot even more. I'll stand up in favor of women's rights. I swing more than just a little weight in the two committees I'm on." He smiled indulgently at her.

Diane felt ill. "Sorry, Chad. I'm committed to the B-1 as the best available solution to our national defense problems. Education will sell women's rights, just as educating your constituents will convince them the B-1 is a good buy."

Stockwell looked absolutely crestfallen. "My influence isn't minimal, you know. I could do your women plenty of good where it counts."

Pursing her lips, she allowed her linen napkin to drop on her plate. "I'm sure you could," she answered smoothly, "but this is one issue that can't be negotiated."

"You drive a hard bargain, Senator," he muttered.

She smiled, realizing she had won the confrontation. "As I said, I believe education is the key. As soon as the voters are given all the facts concerning the B-1, I think they will come to understand its purpose. Let's face it, Chad, giving out half truths or half answers may be beneficial to you and your lobbying interests, but I find it morally unconscionable."

"Morals?" he asked, a wry smile fleeting across his mouth. "Whose morals? Come on, Senator, we could spend the entire day discussing right, wrong, and the gray areas in between."

Diane blotted her lips with the chocolate-colored linen napkin. "News reporting is not a gray area," she noted sharply. "Reporting is supposed to be substantiated by facts."

Stockwell leaned back. "Tess Hamilton at Rockwell gave me all the facts."

Browning gave him a jaded, wary look. "Somehow," she drawled, "I don't think you gave Ms. Hamilton enough time to explain the ramifications of her initial statements. Anyway, my office is contacting her today to verify the 'facts' in the paper."

Stockwell rose, smiling. "Well, let me know what story they're using today. Hey, how about lunch sometime next week at one of my watering holes in the District? You can fill me in on their latest excuse at that time."

She got up, appearing unruffled by Stockwell's crude invitation. "Can you afford a day away from all those good-looking lobbyists?" she asked pointedly.

He laughed. "Can't help it if I'm such a good-looking, influential male animal. Don't tell me you're jealous, Diane?"

She tucked her lower lip between her teeth in an effort not to laugh outright. Stockwell was called "Shorty" by those who didn't care for his Napoleonic streak. He barely stood five-foot-six inches tall.

"I don't think I'd call it jealousy, Chad. Besides, I don't want to waste any more of my time than necessary. And it's obvious you're not a supporter of women's rights."

The insults floated right over Stockwell's head. "At least let me pay for lunch. It's the least I can do."

You bet it is, Diane thought grimly. I'll need two Alka-Seltzers the minute I hit that office. God, I hope Greg knows where they are. . . .

If I don't get out of here, I'm going to go buggy, Tess thought distractedly. She ran her fingers over her tightly knotted hair in a gesture of frustration. The day had started going wrong when she received a nine A.M. call from Senator Diane Browning's office. Her wristwatch now read five thirty. Her stomach growled ominously because she had skipped lunch to work up the needed information for the Senator. She heard a male voice outside her office, someone talking with her secretary. Frowning, she concentrated on the work before her, another material purchase order needing her signature.

"The word's out you're a bear today."

Tess jerked her head up. Her heart took a plunge. "Shep!" she breathed. Her eyes widened and the frown disappeared from her brow. "How—"

He sauntered into her office, looking neat and incredibly self-assured in his dark blue uniform. He grinned affably, his gaze taking in her tense features. "Didn't you know? There was a meeting of all test pilots and the flight control design team today." He stopped at her desk, his gray eyes warm as he gazed down at her. "And, lady, you're a sight for sore eyes."

A small shiver went up her spine as she lost herself in his eyes. A small, tired smile pulled at her full lips. "They were right, you know. I *am* a bear today." She blew out a long breath of air and fell back against her chair. Had it been a week since that wonderful day in the sequoias? How many times had she replayed that kiss? Her glance lingered on his mouth. It evoked a sensual feeling that coiled outward from the center of her body.

"Maybe you need to be fed," he teased, making himself comfortable on the edge of the desk.

"I am starved." She gave him a wicked look. "Are you offering to feed me?"

He gave a slight shrug of his broad shoulders, a smile playing at the corners of his mouth. "I just happened to bring along some civilian clothes in the hope that I might be able to talk a certain very desirable woman into having dinner with me."

"Ah, I see," she murmured, enjoying the verbal fencing. Somehow, Shep made the pressures of the entire week dissolve. "I think you had this planned."

"Could be," he murmured. "I have a motto: never go into any situation unprepared."

Tess laughed softly, rising. "In that case I won't disappoint you, Ramsey. Dinner will be just fine."

He raised one eyebrow in inquiry. "And dancing?"

The thought of being in his arms once again made her giddy. She paused at the corner of the desk, holding his intense gray gaze. Unconsciously, her lips parted. She was aware of his maleness as never before. It was as if he were mentally picturing them in one another's arms at the same moment she envisioned it! A heady, delicious feeling went through her. "I—well, let's see," she murmured unsteadily. Old feelings of guilt were stirring to life. She still hadn't forgiven herself for that night on the balcony. Cy would still be alive if. . . . She brushed away the gloomy thoughts as best she could. Forcing a smile, she tilted her head as she halted near Shep.

"Feel like sinking your teeth into some prime ribs?" she asked.

Shep turned, placing his hand on the small of her back, and escorted her to the outer office. "Hmm, juicy, rare prime ribs—I can just about taste it!"

She made a face. "Ugh! Rare? What are you, an animal?"

He gave her a warning glance. "On some levels, lady, I'm very much an animal," he murmured.

Chapter 9

TESS SIPPED THE DRY BURGUNDY WINE, WATCHING SHEP over the rim of the crystal glass. The dinner had been delicious, the company superb and the atmosphere in the darkened, intimate restaurant made her feel as if they were the only two people on earth at the moment. They had stopped by her home earlier so Shep could change from his uniform to a tan sportcoat and dark brown slacks. The civilian clothing did nothing but make his broad shoulders look even more capable of carrying heavy loads. She smiled to herself. In uniform or out, Shep Ramsey was a commanding figure.

"What are you smiling about?" he asked softly, interrupting her meandering thoughts.

Startled, Tess gave him a wide-eyed look. "Was I smiling?"

Shep nodded his head, downing the last of the wine. "Your eyes were sparkling."

"You don't miss a thing, do you?"

"Not where you're concerned, lady."

The timbre of his voice sent a shiver through her. She turned the delicate crystal goblet between her slender fingers. Her face must have broadcast her sudden moodiness because Shep reached out, gently pulling one of her hands from the glass.

"You're spiraling into a dive. What's wrong?"

"Nothing," she said, giving him an unsteady smile.

"Lady, you aren't very good at lying," he drawled.

His fingers were strong and warm against her skin. She loved his touch, and found herself hungering for it once again. What was she thinking? Cy had only been gone seven months and already she was finding another man enticing . . . exciting in a way she'd never known before. Tess extricated her hand. "You really want to know what I'm thinking?"

He leaned forward. "Always," he answered gravely.

She moistened her lips, giving him a frightened look. "I'm unsure about myself, Shep. About us. I'm scared. And feeling guilty. . . ."

"Guilt is a poisonous emotion," he responded quietly, scrutinizing her. "You feel guilty about our kissing on the balcony and its getting back to Cy?"

"Yes."

Shep placed his elbows on the table, watching her with a tender expression on his face. "The very thing that makes you appealing to me, Tess, is like a curse for you," he murmured.

Tess looked up, a quizzical expression written on her face. "What do you mean?" she asked, her voice nearly inaudible.

"Your vulnerability. Your childlike way of seeing things in this very complex and complicated world of ours. I wish there were some way for me to help you understand the type of guilt you're experiencing. If you were older or more experienced, you'd probably understand your feelings better and you wouldn't let this guilt you're feeling dominate your life." He pursed his mouth, frowning. "Don't take what I've said as an insult, Tess. I'm older than you are. My experience has enabled me to put what happened between us in its proper perspective.''

Tess knotted the napkin in her lap. "Haven't you ever felt guilty about that night?" she asked, her voice tight with emotion.

"Yes and no," he answered hesitantly. "I've felt bad because the whole thing still has such an impact on you. But no, I'm not sorry I kissed you. I'll never regret that."

She gave him a disbelieving look. "You were married at the time! You were cheating on your wife. Just as I was cheating on Cy! You mean to tell me you didn't feel guilt over that?"

Shep stirred, uncomfortable with the course the conversation was taking. "Honey, don't get upset over what I said. That kiss was pure and honest. It wasn't calculated, but an act of the heart. I'm not trying to make excuses for myself, Tess. But you're trying to extract some penance from life to pay for the one mistake you can't forgive yourself for."

Her eyes flashed with azure fire. "Just because you can be cold and callous about it or—or selfish, I can't!"

He stared at her grimly. "All I'm trying to say is put your grief behind you, Tess. Don't hide behind it."

She gasped. "Why—"

"Look, there have been times when I've wanted to take you out over the last several months, Tess. I've stayed away because I knew you needed the space. But it's been seven months now. You need to start living again."

"For whose sake?" she gasped. "Yours? It would seem so!"

Shep sat back, feeling the rage of her disbelief. He hadn't meant to bring up the subject. And it was obvious he had approached it from the wrong direction. Or had he? He had been searching for a way to make her want to live again. He wanted her to reach out, adjust and discover new facets of herself. Perhaps anger was the necessary catalyst. Still, his heart wrenched when he saw tears filling her blue eyes, making them look like large, liquid sapphires. He leaned forward, reaching across the table and gently wrapping his fingers around her upper arm.

"Come on," he urged gently, "let's go. There's a nice park nearby where we can talk more."

Tess grabbed the beautiful Irish lace shawl, throwing it around her shoulders. His fingers burned like a brand into her flesh as he led her out of the restaurant to his car. She took a step away from him when he leaned down to unlock the door.

"Just take me home, Shep," she ordered quietly, gripping the shawl against her breast.

He opened the door, helping her in. "That may end this confrontation, Tess," he said, releasing her elbow, "but it's not a long-term answer."

She clenched her teeth, her jaw pushed out stubbornly as he drove away from beneath the lights of the restaurant into the darker reaches of L.A. A small park, no more than two blocks away, lay like an oasis among the crowded confines of the city. Palms towered over grassy knolls that were dotted with hibiscus bushes here and there.

She remained tense as she slowed the car to a halt, shutting off the engine. The silence widened the gulf between them. Shep slowly placed his hands on the steering wheel, studying her in the semidarkness. "I wonder if you'll ever get rid of that anger you've been carrying around with you over this whole incident," he said slowly, measuring her with a steady stare.

Tess pursed her lips, refusing to meet his eyes. Her heart was pounding unremittingly and her nerves were raw with tension. "I don't recall Cy's passing with anger," she snapped.

"No, but you're holding back anger over how it came about."

She jerked her chin up and glared at him. Her eyes were narrow slits of fury. "Dammit, Shep, I've had the toughest week of my life at Rockwell! I don't need you playing amateur psychologist and badgering me tonight." Her nostrils flared. "Just take me home! I don't feel like putting up with the Spanish Inquisition from you."

His mouth became firm. "I'm going to quit feeling sorry for you, Tess. What you need is some clear thinking to get back on track. Let's face it, you hate Derek Barton. As long as you cling to your guilt feelings you don't have to work through anything!" His voice lowered. "You're only half alive, Tess! You're moving through the days in some sort of fog. I want you to start living again. Quit worrying what other people are going to think."

Tess uttered a small cry and jerked open the door. Before Shep could reach her, she fled from the car, running across the dew-laden grass of the quiet park. A sob tore from her throat and she clutched at the shawl, continuing to run, hearing his heavier footfalls coming up rapidly behind her.

Just as Shep reached out to pull her to a halt, her hair lost the last of the pins which held it in a chignon. The rich, auburn mass tumbled across her shoulders as he pulled her around, bringing her against him.

"No!" she wailed, throwing her hands out to stop her forward momentum. Her palms met the hard, uncompromising wall of his chest.

"Stop it!" he breathed savagely, gripping her arms and giving her a small shake. "Tess!"

Tears streamed down her cheeks as she tried without success to break his hold. He was so close. So tantalizingly male. Even in her avalanche of grief Tess was aware of his natural scent. It dizzied her spinning senses, and she fell against him, sobbing helplessly.

"Oh, God," he groaned, sweeping her into his arms. Shep rested his head against her hair, inhaling the sweet scent of jasmine. He ran his fingers through the auburn strands, his desire inflamed to an aching intensity. Kissing her wet cheek, he murmured soothing words in her ear, trying to comfort her. Holding her more tightly, Shep rocked her gently back and forth in his arms.

"It's all right, honey," he soothed, "go ahead, get it out. God, Tess, I'm so sorry to cause you this kind of pain." He finally coaxed her chin up with his finger, forcing her to look up and meet his eyes. Her lashes were thick and tear-drenched, framing incredibly large blue eyes. He sucked in a sudden breath, unprepared for the fragile beauty of her expression. Cupping her face between his large hands, he leaned down, gently touching her salty lips. At first she resisted, her lips still and unmoving. Tracing the outline of her lips, he felt her quiver imperceptibly. When he deepened the kiss, her lips parted beneath his own. A small moan fled from her slender throat and Shep felt her lean heavily against him.

Rage mingled with despair and desire within Tess as she collapsed against his steadying form. Tears seemed to join their lips into a fiery, consuming kiss. In that instant, Tess felt all the strength and courage he wanted to give her. Finally, she pulled away from him, her eyes reflecting her agony.

Shep reached up, gently pushing a thick strand of hair away from her flushed cheek. "It's better this way," was all he said, his voice raspy with unshed tears.

Tess regarded him in the silence. "Pain is better?" she asked hoarsely.

He gave a slight nod. "In the long run it's better to

face up to the loss and accept it. That way," he sighed, "you can go on living."

"I—I feel at a loss, Shep. I don't know how to reach out." She gave a slight shrug of her stooped shoulders. "I'm tired. And I'm finding out I'm so damn naive." She covered her trembling mouth with her hands. "Where have I been all my life?" she cried softly. "I feel at such a great loss when dealing with people emotionally."

His gray eyes grew tender as he searched her features. "Honey, don't be too hard on yourself. We all learn in different ways. You couldn't help it if your parents made you feel as if the only thing that mattered was getting good grades. School was your whole life. It stunted your natural emotional growth."

He offered her a gentle smile. "You come from strong Irish stock, lady. And you've got what it takes to pull yourself up by the bootstraps."

Tess gave him an uncertain look. "I can't promise you anything, Shep."

"I'm not expecting promises. All I'm asking for is a chance to get to know you. For you to know more of me. But I don't stand a chance if you're walled up with your past." He gripped her arms, gently. "I can tell by the way you return my kisses that you care for me," he whispered, a new urgency in his tone. "And I think you know a little of how I feel toward you, Tess."

She swallowed against a lump in her throat and gave a nod of her head. He was right on all counts. Shep had awakened passions and desires she never realized existed. But more importantly, she felt comfortable around him. "We live two hours apart."

He gave a nonchalant shrug, lifting his head. "So? I'll see you on weekends. Maybe sometimes during the week when we've got meetings scheduled down here."

Tess touched her forehead. "My life seems to revolve around Rockwell so much of the time. . . ."

"Spoken like an over-responsible woman in a management position," he drawled. "Honey, don't you see that because you're a female in a very male-dominated company, you're working twice as hard as any one man? You're trying to prove you've earned the right to be an administrative assistant on this project." He gave her a small shake. "You don't need to prove a thing, Tess. Don't look for approval in other people's eyes, only your own. Do the best you can and be content with how you feel. And leave your weekends for yourself. Not for the company."

She tilted her head, searching his face. "Listen, after this last week, I'm not so sure my position is stable. Senator Stockwell attempted to crucify me with the press." She met his gray eyes. "You read the papers. You saw my name smeared all over the article on the B-1. He made me out to be an incompetent." Tess sighed raggedly, remaining in the safety of his arms, all her fears tumbling out. "I've fought hard to retain my position at Rockwell after Cy died. And now Stockwell has eroded my position by quoting only half the truth!"

Shep leaned down, placing a kiss on her brow. Her skin was warm, stirring his senses. "Sorry, princess. I read those newspapers too and talked with the Air Force public affairs people. Believe me, not everyone sees you as an incompetent."

Tess expelled a breath of air. She felt his arm tighten protectively around her shoulder. "Anyway, I've got to go in Saturday and work on a paper for our PR department. Senator Diane Browning's office called this morning. A chalk-talk has been scheduled for Tuesday with the news media to offset Stockwell's allegations. We feel that the public will see the reasons for the B-1 if they are given the facts."

"And Sunday?" he asked huskily, loving the warmth of her body next to his own. Even in the weak moonlight her auburn hair shone with copper and gold highlights. "Well?" he prodded gently.

Tess gazed into his gray eyes, feeling the natural warmth that emanated from him. How could she ever have thought he was machinelike? That mask he wore was only reserved for those who would not take the trouble to look beneath it. "I should take a day off, shouldn't I?"

A smile touched his mouth. "Absolutely."

"Any suggestions?"

One eyebrow rose in response. Tess fought back the urge to smile. "I have plenty of suggestions. But at this point, I think only one or two of them are applicable." His gray eyes sparkled with mirth.

"What are my options?"

"It's supposed to be ideal weather up in the desert. How about a picnic?"

"Isn't it a bit chilly up there? I hear the wind blows all the time."

Shep nodded thoughtfully. "You're right." He cocked his head, drinking in the sight of her upturned face. His body tightened with desire and he had to stop himself from taking her back into his arms and simply crushing her against him. "How about a trip to the beach Sunday, then?"

"Okay," she agreed softly.

Tess glanced up at him. His face was bathed in moonlight, his features softened and relaxed. She felt a mixture of emotions within her. She had to leave the past behind. Shep was right about that. She closed her eyes, suddenly very tired. Tomorrow would be a new day. A new beginning.

Tess groaned, the loud ringing of the telephone waking her from the badly needed sleep. She groped for the phone, squinting to look at the clock. It was seven thirty Sunday morning.

"Hello?" she mumbled, sitting up.

"Tess, this is Fred. I'm afraid we need your help over at the office right away."

She rubbed her face tiredly. "What now?"

"The leading newspapers back east just broke a story this morning about the B-1 damaging the environment. We've got environmental impact groups screaming bloody murder. The phones have been ringing off the hooks since six A.M. and the press is hounding the hell out of me. Dan is out of town and I need somebody from engineering to help me with this. Can you get down here right away?"

Fred sounded harried and concerned. Tess blinked, trying to clear the cobwebs from her groggy mind. Shep would be coming down at ten A.M. to pick her up. Did she have a phone number where she could reach him? Even though sunshine filtered through the curtained windows on her right, her whole mood changed into a gray despair. She gripped the receiver. "I'll be right down, Fred."

"Thank God. Hurry. I'm not sure I can keep the press at bay with my round table answers."

She took a quick shower and grabbed an apricot-colored dress. Her mind bounced between Shep and the newspapers' allegations about the B-1 being detrimental to the environment. She had to get hold of Shep! She also wondered if it was Senator Stockwell who had dropped this latest bit of information. Disconnected thoughts whirled through her mind as she grabbed her purse and headed out the door.

Fred gave her a look of profound relief when she stepped through the office doors. His face was tight, and she could see small dots of perspiration on his upper lip and furrowed brow.

"Fred, do you have the phone numbers of the test

pilots on this program?" she asked immediately, before he could say anything.

"Why—uh, no. Why?"

"I've got to get hold of Major Ramsey."

Fred walked to another desk as one of the four phones began ringing. "Ellie, my secretary should have the number. Here, you take a look for it while I get that phone."

After an exhaustive search through Ellie's desk, Tess finally found the phone numbers of the Air Force test pilots. Her pulse leaped as she rang Shep's home in Lancaster. Her blue eyes darkened with worry when no one answered after six rings. Reluctantly, she replaced the receiver, her stomach knotting with apprehension.

As soon as she had hung up, the phone rang again and from then on it was five hours of nonstop calls. Near one o'clock Tess wearily looked over at Fred. Earlier, between calls, they had formulated a standard statement. The phone rang again and Tess felt the urge to ignore it. Her head was aching and she didn't think she could stand to speak to one more person.

"Rockwell Public Relations."

"Yes, this is Greg Saint from Senator Browning's office calling."

Tess rolled her eyes upward. "Yes, Greg. Can we help you?"

"We've got a real hornet's nest building over the environmental impact of the B-1. You and I know the plane isn't going to emit any more pollutants than the B-52, but how are we going to convince the press? Stockwell threw the environmental lobbyists a bone on Saturday and the furor today is very real. Senator Browning is coming back from Camp David later on this afternoon to try and stop this panic," Greg continued.

"What does Stockwell want?" Tess growled.

"Nothing less than to stop the funding on the B-1 and get it scratched from the budget," Greg answered just as seriously. "Look, are you people going to be there to man the phones the rest of the day?"

Tess gave Fred a glance. "Yes," she said without enthusiasm, "we'll be here until Senator Browning feels we've stopped the leak in the dike."

Greg laughed. "Stockwell's just up to his old tricks. He's a past master of manipulating the press for public opinion."

"Somehow, I wish we could anticipate his moves so that we could respond and neutralize his claims. As it is, we're always playing catch up, Greg. It makes Rockwell look bad all the way around. We're constantly on the defensive. I believe Fred is in the process of preparing a brochure on these questionable areas in order to deal with such wild, unsubstantiated claims by the other camp."

"That's great, Tess. Look, I'll be getting back to you in a while."

Tess hung up the phone, tiredly meeting Fred's bloodshot stare. He sat down in a chair next to her desk. "We are preparing several pamphlets to answer our critics, Tess."

"Good. When Greg calls back, maybe you two can set up some sort of publicity strategy to start getting that information out so that we don't look like sitting ducks."

He grinned tiredly. "I owe you a big thanks. You didn't have to come in and do PR for me today." He studied her for a long moment before saying, "You know, I've heard the other execs gripe about your performance since Cy died." He gave her an enigmatic smile. "And I think they're definitely wrong about you." He rose. "I'm going to order us some lunch. While I go out and get it, will you stay here and hold down the fort?"

Tess nodded her head. When Fred had left the room, she again consulted the listing of phone numbers of the Air Force test pilots. Between phone calls she had tried Shep's number over and over—to no avail. Chewing on her lower lip, she picked up the phone and dialed a different listing.

"Major Cunningham," a voice answered.

Tess closed her eyes. "Tom? This is Tess Hamilton. I'm trying to locate Shep. Is he there?"

"Why . . . no. I thought you two had a date for the beach today?"

She swallowed hard. "We did. I mean, we were supposed to." She rapidly explained the situation to the major. "I need to find him, Tom. I—I'm afraid he'll think I backed out. That I—"

"I'll do what I can, Tess," Tom reassured her. "Let me make a few calls to the base and see if I can locate him. If I do, I'll have Shep give you a call."

Shakily, she brushed a tendril away from her temple. "Please," she said softly. "I don't know how long I'll be here at the office." There was regret in her voice. What must Shep be thinking? That thought alone had haunted her all day. Did he think she had weakened and run away? Again? If he thought she had run away, how must he feel toward her? Suddenly, she felt real fear. Fear more awesome and terrifying than she had ever experienced. She wanted the chance to know him. And now, because of Stockwell's latest ploy, her personal life had just been turned into a full-scale disaster.

"Why don't I take your work number?" Tom suggested in his easy southern drawl. "I know Shep has your home phone."

"Tom—" she began, and then hesitated. "I—we had a terrible fight last night and I'm afraid he'll think the worst of me because of this no-show."

There was silence at the other end and it scared her. Finally, the major spoke, his voice subdued. "Shep cares a hell of a lot for you, Tess. And I'm not saying you've been wrong in your actions. He's been waiting for you to break free of the past." He gave a small laugh. "Listen, test pilots have this romantic image to combat. We're not all womanizers or out for one-night stands."

"I never thought that!"

"Well, he thinks you do. Shep feels his initial meeting with you and then the suddenness of his divorce from Allyson put him in a bad light. It appears that he's willing to drop one woman for another."

"But—"

"Hear me out. Shep's marriage to Allyson was doomed before it ever got started. He hung in there and tried to make it work. But Aly was always a social butterfly looking to move up one more rung on the ladder of success. She used Shep as a step up that ladder. When it became evident Aly didn't really love him, he tried to renew the relationship with her. After my wife, Maria, died, something inside Shep snapped. I don't know what happened, I can't explain it. He saw the kind of marriage Maria and I shared. Shep helped me through the hell of losing her. I think he saw what real love was for the first time in his life by experiencing the devastating pain involved in its loss. Shep believes in marriage." Tom hesitated, as if searching for the right words. "But it takes two to have a marriage, and when one party quits, Tess, something dies in the other person. Shep reacted from the heart when he kissed you. Aly had killed the real meaning of their marriage years before."

Tears gathered in her eyes, and she swallowed against a forming lump. "God, Tom, I didn't know what was happening either," she said softly, covering her eyes with her hand. "Why didn't Shep tell me this before?"

"How could he? Your husband's death was due to

the strain of hard work. And you were on a guilt trip that was started by that subcontractor. You swallowed it hook, line, and sinker. Shep had no choice but to sit back and wait."

She sniffed. "What can I do? Please, Tom, you're Shep's best friend. What if he thinks I don't care about him anymore?"

"Do you really care for him?"

The words sliced through her and she inhaled sharply. "Of course I do! How could you ever doubt—"

"Because, Tess, your actions haven't proven what I'm hearing you say," he returned.

He was right. Facts were facts. A new ache began in her heart as she raced to think of the options left open to her. To Shep. "You're right," she murmured. "What do you think would convince Shep that I am serious about our relationship?"

"You really want to know?"

"Yes."

"Drive up here and meet him head-on. Don't pussyfoot around with a phone call. I haven't seen him at all today and I've been over to the Officers' Club, at the office, and the base exchange earlier. I'm sure I'd have run into him. Or at least seen his car."

"Well, if he isn't on base or at home, where is he?"

Tom snorted softly. "You tell me, Tess. For all I know, he could be driving around doing a lot of thinking. Maybe he went to the beach to walk around. I just don't know."

Tess clenched her fist on the desk. "What does a man do when he's hurt badly, Tom?"

The major gave a low laugh. "You start out by taking a good stiff drink. Maybe getting slightly drunk to dull the pain. And when your head clears, you try to sort out what's left of your life. Look, I don't want you to worry. That's not my aim in telling you this. Shep's probably out driving around somewhere wondering why you weren't at home this morning."

Tess mentally cursed Rockwell and her responsibility to the company. Which was more important? Her personal happiness or her career? "As soon as I can get someone to take my place here this afternoon, Tom, I'll drive up to Lancaster."

"Okay, but it's almost two o'clock and it's a two-hour drive from L.A."

"That's a moot point, isn't it?" she commented, her voice hushed.

"That's the spirit. You got a paper and pencil?"

Tess reached for the articles. "Yes."

"Here's Shep's address. We only live a couple of houses apart here in Lancaster. I'll give you mine, too, just in case he hasn't shown up by the time you arrive, you can stay over here."

She nodded, busily scribbling down the information. "I'll be there just as soon as I can, Tom. I owe you one for your help on this."

"You can make it up to me by getting together with Shep. You two haven't really had a chance yet to see if you both have what it takes to go the distance. See you in a few hours, Tess."

Tess hung up, worry written on her features. Fred returned moments later with two Styrofoam food containers. He grinned. "Feel like Chinese food this fine Sunday afternoon?"

She managed a smile. "Sure. Why not?"

Tess wearily looked at her wristwatch—it was just after eight P.M. Between bites of food, the phones had begun to ring in earnest once again. Fred had tried to reach a few other of their coworkers, but he had had no luck. Besides, only one other person could deal with this crisis: Dan. On four different occasions, she had tried to reach Shep. He had not answered the phone.

Sighing, Tess slid into her small Toyota and closed the door. Fastening her seat belt, she turned the key. The Toyota purred to life, Tess began the drive up to Lancaster.

Chapter 10

THE ROAD WAS DARK AND LONELY. THE WINDS COMING off the Mojave Desert whipped through the mountains with a vengeance, and it took all her concentration to keep the silver Toyota on the road. The lights of Lancaster were bright and clean against the darkness. She drove eight more miles through the Antelope Valley region before coming to the neatly laid out town. Her unfamiliarity with Lancaster cost her nearly a half an hour before she found Shep's street. The houses, stucco and single story, all looked alike.

Close to exhaustion, Tess almost gave way to tears when she saw there were no lights on at Shep's home. A sense of relief washed over Tess as she saw the lights burning brightly at Tom's residence. Pulling into his driveway, she shut off the car engine and sat there a moment, trying to pull herself together. Wearily, she climbed out of the car, bringing her purse and coat along.

Tom answered her knock almost immediately. She could see the concern on his face. "Come on in, Tess," he invited, opening the door. "I was starting to get worried about you."

124

Anxiously, she searched his features. "Have you found him?" she asked, her voice breathless.

"No. Come on in. Let me get you some coffee."

"Thank you."

He took her coat and hung it up. "I've looked everywhere. Made a few more phone calls. No one's seen him, Tess." Tom gave her a reassuring smile. "He'll be back. He's scheduled for an eight o'clock flight tomorrow morning, so he has to show up pretty soon. He's real good about getting rest before a flight."

"Even in circumstances like this?" she asked, following him to the kitchen, where he poured them each a cup of coffee. There was a comfortable warmth to Tom's home. Although he was a bachelor, the place had a lived-in look that Tess appreciated.

"Well, that's a horse of a different color," he agreed, leading her into the living room.

Tess sat down in an overstuffed chair and took a sip of coffee. As she balanced the mug in her hands, she looked across the living room at Tom. "I'm going to wait for him," she said. "Is there any way I can stay over at his house?"

He gave her a slight grin. "What if he brings home another woman?"

Tess stared at him, incredulous. "It doesn't matter," she murmured firmly.

"I doubt if it would happen, Tess. But I thought I'd better make you see the whole picture."

Her fingers tightened around the cup. "Does he have someone else?"

"No, but a man can do dumb things when he's feeling hurt. Look, I have a key to his house. How about if I walk you down the block and get you settled in? He's bound to come back pretty soon."

"I'd appreciate it."

Tom made her comfortable at Shep's home and then

left. She noticed a distinct difference between the
interior of the two houses. There was an obvious
richness to the furniture here. She recognized the
sophistication of Allyson's touch everywhere. The living room was tastefully decorated with a taupe carpet,
modern white furniture, and a glass coffee table on
brass legs. The end tables were crafted of dark mahogany, matching the huge hutch against one wall. Fig trees
were strategically placed in two corners, lending a sense
of vitality to the careful creation. She hovered at the
entrance. Did Shep spend much time here? It looked as
if no one really lived in this portion of the house. For
some reason she felt uncomfortable, as if she were
trespassing.

Eventually she sat on the edge of one of the two
couches, her back straight, her hands folded tightly in
her lap. The room looked as though it came out of
Town and Country magazine, but it left her cold. It
was not the sort of room that invited one to kick off
one's shoes and bury one's toes in the lush carpet. Did
Shep enjoy living in this plastic world that Allyson had
created? Her fingers were growing damp from nervousness. Glancing at her watch, she saw that it was eleven
P.M. Tiredness was encroaching on her rapidly, and
Tess felt as if her eyelids were weighted. She should try
to stay awake. But the huge white pillow beckoned to
her and against her better judgment, Tess slipped off
her shoes and stretched out on the couch. The folds
of her dress fell about her slender form, emphasizing
the shape of her hips and long thighs. She tucked her
legs close to her body, closing her eyes, utter fatigue
robbing her of everything except the desperate need for
sleep.

Shep pulled his car into the narrow driveway, shutting off the engine. He frowned, immediately noticing
that lights were burning in the kitchen. Had Tom come

over? He gathered up his jacket and the unused picnic
basket that sat in the other bucket seat. It was a typical
Mojave night, the winds cutting and chill. Somewhere
in the distance a coyote yapped mournfully. At midnight Antelope Valley slept like a huge, undisturbed
ghost in the high plain region of the desert. Ordinarily
the sights, sounds, and smells would register sharply on
his senses. But tonight he was aware of only the heavy
feeling in the region of his heart. He hoisted the basket
out of the car and shut the door.

The back door was unlocked. "Tom?" he called.
Shep climbed the three concrete interior steps. The
noise seemed amplified in the quiet confines of the
house. If Tom wasn't here, what was the door doing
unlocked? He put everything on the table and walked
through the dimly lit dining area into the darker living
room. Shep's heart pounded wildly, his pulse becoming
erratic. He froze, staring into the murky darkness of
the living room. Was he seeing right? His mouth grew
dry as he allowed his eyes to adjust. Tess? Tess was
here?

A hundred thoughts whirled through his mind as he
stared over at her sleeping figure barely fifteen feet
away. Even in the semidarkness she looked beautiful.
Why had she stood him up and then come here?
Despair interlocked with hope. Anxiety wrestled with
chilling anger. His mouth thinned, and he rested his
hands tensely on his lean hips. Had she come to
apologize because she felt guilty? That would be typical
of Tess. His heart wrenched violently in his chest. God,
how he loved her! Shep swallowed hard, his eyes
narrowing as he hungrily drank in her form. He had to
fight himself. He couldn't run to her side and pull her
into his arms. No. Too much damage had been done.
Why? Why was she here?

Slowly, the tenseness drained from his body, his
shoulders drooping. Shep's gray eyes revealed the

private hell of his anguish as he continued to stare at her. His emotions couldn't be relied upon. Part of him wanted to shake some sense into her, another part wanted her to realize exactly what she had done to him on this day. He released a shaky breath, allowing his hands to drop to his sides. Anger warred with joy within him. He wasn't sure what to do or how to feel.

He would never forget the anguish he'd gone through when he arrived at her home at exactly nine o'clock and no one answered the door. Why hadn't she at least had the decency to leave a note? To explain her position?

Without a sound, Shep walked into the living room, coming to a halt inches from the couch on which Tess slept. His gaze missed nothing. How could she have grown more lovely? Yet she had. At least in his eyes. He was trained to see every minute detail. He noted the exhaustion shadowing her peach-colored skin. Darkness lingered beneath the thick, fan-shaped lashes of her closed eyes. Her hair, once tamed into the severe chignon, had pulled loose. The auburn strands framed her face, softening the natural angularity of her high cheekbones. Shep groaned inwardly, controlling himself. Her lips were parted, looking so damned vulnerable and so kissable.

He leaned over, hand extended to give her a small shake on the shoulder to wake her. Fingers outstretched, Shep hesitated, his breath lodging in his throat. An imperceptible tremble coursed up his arm. Instead he lightly caressed her cheek, delighting in the smooth texture of her skin. His heart began a slow pound as he watched Tess rouse herself. Against all his better judgment, Shep crouched down, mesmerized. Tess stirred like a lost kitten, snuggling more deeply into the pillow she slept upon. Her red hair framed her face as in an old Celtic legend. Was she a druidess awakening within the embrace of the trees which held her safe? Shep shook his head to clear his fatigued mind. He reached out, placing his hand on her shoulder this time, his fingers sinking into her arm and giving her a small shake.

"Tess?" he called, his voice more stern than he meant it to be.

The auburn lashes lifted, revealing drowsy blue eyes. Shep inhaled softly, stunned by the richness of their color. For the first time it occurred to him that they reminded him of the sky he loved so much. He felt himself spiraling into her lovely sapphire gaze, helpless to halt the feelings welling up from the depths of his wounded heart. Her eyes widened slowly. He saw the exhaustion in them and felt guilty for waking her.

"Shep!" He rose, forcing himself away from this weaver of spells. Away from whatever it was that still existed between them. If he hadn't moved, Shep would have leaned over and kissed her parted, flower-perfect lips. Slipping his hands into the pockets of his jeans, he moved around the coffee table. Tess roused herself immediately into a sitting position, strands of hair falling across her shoulders, resting against her breasts.

He stared down at her, ignoring her natural beauty. Ignoring the tiredness that was so evident in every drowsy movement of her body. "You're a little late," he bit out in a cold, hard voice. "We were supposed to meet at nine o'clock this morning."

"Shep," she begged, "please, don't be angry. You have every right, but—"

"Just what the hell are you doing here?"

Tess jerked her head up, eyes wide with shock. The hostility in his voice was like a knife slashing into her. "I—" she stumbled, stunned.

"What's the excuse this time? Don't you think I know why you were afraid to see me today?"

She winced, dropping her gaze. Silence built like a fortress between them. Compressing her lips she whispered, "I guess I had that coming."

"You know how to dish it out too," he reminded her, fury evident in his tone. "Well, if you're going to dish it out, Tess, you're also going to take it." He ran his long fingers through his hair, glaring over at her. "You really disappointed me this morning. It's not that you didn't show, but the simple fact that you didn't even have the decency to leave a note or make a phone call. I never expected that of you." He gave her a cutting smile, his gray eyes glittering. "Of course I built you up as something special. I put you on a pedestal, which was wrong. Put people on pedestals and they sure as hell are bound to fall off."

Tess raised her chin, meeting his cold fury. "Aren't you even going to—"

He raised his hand, jabbing it in her direction. "You sit right there and take the heat, lady. By God, you've had this coming and you're going to get it. I've done a hell of a lot of thinking today, Tess. About you. About me." His voice became flat. "About us." He turned away from her. "Thanks to you, I had time to think about plenty of things." He turned, looking back at her. "You were always special in my eyes, Tess. I saw so much in you. So much of what I needed. . . ." He halted, the corners of his mouth drawing in with pain. "Maybe I pursued you too soon. Maybe I pushed you too hard. I don't know. All I wanted was the right to get to know you better. And you kept backing off. And I know you feel something for me. I could see it in your eyes, hear it in your voice." His tone dropped to a raw whisper. "I felt it every time I kissed you."

Tears gathered in her eyes. Tess got to her feet, unsure of where or how to unravel all that had been done. She opened her arms in a gesture of peace, a plea for understanding. "God, Shep, give me a chance to explain!" she cried softly. Tears made silvery paths down her drawn, pale cheeks.

He gave her a cynical look, walking back to where

she stood. He halted inches away. "There's nothing to explain," he growled. "You're a little late with apologies, Tess."

Her face contorted. "What about justice?" she cried. She clenched her hands at her sides, balling them into small fists. "You've already sentenced me, haven't you?" she hurled back, her voice high pitched with fury.

"You sentenced yourself with your own childish behavior!" he snarled.

Tess uttered a small cry, bringing up her hand without thinking. The sharp crack of her palm catching him on the cheek resounded like a shot through the room. A sob broke from her lips. She stared up into his dark features, stunned by her own action. She had never hit anyone in her whole life! Never! Tears streamed down her cheeks.

Shep reached out, his fingers sinking deeply into her arms, gripping her. "So," he breathed, his face inches from hers, "this is where your hotheaded Irish temper comes out?"

Tess beat her hands against the wall of his chest. "Let me go!" she cried, struggling to break his grip.

"Stop it!"

Tess shook her head, hair spilling across her shoulders as she tried to twist free. His grip tightened. Her heart pounded, the last shreds of control slipping. "You don't care!" she screamed. "You just don't care what the truth is! Let me go! Damn you!"

Shep gripped her hard, forcing her against him. He was aware of the yielding softness of her breasts against him, the sharp, short breaths escaping from her. "I don't care?" he said in hushed fury. "*I* don't care? Dammit, I'll show you just how much I care!" His mouth smothered her lips, ripping her breath away, melting her anger. His mouth moved with masterful insistence across her salty lips, forcing her to respond.

Anger was purged from Tess as an uncontrolled fire swept through her. The roughness of his beard against the softer plane of her cheek, the smell of his body, the awareness of his muscles, taut and tense, overwhelmed her senses. His grip loosened, and she felt his left hand pull her hips possessively against his straining body. A low moan of need escaped from her throat as she returned his demanding kiss.

Almost instantly his mouth grew more gentle, searching. Tess gave a little cry of defeat, leaning completely against the strong framework of his body, her arms slipping around his shoulders. Her heart pounded unrelentingly in her chest. She had hurt him deeply, and he had meant to hurt her. But the instant his mouth molded against her lips the need to hurt was suddenly transformed into the need to love. Now his mouth moved in small circles over her parted, waiting lips. Suddenly nothing else mattered. She pressed her lips against him, wanting him to realize how much he meant to her. A low groan came from him and he pinned her against him. He tore his mouth from her throbbing lips. "God, I need you," Shep whispered raggedly, his eyes silvered with barely restrained desire.

Tess stared mutely up at him, wildly aware of him as a man. A collision of thoughts left her speechless, only her mobile features telling Shep what she wanted and desired. Without a word he picked her up, taking her to the darkened confines of the spacious bedroom. Tess sighed brokenly, leaning her head on his shoulder.

As he laid her on the bed she whispered, "I didn't mean to hurt you, Shep . . . please . . . let me explain—"

He leaned over, placing his fingers against her lips. "Ssshh," he murmured huskily, "later."

Mutely, she looked up into his strong, tender face. Her heart blossomed with newfound feelings as he began to undress her. The apricot-colored dress fell

away, revealing a pale pink camisole of silk and lace.
She heard him take in a deep breath, his fingers
trembling slightly as he outlined the curve of her
breasts with his hands. Fire leaped along her flesh, and
she reached up, pulling him down upon her. She
wanted to drown in the beauty of the unfolding moment. No longer was Shep demanding or brutal. Instead, he coaxed her totally into communion with
himself.

"God, you're beautiful," he breathed against her
ear.

Tess closed her eyes, responding to the caress in his
voice, pressing her naked body against the planes of
his. His hand traced the outline of her slender neck,
then followed the curve of her taut breast. Her lips
parted, the breath stolen from her body as his hand
circled the hardening nipple. "Please . . ." she begged,
her voice a ragged whisper. She waited in agony for his
touch. She felt him lean over, aware of his breath
against her heated, straining flesh. His mouth closed
about her nipple. A low moan of pleasure broke from
her lips, and she arched unconsciously into his arms.

Time dissolved into a world of throbbing sensation.
It seemed only seconds later that she was aware of his
naked form against her. Meeting the warm hardness of
his muscled body, she felt new fires spring to life within
her. She ached to fulfill that fiery need. Just the slight
touch of Shep's hand brought her to new heights of
sensuality. His mouth teased her unmercifully, asking
her to participate without inhibition. She delighted in
the feel of the dark mass of his chest hair against her
breasts.

She was aware of shuddering, delicious sensations
surging throughout her straining body. She allowed her
fingers to trail across the expanse of his broad chest, to
follow the curve of his flat stomach. Shep tensed beside
her, pulling her possessively against him. Her eyes

looked upward, meeting his burning gaze. Then Shep
brought her chin up further, his head descending to
meet her parted lips. At that moment she felt very
inexperienced, a woman who had only known one
man's love. Shep seemed to sense her nervousness.
Cupping her face, he pressed a tender kiss upon her
lips, forcing those feelings away. It was as if he realized
that she was still part child, part blossoming woman.

Gently easing her back on the bed, Shep rose above
her, parting her thighs, and settling his knee between
them. She breathed deeply, wildly aware of the electrical current that jolted through her each time their
bodies touched one another. His breath was hot as he
leaned down to capture her lips. She moaned, her body
taut, ready for his entry. She arched upward, meeting
his forward motion. A wild, earth-tilting explosion
invaded the very depths of her soul. A cry of pleasure
broke from her lips, and she gripped his broad shoulders, carried upward on an untamed vortex of heat and
rhythmic pleasure.

She tasted the sweat of his tense body, and moved
with him, her mind swirling. She reached higher,
higher, intensely aware of the culmination that melted
her body against Shep's. Moaning, she fell back into his
arms. Time did not exist; only the wonderful sensation
of his arms about her damp, spent form, as he held her
near, kissing her nose, eyes, cheeks, and mouth very
gently.

It was still dark when Tess slowly awoke. She unconsciously nuzzled against Shep's shoulder, inhaling the
musky scent of his body. His arm tightened momentarily around her in response. Just then, the alarm went
off, cutting through her grogginess. Shep muttered
something. Pulling his arm from beneath her, he
reached for the noisy clock. Tess blinked, realizing it
must be near dawn. Gray light filtered in through the

large, curtained window. She opened her eyes. Her
heart wrenched with newfound joy as she stared up at
Shep's serious, handsome face. His hair was tousled,
lending him a boyish, vulnerable look. The soft curve
of his mouth gave a gentle expression to his face. And
his gray eyes . . . she lost herself within their lambent
gaze, realizing how much he cared for her. Her lips
parted as Shep leaned down, tasting them tentatively.
She responded, reveling in the strength of his mouth.
He groaned softly, caressing her cheek. Shep raised his
head, only inches from her face, studying her wide
eyes.

"Lady, you look more beautiful now than you did
last night, if that's possible," he breathed huskily. His
eyes narrowed slightly. "Look, it's time for me to get
up. I've got a flight scheduled at eight o'clock this
morning and a pre-ops briefing in an hour."

Tess frowned, reaching out and hesitantly touching
his face, aware of the sandpapery feel of his unshaven
skin beneath her fingertips. "Shep, we have to talk.
You didn't let me explain what happened yesterday."
Her voice was thick with sleep, sultry sounding. Tess
saw a fleeting look of pain in his eyes. She rose on one
elbow, trying to gather together her thoughts.

"Look," he said heavily, placing a hand on her
shoulder, "before you go any further, do you realize
it's Monday morning? It's five o'clock. Why don't you
call in to your office and take the day off?" Shep
longingly stroked her hair, delighting in its silken
texture between his fingers. "Tess, if you're really
concerned about us, stay. Stay and wait until I get done
with this flight. It'll only be two hours. Then we can
talk."

Her eyes widened in surprise. "Monday?" she uttered in disbelief.

A lazy grin played across his mouth as he sat on the
edge of the bed watching her. "Yeah. You lose a day or

something? Remember yesterday? It was Sunday. Today is a working day."

Her mind whirled with various options. Her heart had already made its choice; she wanted to stay and talk out the misunderstandings between them. But Dan would be away for the rest of the week. That meant she had to be in the office to take the helm. Swallowing hard she met his curious eyes. "Shep, I can't stay . . ."

His face became less readable and he got up. "Duty calls, doesn't it?" he asked coldly.

Her pulse leaped in fear and she sat up. "You don't understand."

He gave her a troubled look and walked to the door of the bathroom. "I guess I don't."

Everything was going wrong again. Why couldn't they communicate? Why did he have to jump to conclusions? "You can't get out of that flight and I can't get out of my responsibility at the office," she challenged. "So duty calls for both of us. Not just me."

Shep compressed his lips. Finally, he nodded, his face becoming unreadable. "Point well taken, Tess. I'll take a shower and shave. Then, the place will be yours."

She sat there in bed morosely listening to the sound of the shower. He had been crushed by her logic. Duty. Was it always duty? Tess ran her fingers through her hair, at odds with herself. She wanted to stay. The secure warmth of his body against hers during the night had brought a good feeling to Tess's healing heart. He had loved her so totally that she was still wrapped in euphoria even now. Cy had never made her feel like this . . . so joyful . . . so free and uninhibited. She felt a tendril of hope. Tess lifted her head, a new spark of life in her eyes. Anxiously, she waited until Shep reappeared.

His hair was dark and glistening, his face clean shaven. Pulling a dull olive green flight suit from the drawer, he slipped it on, zipping it up in one sure motion. A black leather square with his last name and rank emblazoned in gold was positioned above the left breast pocket. Patches showing that he was part of the B-1 test team adorned each of his shoulders. He glanced up at her as he sat on the edge of the bed, pulling on his socks.

"Your turn."

Tess drew up her knees, resting her chin on them and watching him. "I think I have a compromise, Shep," she began softly. Her heart quickened as he caught and held her eyes. He looked incredibly handsome and masculine.

"What kind?"

She licked her lips, praying her words would come out right. "I'm going to call my office and tell them I'll be in early this afternoon. Since your flight is this morning, I thought I might tag along with you. When it's over, I'll spring for breakfast."

A glimmer of life flickered in his eyes. "How about brunch? And I'll buy."

She reached out to touch his left hand. "Okay." Her blue eyes darkened with uncertainty. "It's the best I can do under the circumstances, Shep."

He finished putting on the second sock and turned to her, gripping her gently by the shoulders. He gazed deeply into her eyes. "It's more than enough, honey," he whispered huskily. "Come on, you've got a half hour before we have to leave," he coaxed, leaning over and lightly kissing her mouth.

There was a ribbon of pink above the mountains in the distance, suffusing the bone-white desert with a pale wash of rose-colored light. Tess sat in silence as Shep drove across the deserted highways toward the Operations building. A huge control tower rose out of it, looking oddly out of place on the dry desert lakebeds that surrounded Edwards. The only other creatures moving in the early morning were an occasional jack-rabbit or cottontail. Shep had loaned her one of his Air Force flight jackets to keep her warm in the predawn hours. He had made coffee for both of them and she cradled the mug in her hands as he drove.

"I'll have to call in to Rockwell at eight o'clock."

Shep nodded. "Tom is going to meet me over at Ops. I'm sure he won't mind escorting you around while I do my two hours of proficiency flying. He'll show you where the phones are located so you can make the call."

Tess nodded. How could she begin to explain to Shep how comfortable she felt in his presence? Her body still felt warm from their passionate lovemaking. Each time he looked at her with those knowing gray eyes, she melted inwardly to the core. She had never trusted anyone as much. "I owe you an apology," she murmured, thinking of the angry slap she had delivered the previous night.

He glanced over at her, a wry smile touching his mouth. "No, you don't. You owe it to yourself to start living again. And you're starting to do that."

A blush spread across her face. "I didn't mean to slap you. . . ." Her voice became inaudible. "I've never hit anyone, Shep—"

"I wanted to paddle you," he admitted. There was amusement in his tone. "I can see why you have red hair now," he chuckled.

Tess stared over at him. "That isn't funny, Shep. I hurt you."

He laughed fully. "You hurt my pride more than my face. I didn't think you'd really do it. I saw it in your eyes and I said, no, she won't do that. She wouldn't have the nerve." His eyes crinkled. "I was wrong. It forced me to quit treating you like some lost waif. I figured if you were woman enough to strike out like

that, you were woman enough to take the conse-
quences."

"I'm just glad you didn't hit back," she murmured,
relief in her voice.

"I may do many things, Tess," he answered gravely,
"but I'd never hit a woman."

"I didn't mean to imply that," she said quickly. "It's
just that you were accusing me of running away, but I
didn't. I was so angry at you. You never let me get a
word in edgewise."

Shep reached out, capturing her free hand and giving
it a squeeze of reassurance. "I had all day to think
about it, Tess. And I sure as hell wasn't prepared to see
you on my couch asleep when I got home. I thought
you had deserted me. I didn't know what to think when
I saw you there."

Her voice became softer. "Shep, I got called in to
Rockwell on an emergency at seven A.M. Sunday
morning by the PR department. Stockwell dropped
another of his unfounded allegations. We had every
major East Coast paper calling us. And then we
handled at least twenty-five calls from each time zone."
She shook her head. "It was horrible. I wasn't prepared
to help Fred do something his department should have
handled. But everyone was out of town and I ended up
getting stuck with it." She chewed on her lower lip. "I
tried to call you so many times, Shep. I finally got in
touch with Tom and explained the situation. He
thought it would be best if I came up here to try and
straighten things out." Her voice trembled. "I was so
worried about you, Shep. Tom was worried too. I could
tell."

His hand tightened about hers. "I just drove around
all day thinking and spent a lot of time talking to
myself," he admitted quietly. He gave her a piercing
look. "You mean a hell of a lot to me, Tess. I thought
I'd lost you. I felt so damn helpless."

Her heart was buoyed up by his admission. The strength of his love was undeniable. A pulse leaped at the base of her throat. Love? Tess gave him a brief, startled look, trying to hide her reaction. Making an effort to quell her pounding heart, she said, "I understand that now."

Chapter 11

It was one of the few times Tess had been to the Operations building. "Ops," as it was commonly called, housed a briefing area and a meteorology office as well as a control tower. It was from this building that the test flights originated. Shep escorted her through the doors, his left hand on her elbow. He carried a duffel bag that contained his helmet and oxygen mask in his right hand. Tom Cunningham greeted them in the spacious entrance attired in his blue uniform and flight cap.

"See you made it home last night, buddy."

Shep shared a brief smile with his friend. "I don't know whether I should shake your hand or call you a few choice names," he said.

Tom grinned mischievously, coming over. "You'll thank me sooner or later," he said.

"Tess is going to stick around until I get my proficiency flight out of the way. Mind keeping her company?"

"Not at all. You go ahead and pick up your flight plan." He looked over at Tess. "Come on, I'll show you how test pilots keep their skills up to par while he's getting briefed."

141

Shep leaned over, placing a kiss on her lips. As he drew away he said, "You'll be bored as hell watching me bump and go."

She liked the lingo of the Air Force pilots. *Bump and go* simply meant that the aircraft would land on the runway and then take off moments later. Her lips tingled warmly beneath his mouth and she said, "I don't think anything you do is boring."

Shep gave her a long, appraising look, a smile lingering in his gray eyes. He looked up at Tom. "Hey, buddy, you might see if they'll let you up in the tower to listen to transmissions."

Tom's brows raised. "Good idea."

"I've got an hour's worth of high altitude flight to do first. You might take Tess to get a bite to eat over at the cafeteria. See you two later." He waved to them and walked down the highly polished hall toward the briefing room. Tess fell in step beside Tom as he ambled toward the opposite side of the building to the lounge.

"Well?" Tom asked, glancing over at her. "How'd it go?"

"It was rough," she murmured, glad to be able to confide in him. "I fell asleep on the couch and didn't hear him come in. I don't know who was more shocked. Him or me."

Tom allowed a small grin to surface. "You both look pretty happy now. Matter of fact, Shep looks like he's on top of the world."

She slowed her pace as they neared the glass doors. The rose wash that had given the white lake beds a pink hue was now gone. The sun was edging above the desert horizon, its rays creating long shadows across the bare landscape. Jets of all sizes and types stood silently on the ramp to the left of the tower. Some were camouflaged green and brown, others were white. Ground crews worked around several preparing them for flight. Tanker trucks filled with JP-4, the fuel used by jet aircraft, traveled up and down the line, filling the awaiting planes. The sun's rays warmed the lounge area. Tess crossed her arms, watching the scene before them.

"He thought I had run away," she murmured, "again."

"And?"

"He was pretty angry," she admitted, and then frowned, remembering the confrontation the night before. "I don't blame him."

"Shep cools off pretty quickly, though. I'm glad to see you could stay around today."

"I have to call Rockwell at eight and tell them I'm coming in this afternoon."

He pursed his lips. "Something's better than nothing under the circumstances," he said.

"Yes," she agreed fervently, "it is."

At seven thirty, Tess saw Shep emerging from Ops. One of the crew chiefs escorted him to a T-38. Tom pointed toward the sleek supersonic jet aircraft. "The T-38 is utilized as a supersonic trainer and chase plane for test flights. Normally the instructor sits in the rear seat and the student in the front."

"But he's going to fly it alone," Tess said, wondering if he should have a copilot in case something went wrong.

"When a test pilot isn't getting enough flying time in because things are slow, we all fly the T-38. It's a standard trainer. It's a twin jet-engine aircraft that handles real nice. You look worried."

She shrugged. "I thought if there were two seats, that automatically meant two pilots."

"It's not mandatory to fly with a copilot. Relax, he'll be all right. This is just standard flying." Tom smiled. "God, what will you do if he's picked to be the first Air Force officer to make the test flight of the B-1?"

She laughed. "Be a basket case." The ladder was

placed on the side of the T-38 and Shep gingerly
climbed into the front cockpit seat. The crew chief
helped him strap in, giving Shep some last-minute
information. Tess had to admit the T-38 was a sleek-
looking aircraft. Still, she thought that the B-1, for its
size, looked even more beautiful.

Tom's comment about Shep possibly being chosen to
fly the B-1 sent an unexpected jolt of fear through her.
She absentmindedly chewed on one of her nails as she
watched the ground crew remove the ladder and pull
the parking chocks out from beneath the wheels of the
T-38. Even through the thick windows of the lounge
area, they could hear the high-pitched whine of the
engines on the aircraft. With the white helmet on his
head and the dark green sun visor drawn down against
the oxygen mask, Tess couldn't tell Shep from any
other pilot. She watched as the canopy slowly closed
down over him. Shep gave a thumbs up signal to the
crew chief, moving the T-38 out of the confines of the
ramp and onto the taxi strip.

"Can we go outside and watch him take off?" she
asked Tom, a tremor of excitement in her voice.

He smiled indulgently. "Sure. Knowing that you're
watching him, Shep will probably light the afterburners
and give us a real bang."

There was more jet traffic than Tess would have
expected at that early morning hour. At least five types
of Air Force jets, ranging from another T-38 to a huge
cargo plane known as a C-130 Hercules, were flying at
different altitudes around the huge base doing bump
and go landings. The sun warmed Tess as she stood on
the balcony in the clear morning air. She loved the
clean, fresh air of the desert. Sunlight glanced off the
glistening white skin of the T-38 that Shep piloted. At
the end of the taxi strip, he brought the plane to a halt.
The C-130 dropped in like a mammoth seagull, its four
turboprop engines whining as it sped past them, briefly

landing. Halfway down the airstrip the cargo plane's engines revved up as it took off once again, pointing its nose upward into the crystal morning air.

Tom leaned over. "Shep should be next to take off. The tower will wait about a minute before letting him go. The backwash of those propeller jobs creates a whorling wind effect. If you take off too soon afterward, it can flip a plane on its wing and cause a crash."

"Is that why they always have a few minutes between takeoffs and landings?" she wondered aloud, shading her eyes against the sun's brilliance.

"Yes, ma'am. Now listen. You'll hear those engines in the T-38 start shrilling in a moment. Those babies can cause you to go deaf if you don't take proper precautions. That's why the crews all wear protective ear gear around them. There. He's got the go ahead from the tower."

The T-38 moved onto the end of the runway. Tess could hear the engines becoming shrill as Shep held the plane with the brakes. The morning quiet was shattered as he started the T-38 rolling down the strip. The afterburners, which provided sudden forward thrust, were lit. With an explosion of sound, the jet leaped forward like an unshackled eagle. Tess watched in awe as the arrowlike jet covered only a few thousand feet of runway before lifting off. She heard Tom laugh.

"That showoff! Watch him. He's gonna take that plane straight up at the end of the runway!"

Her breath lodged in her throat as the plane suddenly lunged skyward at an almost impossible angle of attack as it hurtled into the blue. She had no idea how many thousand of feet per second the agile T-38 could climb. Rapidly the plane became a small speck, the thundering sound of the afterburners dying away very quickly. Tom turned to her.

"Pretty impressive, isn't it?"

She nodded. "Very. And you do the same thing?"

"If I had my girl watching, I would," he returned, grinning. "Come on; I'll treat you to breakfast. It will be at least an hour before he comes back to complete the bump and go's."

She was surprised at the number of people in the civilian-run cafeteria. Clusters of mechanics, pilots in their olive green flight suits and various other uniformed personnel sat grouped at the tables. Tom escorted her through the line and then chose a small table in one corner near the window.

Tess had just sat down and was getting comfortable when she gazed across the room and turned pale. Tom sat opposite her, his tray piled high with enough breakfast for two people. A strangled sound emerged from her throat as her eyes met those of Derek Barton. Her heart began to beat rapidly; her fingers turned cold.

"Tess? What's wrong?"

She couldn't tear her gaze from Barton's. He had been watching her all along. Her stomach knotted and blood pounded through her head, cutting off all other sounds.

"Tess? God, you're pale. What's wrong?" Tom leaned across the table, reaching out to touch her arm.

The warmth of his fingers broke the shock. Automatically, she pulled her arm away from him, lowering her eyes to her tray in confusion. Derek Barton was here! Oh, God. Her sudden shock was overcome by anger. He had helped kill Cy, she screamed silently, fighting back tears. The filthy little rat of a man had told a lie. A lie that had killed her husband. She was vaguely aware of Tom talking to her. His voice was low, filled with concern. Biting down hard on her lower lip, Tess raised her head, meeting Tom's worried eyes.

"Barton's here," she rasped, clenching the napkin tightly in her lap, her fingers whitening.

Tom cocked his head to one side. "Barton?" His eyes

suddenly narrowed. "That bastard's here?" he muttered. "Where?"

Tess was shaken by the major's vehement reaction. Thank God Shep wasn't here.

"Never mind!" she breathed. Tess closed her eyes for a second, willing her pounding heart to stop beating so heavily. There was nothing she could do about Barton seeing her here. But what would he think? What slimy new gossip would he spread about her? She opened her eyes, staring down at her tray. Suddenly, she wasn't hungry. She was angry. Angry in a way she had never been before.

Tom had turned, looking out across the crowded cafeteria. When he turned back, his normally easy features were hard. "I see him," he snarled. "It's okay, Tess. Just ignore the little creep. He can't hurt you anymore."

She had an urge to look back over at Barton to see if he was still staring at her but fought the impulse. She took an unsteady gulp of air. "He killed Cy," she whispered tautly. "He killed him with lies, Tom. Oh, God, I don't know if I can sit here. . . ."

"You have as much right to sit here as he does," Tom reminded her. He glanced up at her sharply. "You staying or running?"

Tess jerked her chin up, eyes wide. "No more running, Tom," she rasped. Her voice sounded strained to her own ears. She had promised herself to start living again. To grow up. It was an uncomfortable situation at best, but she forced herself to pick at the toast and jelly.

"Atta girl. Barton's going to get his," he promised grimly. "It's just a damn good thing he didn't run into Shep. He'll deck him if he sets sights on him."

"I feel so much anger toward Barton, Tom. I—I can hardly sit here and eat."

He gave her a tight smile. "I know. It must be hard

under the circumstances, knowing Barton lied and
helped trigger your husband's heart attack. But sooner
or later, you've got to face him. Either here or at a
meeting with Rockwell contractors."

"I want to wrap my hands around his throat," she
confided.

"Hey, ease up, Tess. We'll finish our breakfast and
mosey back to Ops." He glanced at his watch. "We
should be going in another ten minutes."

Tess sat there, inwardly amazed at the strength of her
feelings.

"I wonder what he's going to do with this newest bit
of gossip?" she asked under her breath.

"Probably say that you and I are now having a
red-hot affair," Tom suggested, smiling more easily this
time.

Tess couldn't help but frown. "He's an ugly man,
Tom. I hope you don't get caught in the middle of this."

"I know at least twenty other officers who would turn
green with envy if they thought I was going with you."
His brown eyes sparkled. "There are worse things to
have people gossip about, you know. Being seen with a
pretty lady is always a pleasure, believe me."

Tess blushed at the compliment. "Shep and I are
both lucky to have you as a friend," she whispered,
meaning it.

He winked at her. "You're both worth it. Come on, it
looks like you're done picking at your breakfast. Let's
go over and watch Shep play in the pattern for a while."
He rose and put on his flight cap. "And don't worry
about Barton. We've got better things to do than let
him ruin our day."

Nonetheless, Tess was relieved to leave the cafeteria.
She began to breathe easier as they arrived back at
Ops. She noticed that several more planes were in the
landing pattern around Edwards. Tom took her up a
series of stairs until she found herself in the control

tower itself. The chief controller nodded in her direction after Tom explained the situation. Tom picked up two headsets.

"He's already in the pattern, Tess. Just put this contraption on and you can listen to them talk. His call sign is Hawk six."

She put the slender headset on and was immediately confronted with the strange lingo of pilots speaking with the tower. There was a rectangular landing pattern at Edwards. After a plane took off from the airstrip, it would make a left turn, then fly less than a mile, and make another left-hand turn so that the plane paralleled the runway. The base leg was reached with the next left-hand turn. After that, the plane would make one last left-hand turn which would line it up to land on the runway. At least seven jets were now in that familiar pattern, practicing bump and go's. Tess turned to Tom.

"Which one is Shep's plane?"

Tom listened intently to the conversations for a moment. He nodded as if confirming his suspicion and pointed through the large, green-tinted windows that encased the tower. "He's on the crosswind leg. The second white T-38 over there. See him?"

There were several planes in that area and it took her a moment to sort them out. Besides two T-38's, there was also a T-37 and a C-130 Hercules at a higher altitude.

"Edwards, Hawk six, turning downwind," Shep's voice carried clearly over the earphones.

Tom pointed. "That's him turning now."

Tess nodded, her heart expanding with an inexplicable happiness. The last thirty minutes of anguish disappeared. She watched, mesmerized by the slender beauty of the T-38 streaking along one thousand feet above the desert floor. She listened as he made another call before turning onto the base leg. Having

seen several other jets land and take off, she watched
with interest to see if he would land the T-38 smoothly.
The jet was like a graceful ballerina, banking for the
final left-hand turn, lining up perfectly with the runway. She watched with pride as he made a smooth landing, the wheels of the jet lightly touching the airstrip.

"He'll hold it on the ground for a couple thousand
feet before applying power through the throttles to take
off again," Tom explained. "Too bad you can't be there
with him. The g's build up on takeoff. There's nothing
like it," he said, excitement barely veiled in his voice.

Inside the cockpit, Shep held the T-38's nose level as
he streaked down the runway. Right hand on the dual
throttle, he inched it forward, listening to the whine of
the engines increase, watching the rpm gauges jumping
upward. The vibration of the tires against the runway
made the jet shiver imperceptibly. He could feel the
quiver throughout his body. It was as if the jet were a
living being surrounding him. Out of long habit, his
gaze swept across the myriad of dials. The sunlight was
strong through the cockpit window even with the dark
visor down over his face.

Pushing both throttles to the maximum, he gently
eased the stick back between his legs, allowing the nose
of the jet to move upward. The gravity of g-forces built
up against his body as he allowed the jet to lunge
skyward. The engines growled with their high-pitched
whine. "Edwards, Hawk six, turning crosswind leg."

"Roger, Hawk six, crosswind leg."

Just as he applied slight left rudder with his left foot
and moved the stick a bit in the same direction, he saw
a flight of birds crossing his intended flight path. His
hand momentarily tensed on the stick. There was a
sudden bang like a muffled pop on his left. The T-38
quivered perceptibly. Flame out! His lips thinned, and
he whispered, "Son-of-a-bitch!" The jet had just lost an
engine! From thousands of hours of training, his reac-

tions were automatic. He yanked the throttle back to the idle position. His eyes shot to the rpm gauge. The needle lay lifeless, indicating the engine had flamed out; the flow of fuel to it had somehow been halted. Why? Had a bird struck the intake of the engine? Was it a simple case of a plugged fuel line? Should he hit the restart button? His mind whirled with options. At the same time, the jet nosed downward with the loss of the power from the engine. He automatically shoved the right throttle to the fire wall, making up the difference, halting the drop of the jet. Simultaneously, he hit hard right rudder to bring the jet back to a stable angle, allowing the right engine to labor under the added load.

"Edwards, Hawk six, I just lost an engine. I'm declaring an emergency," he stated calmly.

Should he hit restart? He glanced at the exhaust gas temperature gauge. It was high and climbing. That meant it was more than a fuel line plug. If he didn't shut the engine off completely, it would mean a fire. And if he shut that engine down, it meant the loss of all hydraulics to the landing gear. As he watched the temperature gauge soaring upward rapidly, he realized he had no choice. His eyes moved to the fire light indicator. So far, it wasn't glaring red to show that fire had begun in the engine. Sweat trickled down his temple.

With his thumb, he cocked the trigger on the left engine throttle, pulling it all the way back and completely shutting the engine down. Glancing out of the cockpit, he didn't see any telltale signs of smoke coming off the dead engine.

"Hawk six, Edwards. What is the nature of the emergency?"

"Edwards, I've got a compressor stall. Have shut the engine down. Will call you on downwind after I manually lower landing gear."

"Hawk six, you are cleared to land."

"Roger," Shep answered. His mind was clear. Shep wasn't aware of anything but the present and what had to be done to get the jet back on the ground in one piece. Leaning over in the cramped cockpit, he gripped a handle, beginning to lower the landing gear manually. All the while he was watching the gauges which monitored the right engine, looking for problems because of the weight overload. He glanced at the fire light indicator on the port engine. So far it remained unlit. One shred of extraneous thought interrupted his concentration—Tess was down below. Did she know about the emergency? Grimly his lips thinned as he continued to work the handle to bring down the landing gear.

Tess stood frozen, her hands across her mouth, eyes wide and frightened. Tom gripped her shoulder.

"He'll be okay," he said automatically, eyes narrowed upon the limping T-38 in the downwind pattern. They had both seen the jet suddenly lag and fall to the left. Tess had gasped. The rest of the men in the tower suddenly went into action. As soon as Shep declared an emergency, the controllers set the alarm for the fire rescue unit. Instantly the trucks were screaming down the taxi way toward preplanned positions, ready to assist when the controllers brought the crippled jet in for the landing. All other traffic was immediately rerouted out of the pattern. Jets of all varieties suddenly scattered like a flock of disturbed birds in all directions, giving their wounded comrade all the airspace necessary to deal with the emergency.

Tess felt her knees jelly as she stared horrified at the jet whose landing gear was slowly being lowered. She was barely aware of Tom's fingers gripping her shoulder to steady her. Shep, she screamed silently. Oh, God, don't die! Don't die!

Memories of losing Cy overwhelmed her. She had

loved him and had lost him. She had fallen in love with Shep. Was he going to crash and die before her eyes? A small sob escaped from her and she buried her face in her hands, unable to cope with the grisly thought. Tom moved closer, putting his arm around her shoulders.

"He'll bring it down nice and slow," he said. "Don't cry, Tess. He'll be okay. There's no sign of fire on that left engine. He's landed more than one jet with just a single engine."

Her heart was filled with anguish, regardless of Tom's confident tone. Shep's handsome face danced in her mind. She heard his laughter, remembered poignantly how he had made love to her, and how she had loved him in return. It was too much, and tears fell down her pale cheeks.

"Edwards, Hawk six, gear down. Will contact you on base leg."

"Roger, Hawk six, landing gear down and in place. Runway is clear and ready. Winds calm, visibility unlimited."

"Roger, Edwards. Gear down and locked."

Tess hung on his every word. He sounded so calm! She looked up at Tom. "He doesn't even sound worried!"

Tom smiled for her benefit. It wasn't much of a smile, but it was the best he could muster under the circumstances. "He's a test pilot, Tess. He's trained to think calmly under emergency situations just like this one."

"He's got to be frightened!" she whispered, watching the white jet slowly descend.

Tom shrugged. He didn't say it, but he was worried. Shep hadn't tried to restart the engine, which was the normal procedure. Most pilots of jet aircraft had experienced flame out. He didn't explain the ramifications to Tess, sensing how frightened she was. Something had gone wrong with the engine or Shep wouldn't have shut it off completely. He strained to see if the

least little indication of black smoke was trailing after
the left engine. If a fire started—he didn't even want to
consider the possibilities. Instead he shifted his attention to the fire trucks that sat at thousand-foot intervals
along the runway.

Each fire truck carried thousands of gallons of foam
which would be utilized if there was a fire. They looked
like lime green monsters. The firefighters stood ready
in their asbestos-lined silver-hooded turn-out gear,
looking like spacemen.

"Edwards, Hawk six, making final approach."

"Roger, Hawk six. You are cleared for emergency
landing."

"Roger, flaps down, gear locked."

Tess held her breath, hands clenched into tight balls
of tension against her breast. The jet made the final
turn, lining up with the runway. The *what if*'s careened
through her frightened mind. The sun had risen high
enough to begin burning the land once again. It created
up and down drafts, large columns of air rising vertical-
ly thousands of feet into the atmosphere. As Shep
guided the T-38 toward the end of the runway, several
drafts made the jet bounce wildly. A lump threatened
to shut off the air in Tess's throat as the plane staggered
drunkenly. A strangled cry was torn from her as the
nose of the jet suddenly came up. The T-38 flared
out only a few feet from the beginning of the runway, its flaps fully extended downward. It looked
like a huge predatory bird hovering momentarily
before it landed. Suddenly, the jet was safely on the
ground, shrieking past them. The fire trucks moved
into action, following the jet's progress down the
airstrip.

Tess turned to Tom. "He made it!" she cried.

He nodded grimly. "Come on, let's get downstairs.
They'll park that jet away from here just in case of
fire."

Shep throttle cocked the right engine, shutting it down and bringing the T-38 to a complete halt. Three fire trucks hovered nearby. He completed his post-flight check and watched as the canopy slowly yawned open. Unhinging the oxygen mask, Shep pulled the helmet off his head. His hair was damp with sweat, plastered against his skull. The ladder was brought up and hooked to the side of the plane, and he climbed down to the pavement. He took a deep breath of fresh air as he put the flight cap on his head and walked slowly over to the port wing.

Three crewmen were inspecting the engine, looking into the mouth of the intake. As Shep came up, the crew chief raised his head. "You ate a bird from the looks of it, sir."

Shep looked into the fanlike engine. He grimaced. "There was a flock of birds in the area I flew over," he explained to the crew chief.

"Yes, sir," the older man agreed. "From the looks of those bent fan blades in there, I'd say you sucked one in for sure. We'll know more when we tear it apart for inspection."

Shep nodded. "Let me know what you find, Sergeant."

"Yes, sir. Good landing you made, Major."

He smiled distantly. "I didn't have much of a choice under the circumstances. I'll be over at Ops filling out a report on this."

The crew chief nodded, avidly returning to the inspection of the jet engine. Shep hopped a ride back to Ops. He saw Tom and Tess standing at the bottom of the steps. As he got out, he anxiously searched her face. The terror was written in her eyes and in the lines of her face. He thanked the driver, walking quickly toward them. There was a gathering crowd of people at the doors, but he ignored them, intent only upon Tess. He opened his arms and she flew to him. The soft curve of her body fitted against him and he groaned, embracing her.

"Oh, Shep," she cried, her voice muffled against his shoulder. "Are you all right?"

He laughed gently, kissing her hair. "I'm okay, honey. It's a routine type of emergency," he explained, making less of the incident for her benefit. The moment she raised her tear-stained face, his heart contracted. The fear in her blue eyes was very real. Her lips trembled, glistening with shed tears. Leaning down, he kissed her longingly, tasting the salt, reveling in the pliancy of her lips beneath his mouth. Minutes ago he had been alone in the sky with an ailing jet. Now he held a warm, beautiful woman in his arms. Her mouth tasted sweet, and he inhaled the natural scent of her body. Finally he released her, giving her a reassuring smile. "I didn't plan this emergency just because you were here," he said, worriedly assessing her strained face.

Tess gulped unsteadily, reassured by his arm around her body as she clung to him, afraid to let go. "I certainly hope not!" she said fervently. Giving him a small smile, she said, "I'm just glad you're safe, Shep."

He laughed indulgently, turning and leading her toward the steps where Tom stood. "Makes two of us, lady. Come on, I've got a pile of paperwork to fill out over this incident." He gave her a squeeze. "I'm still taking you to lunch. This doesn't change anything."

Tess looked up as they negotiated the stairs. At least fifteen men stood watching them through the entrance doors.

"What'd you do?" Tom asked. "Eat a bird?"

Shep pushed the drying hair off his brow. "Yeah, I think so. I saw the damn flock rising, and they veered off right into my flight path. I heard a bump and rumble, and that was the beginning of the end."

"I was wondering why you didn't hit restart."

"Couldn't. The exhaust temperature gauge was climbing." He grinned over at his friend. "Believe me, I wanted to. It's a hell of a lot easier hitting restart than flying around on one engine."

Tess felt Shep's arm tighten around her waist momentarily. "You okay?" he asked.

She tore her gaze from the crowd, from one man who was staring at them with more than just idle interest. Derek Barton gave her an evil smile and then turned away. Tess tried to shake the ugly feeling, returning her attention to Shep. "Yes," she said, "I'm fine. Just a little shaken."

Tom opened the door and they filed through it. The small group parted, allowing them to walk toward the debriefing area. "What will you do if I get to be the first to fly the B-1?" Shep teased. The adrenaline that had been pumping through him during the emergency was waning, leaving him feeling momentarily exhausted.

"If you are selected as the first to fly it, I told Tom I'd probably be a basket case," she confided.

Shep feigned shock. "What? You don't trust the plane you're building?"

"We know she'll fly. I'll just worry, that's all."

He shared an intimate smile with her. "That's nice to know," he murmured.

Tess sat in a chair at the back of the room while Shep and the Ops officer went over the series of events concerning the T-38 incident. She couldn't quite understand how Shep could be so casual about the near accident. As he spoke with the other officer, she watched his gestures and listened to the tone of his voice. It was as if he were making small talk about the weather to a stranger. Tom excused himself, saying he had to meet someone for lunch over at the Officers' Club, and left. She glanced at her watch—it was almost eleven thirty. With a sinking feeling, Tess knew she would have to leave shortly in order to make it back to

L.A. on time. She had promised to be in by no later than one thirty P.M.

Tess was deep in thought about seeing Derek Barton at the base when Shep walked over and interrupted. He smiled down at her, holding out his hand. "Sorry to keep you waiting. Ready for a late brunch?"

She took his hand. His fingers were strong and steady. "It's eleven forty, Shep. I have to leave for L.A. in a few minutes," she explained, walking with him out the front door. The sunshine was bright and warm. The wind had picked up briskly off the desert, blowing a few tumbleweeds down the street in front of them. He halted at his car, opening the door for her.

"Then I'd better take you to Tom's house to pick up your car."

Tess glanced over the top of the car at him. If he was disappointed, he didn't show it. "That would be fine," she agreed quietly.

The trip back to his house was mercifully short. He walked Tess over to her Toyota, which sat out in the street next to Tom's home. She opened the car door, turning and looking up into his incredibly handsome face. His hair had been dark with sweat earlier from the near accident. Now it was dry, the wind lifting strands of it, giving him a boyish appearance. "I'm sorry I have to leave."

Shep shrugged his broad shoulders. "Duty calls, like you said before." A wry smile drew the corners of his mouth upward. "If I hadn't had that emergency, we would have had plenty of time for brunch. Can I get a raincheck?"

She warmed to the huskiness in his voice. She didn't want to leave him yet. The accident was too real. It had produced a startling revelation in her—she loved Shep. Did he love her? Digging nervously for the car keys in her purse, she nodded. "Sure you can."

"What about dinner Friday night? I understand the

test pilots have to be down at Rockwell during the day to review some of the latest system designs descriptions."

"I'd like that."

He grinned, his gray eyes twinkling. "Sure?"

"Very sure."

Reaching over, he placed a light kiss on her lips. "It's a damn good thing we're out in the street," he growled. "Or I might not be responsible for my actions. I'll see you Friday, Irish princess. And be careful driving back to L.A. One accident a day is plenty."

Tess fervently agreed, her lips tingling from the touch of his mouth. "Just be careful, Shep . . ."

He stepped away. "Where you're concerned, always. And don't make too much of what happened today, Tess. It's a pretty common flight problem."

She grimaced and shut the door. It didn't matter how many times it happened, she would never get used to it. Driving back, she realized that for over a year she had worked on blueprints of the B-1. And in that period of time she had never doubted that it would fly. It had never occurred to her that she might have an emotional involvement with one of the men chosen to fly it for the first time. That put an entirely different light on the situation. What if the B-1 didn't fly? She had heard horror stories of prototypes barely getting off the ground and then diving headlong into the earth, erupting into balls of flame.

Tess shuddered, trying to block out the picture that hung stubbornly in the back of her mind. Shep was a good pilot; there was no doubt. He had made the landing of the ailing T-38 look simple—almost as if the plane had landed with two engines instead of one. What were his chances of getting chosen as the Air Force test pilot to accompany the two Rockwell test pilots on the B-1's maiden flight? She made a mental note to find out. If she had her way, Shep wouldn't fly.

Frowning, Tess knew that the decision rested with the
Air Force and not her. On Friday she would ask him
more about his flying credentials and try to determine
the odds of his getting that prestigious position. Blueprints, for the first time, had become more than just
inanimate white lines on blue background. The man
she loved might be flying that untested bomber in a few
months. Was her life falling into a pattern? Was she
destined to lose Shep to the bomber as she had lost Cy?
A shiver of dread washed over her, and Tess tried to
shake the feeling.

Chapter 12

ON FRIDAY, A LARGE GROUP OF ROCKWELL ENGINEERS, contractors and subcontractors milled around in the conference room waiting for the meeting to begin. A contingent of Air Force officers was also included in the crowd. Coffee and doughnuts were being passed around for the late morning meeting. Shep glanced over at Tom Cunningham who had walked in with him.

"Knowing the usual course of things, I'll have time to go see Tess before this starts. Be back in a few minutes."

Tom nodded, studying the civilians in the room. "Okay, buddy. Make your ETA about fifteen minutes. Looks like this group is serious about getting down to business."

"Roger."

He turned, nearly bumping into three men entering the room. Shep froze, eyes narrowed upon one face. Derek Barton's black eyes lifted, meeting Shep's. The thinness of Barton's face became more pinched as he walked quickly past. Adrenaline pumped strongly through Shep, and he fought the urge to turn and grab the small man by the collar. There was an air about

Barton that made Shep simply want to throw a punch
into his smug face. Fighting the urge, Shep resolutely
headed out the door. He'd always known he'd run into
Barton some day. A grimace pulled at the corners of his
mouth. Naturally it would be in a meeting like this
where civility was a must. Shoving away the whole
messy problem, Shep stepped into the nearest elevator.

Tess looked up just as Shep entered her office. A
pink blush spread beautifully across her face, giving her
cheeks a rose hue. The week had dragged on as though
Friday would never come. She had had time to think
about the in-flight emergency and the possibility of
losing Shep. He smiled, a lazy grin curving the corners
of his mouth upward as he quietly entered her office.

"Lady, you look beautiful," he said, coming to a stop
at the edge of the large oak desk.

She had decided to wear her hair down today for the
first time since joining Rockwell. The auburn strands
lay across her shoulders like molten copper against the
midnight blue of her dress. She had taken great pains to
look as feminine as she felt. And it was all because of
Shep. Earlier, as she had traversed the halls, more than
one male employee had gawked or given her a second
look. Normally she wore a conservative pants suit and
her chignon as a symbol of authority. Not anymore.

She smiled up at him. "Thank you," she whispered.
Her heart beat in heightened awareness of Shep. How
did he manage to look so incredibly handsome? Was it
the cleanly cut lines of the dark blue Air Force uniform? Or the intensity of his eyes as he devoured her
with his full attention? She wasn't sure. "At least
you're not giving me a shocked look," she laughed.

Shep made himself comfortable on the edge of her
desk, taking in the overall effect. "Lady, you're stun-
ning. I am in shock. Just not showing it." Her blue eyes
were large and incredibly beautiful. He felt himself
becoming lost within their azure-gold depths, his body

tightening with need of her. How many times during the past week had he replayed the night they had made such passionate, wildly pleasurable love? He wanted to kiss her lips again, taste them, mold them against his mouth in hungry adoration. "Tonight can't come too soon," he murmured huskily.

Tess felt a wave of nervousness intertwined with expectation. She lowered her gaze, her long, thick lashes resting against her cheekbones. She groped for some flip reply to cover the sudden flutter in her heart. Gathering the few threads of sense still remaining to her, she murmured, "Did you bring civilian clothes?"

"Yes, ma'am." He gave her a wink and straightened up, squaring his broad shoulders. "Well, that meeting ought to be starting by now. It promises to be a long one."

"Better you than me."

"Thanks."

Tess met his smiling gray gaze. "I've had four meetings this week. I've met my quota."

"See you sometime late this afternoon, honey."

She nodded, resting her chin against her folded hands. Her heart filled with happiness as she watched Shep leave as quietly as he had come. There was a cougarlike grace to his walk, a smoothness that belied the power that was coiled and waiting within his lean body. It was a loving, giving body, she thought.

Tess had to force herself to return to work. Dan would be back early in the afternoon, which meant she could leave on time for once.

Derek Barton watched Major Ramsey's progress into the meeting room. The secretary had finished distributing a thick folder in front of each man. He fingered the cover absently, never taking his eyes off the Air Force officer. The names of the men who would be taking the B-1 on its initial flights would be announced today.

Derek Barton had an old grievance with one of those men—Major Shep Ramsey. It had been the major's adamant contention after one test flight that the bearings his company manufactured were responsible for the fracture of the starboard wing. X rays were taken, revealing that the bearings were indeed the culprit. A coldness swept through Barton. The Hamilton woman was still checking performance test results on every damn bearing going into the B-1. Was it her way of taking vengeance on him for telling Cy Hamilton about her affair with Ramsey? He glared down at the rich walnut-colored table for a moment. He was going to have to apply more pressure to get her out of that office. He raised his head, staring directly across the table at Ramsey.

Charlie Starling, the Rockwell representative, got up and lumbered toward the head of the long rectangular table. He placed the vinyl-covered notebook on a lectern that had been strategically placed before him.

"We've got quite a bit to cover on today's agenda," he began in his rumbling voice. Cocking one graying eyebrow at the left side of the table, he said, "But first things first. I'm sure the test pilots would like to know who's been assigned to the first flight test crew." He pulled out a paper from his breast pocket, unfolding it with characteristic meticulousness. Spreading it out before him, he straightened the wire rim glasses that perpetually slid down his bulbous nose. "Okay, for Rockwell, we have Dave Faulkner as pilot and Pete Vosper as engineer." He glanced over at the Air Force contingent. "And for copilot, Major Shepherd Ramsey. Congratulations to the three of you." He allowed a hint of a smile. "This team will be responsible for the first flight, the gross weight tests, wing movement and supersonic tests. Providing all goes according to the schedules we've worked up, we'll be feeding in the following test pilots or engineers: Major Tom Cunningham, Colonel Jim Munkasey, Brett McMorrison, and Taylor Holmes."

Barton squirmed uncomfortably in his chair. That damn Ramsey. Again! The officer had eyes like a damned eagle. Barton rubbed his brow slowly, feeling an impending headache coming on. At the same time, a dark shadow began to take shape, a plan forming in his mind.

"Ah, excuse me, Charlie," Barton interrupted.

Charlie's brows fell downward. "Derek?"

Barton rubbed his nonexistent chin in what he hoped looked like a thoughtful gesture. Then he gave a quick, cutting smile that didn't reach his eyes. "Yes. I was just wondering how you came up with the test pilot assignments."

The room fell into silence. Shep Ramsey's face remained expressionless as he coolly watched Barton. "Without sounding terse about it, Derek," Charlie responded, "Rockwell picked their people based upon past flight performance and skill. For instance, Dave, here, had over two thousand hours in B-52 bombers before leaving the Air Force and joining Rockwell as a test pilot. He's got a lot of experience in that area."

"Was that the criterion? Time in bombers?" Barton asked, his dark eyes narrowing speculatively.

"For Rockwell it was."

Barton turned to Colonel Preston, the man responsible for the Air Force contingent of test pilots. "And how much time does Major Ramsey have in bombers, Colonel?"

"A little over a thousand hours."

Barton feigned surprise. "Only a thousand?"

The colonel, a tall, spare man of forty-five, shrugged. "We felt the quality of Major Ramsey's experience made him the strongest candidate in the B-1 program, Mr. Barton."

The subcontractor gave an eloquent shrug of his thin

shoulders. "That's only half the number of hours Mr. Faulkner has to his credit."

Shep slowly leaned forward on his elbows, pinning Barton with his gray eyes. "Are you implying that I'm less competent than the other pilots, Mr. Barton?" he asked, his voice almost friendly.

The contractor gave a slight laugh. "Hardly, Major. I'm just curious about how the members were selected. That's all." He looked up at Starling. "But it would seem to me that if the press gets hold of this kind of information it might make the Air Force look bad. I mean, what if we do run into problems with the B-1 in flight? We all know the American public is jumpy about spending so much money on the program. What if there's an emergency? The press might be inclined to question the selection criteria." He shook his head. "None of us on the project want to encourage bad press."

Shep controlled his anger. He stared across the table at Barton. He knew exactly what the man was trying to do. "Tell me something," Shep interrupted, breaking the brittle silence. "How much money would your company stand to lose if the project was cancelled?"

Barton nervously met his gaze. "Seventy million. Not much when you consider that each plane costs sixty-one million."

Shep nodded, forcing a polite smile. "Correct me if my memory is wrong, Mr. Barton, but as I recall, the Air Force had trouble with your company's ball bearings on another plane I tested. Isn't that true?"

Barton flushed to the roots of his black hair. "Aren't we getting off the subject, Major?"

Shep shrugged. "I don't think so. If you're questioning my hours in bombers, I suppose I can question the quality of the ball bearings made by your company. I'm curious about the nature of your concern for my being assigned to these first flights. Last time I flew a fighter that had your bearings installed, there was nothing but trouble."

The entire room buzzed with shocked murmurs. Charlie Starling shifted from one leg to the other, not quite sure what to say. Finally Colonel Preston spoke up.

"Mr. Barton, what the hours fail to show is the quality of Major Ramsey's flight experience. He had two tours of duty in South Vietnam and accrued a very impressive record. He flew one bird home with three engines out. Another time, three-quarters of his plane's tail had been blown away by a SAM missile. On a third bomber flight, flak damage was so great that he had most of his crew bail out over the Gulf of Tonkin. He then used his considerable skills to bring that bomber back to Thailand and land it in one piece. We believe that no one has better hands-on experience with bombers in an emergency."

"We aren't at war now," Barton stated flatly. "There's no tail missing, no holes in the fuselage, and no SAM missiles around, Colonel. No offense to Major Ramsey, but I just don't think his war medals are going to instill confidence in the American public in his being selected as copilot for these initial tests." Barton glanced around the table, realizing that he had blundered into a very delicate situation. But his own fears for his company coupled with his hatred of Tess Hamilton forced him to continue. "Look," he laughed, "I'm just trying to view all sides of the situation. Rockwell has gotten a lot of bad publicity the last couple of months." He glanced across the table at Ramsey, but directed his comments to Charlie Starling, seeking to gain an ally. "Poor Mrs. Hamilton has talked to the press and as a consequence, your whole company's image has suffered."

Tom Cunningham looked sharply at Shep. He sensed his friend's mounting anger. Glaring at Barton, Tom said between clenched teeth, "For someone who has only ball bearings to worry about, you're sure interested in phases of this project that have very little to do with you directly."

Barton gave him a wolfish smile. "I'm merely a concerned team member, Major Cunningham. I have just as much right as any contractor at this table to speak my mind. After all, my business lives or dies by what Congress decides on the B-1. And I'm very interested in making sure the plane has a positive image."

Fred Berger, who headed the public relations department, finally spoke up. "Frankly Mr. Barton, I don't think your insinuation about Mrs. Hamilton is in the least bit correct. She's done one hell of a job. It wasn't her fault the press was encouraged to print only half of what was said. If it hadn't been for her help recently, we'd have another problem on our hands about the B-1 polluting the environment. This past weekend she single-handedly helped me field reporters' questions on the subject. And she did it very well."

Shep toyed with a pencil, listening to the conversation. The urge to physically injure Barton was hard to ignore, but in a meeting of this type only the most professional type of behavior would be tolerated. He lifted his head, staring blackly at Barton.

"Mr. Barton," Colonel Preston said, "I personally approved the Air Force selection. It is my professional judgement that Major Ramsey is—"

"Gentlemen!" Charlie Starling's authoritative voice boomed out. "I'm afraid this is not on the agenda for discussion." His brows dipped downward as he glared at Barton. "If you wish to continue this discussion further, may I suggest that you do so during our lunch break or, if necessary, that we schedule an appropriate meeting on it."

It was during the first break that Shep made a point

of cornering Barton. "I hope," he said with finality, getting Barton's full attention, "that when we start testing the B-1, your company's small part in the construction stands up to specifications, Mr. Barton."

"I'm sure it will, Major."

Shep gave him a cutting smile, his gray eyes glittering with anger. "Like it did in the last fighter?" he asked softly.

Barton glared at him. "Look, dammit, our lab made an error in one spec reading!"

"I understood the problem was more serious than that. It damn near cost me my life as well as a twenty-million-dollar fighter. You can bet I'll have more than just a passing interest in how your ball bearings hold up in the B-1." His eyes narrowed dangerously. "And I know for a fact that the chief engineer's office is vitally concerned as to how they perform. Don't be so quick to make your 'all for the team' speech unless you're fulfilling your part of the bargain."

Charlie Starling cleared his throat, shuffling nervously from one foot to the other. "Okay, gentlemen, let's get back to the meeting."

Shep returned to the table, his lips a thin line. Barton had tried to smear his name as well as Tess's credibility. Shep's knuckles whitened around the pencil he held in his right hand.

By four thirty, the meeting broke up. The Air Force contingent was the last to leave. Finally, when the room was cleared, Colonel Preston turned to Shep.

"What's eating Barton?"

"A couple of things," Shep explained, placing the last of the papers in his leather briefcase.

Preston raised an eyebrow. "Oh?"

"Part of it is personal. But last time I flew that new fighter it was his company's ball bearings that fractured and caused me to almost lose the plane. He's worried that I'm going to pay particular attention to the ball bearings his company has installed in the B-1." He snapped the case closed with finality. "He's right. I am."

Cunningham put a hand on Shep's shoulder. "Barton's a first-class moron."

Shep smiled grimly, picking up the case. "I'm going to enjoy watching him sweat out every test flight briefing. He'll pay for it." Leaving the room, he headed down the busy corridor. Taking a short cut down a minor hallway, he walked toward the area that held the elevators, nearly colliding with Derek Barton. Shep stopped, looking down at the contractor, his face becoming dangerously unreadable.

"What do you know," Shep said softly, turning and facing him. "It must be fate, running into you like this."

Barton took a step away from the Air Force officer, aware of the tightly held anger in him. He had been in the process of congratulating himself on being able to get both Ramsey and Hamilton in one grand play. Although he was not totally pleased with the results of the confrontation, at least his words had put doubts in the minds of his fellow contractors. "I don't believe in fate," Barton growled, taking a better grip on his briefcase.

Shep lowered his attaché case to the polished floor and straightened back up, advancing within inches of Barton. "I do." His voice became low, menacing. "Understand one thing; you won't get away with a thing on this project because I'll be watching your every move."

Barton's nostrils flared as he looked up into the officer's hard features. "I don't know what you're talking about!"

"No? Your company was low bidder on those bearings. I'm not risking my neck for your shoddy workmanship again. Nice try to smear me in there, but it didn't work."

Barton backed through the entrance of the open office. It was a small secretarial office and everyone had left for the day.

"Smear?" he asked weakly. "Hardly, Major—"

Shep advanced upon him menacingly. He reached out, jabbing Barton in the chest with his index finger. "I don't care what you try to do to me, Barton," he breathed, leaning over him. "But I won't let you harass Tess Hamilton." His lips drew away from his teeth. "You spread rumors that we were having an affair, Barton. And it was a lie. You helped cause Cy Hamilton's death, did you know that?"

Derek's eyes widened, the pupils contracting in fear. He backed away from Ramsey until he was stopped by a desk behind him. The briefcase dropped with a bang to the floor. He started to lean over to retrieve it when the Air Force officer reached out, gripping his lapels and jerking him upright.

"Answer me!" Shep snarled.

Barton gave a small cry. "I don't know what you're talking about!" he squealed, caught between the officer and the desk.

"You're lying—"

Anger shot through Barton's fear. His eyes narrowed to slits. "Get your hands off me, Major," he rasped, trying to bluff his way out of the situation.

"No way."

"Please!" he begged. "Let me go!"

Shep smiled grimly. "People like you are afraid of confrontation. You do your best work by spreading cruel gossip. I know your kind." His grip tightened, bringing Barton inches from his face. "If I hear one more filthy word out of your mouth about Tess Hamilton or the job she's doing here for Rockwell, I'll make damn sure—"

Barton suddenly raised both arms, knocking Shep's hands away. He quickly backed around the desk, breathing hard, his face glistening, feeling bolder now that the desk formed a barrier between them. "You'll what, Ramsey? You don't scare me, war hero. Take your goddamn medals and shove 'em. You and that bitch are nothing but troublemakers. You got it in for me, and I want to see you off this project! I'm not letting some lousy Air Force pilot take seventy million away from me and—"

Shep snarled an obscenity, reaching out. Anger roared through him. He jerked Barton forward by the coat, dragging him halfway across the desk before Barton realized he had been caught. Shep brought back his fist. A sense of pleasure seared through him as he connected solidly with Barton's narrow jaw, sending him sprawling on the floor. Barton uttered a cry, scrambling to his knees, holding his bleeding mouth. Before the contractor could scream for help, Shep leaned down, picked him up and slammed him against the wall.

"Don't let me ever hear you call her a bitch." Shep tightened his hold on Barton. He had gripped Barton's shirt, effectively shutting off his air supply. Barton struggled weakly, his face turning redder and redder. "Do you hear me?" Shep snarled next to his ear.

Barton squeaked, struggling wildly. Disgusted, Shep released the little man, letting him drop unceremoniously to the floor in a gasping heap. Shep's knuckles were skinned and bleeding where he had connected solidly with Barton's mouth. He was breathing hard, adrenaline pumping through his tense body as he continued to stand there, waiting for Barton's answer.

Barton glared up at him through watering eyes. "I'll sue you for this!" he mumbled, holding his aching jaw. Blood trickled from the corner of his mouth.

"Just try it. You killed a man, Barton, with your lies.

You hurt a woman for no justifiable reason except for your own damn selfish interest in money. If I hear one word out of that ugly mouth of yours about her from this time on, I'll come hunting you in earnest."

"The courts would be interested in your threats," Barton hurled back.

Shep smiled coldly, forcing down the anger. "There isn't a witness, Barton. It's your word against mine. And after that little political display of razzle-dazzle at the meeting this morning, I wouldn't have any problem establishing that you have it in for me personally. Come after me all you want, but leave Tess out of this. You understand?"

Grudgingly Barton nodded, looking down at the floor tiles. Shep walked quietly to the door, pulling it closed as he walked out of the room. Picking up his briefcase, he continued down the hall toward the bank of elevators.

Tess looked up and smiled as Shep sauntered through the open door to her office. She placed her pen down on a stack of papers. Her smile disappeared as she caught sight of his unreadable features. "What's wrong?" Tess asked, suddenly concerned.

Shep put the briefcase down by the door and walked over. "You about ready to leave for the day?" he asked, ignoring her concern. Shep saw her gaze settle on his right hand. He inwardly chastised himself for not going to the men's room first and cleaning off the scrapes and blood across his knuckles.

Her blue eyes widened enormously as she looked at his uniform, which had become slightly rumpled during the scuffle. "Something happened," she said, making it a statement, not a question.

"A little run-in with Barton," he answered casually.

Tess stood, her face revealing her sudden anxiety. "Your hand is bloody and swollen. What did you do?"

"Hit him."

"Oh, my God . . ."

"It's okay," he explained calmly, "he's had it coming for a long time."

Tess stood there, staring across the desk at him. If something like this had happened six months ago, she would have been unable to cope with it. Gone was the little girl who had hidden behind the protective shield of Cy Hamilton. "Well, I suggest you come home with me and I'll clean it up for you. Some antiseptic is in order."

He grinned. "Yeah, he's poisonous, all right. Maybe I ought to get a rabies shot."

Tess pulled her purse from the bottom left drawer and shut off the office light. "You can tell me what happened on the way home," she said, ignoring his bit of humor.

"Only if you still promise to have dinner with me."

She turned, looking up at him. "Will a quiet dinner at home be okay? I don't feel like going out tonight. It's been one hell of a day."

Chapter 13

Shep sat quietly on the bar stool in the kitchen while Tess cleaned his hand. Her touch was gentle, soothing.

Traffic on a Friday night in L.A. was always a nightmare. By the time they had arrived at her home, both she and Shep were exhausted. He had ambled over to the liquor cabinet, making each of them a stiff drink. Ordinarily, Tess wouldn't have had anything stronger than wine, but tonight she finished off a Scotch on the rocks without hesitating.

As she leaned over to examine her handiwork, Shep inhaled the scent of her hair. He moved the hair away from her neck, placing a kiss on the soft nape. Tess smiled.

"I should play nurse more often."

"You like the reward?" he asked huskily, taking her into his arms.

Tess turned her back against him, content to remain within the protective enclosure of his arms. She rested her head lightly against his, closing her eyes. The Scotch had relaxed her, easing all those tightened muscles in her neck and shoulders. Shep's nearness

only increased her contented feeling of well-being.
"Just being able to see you again is reward enough,"
she murmured.

He nuzzled her cheek. "Yeah?"

"Yeah," she answered, laughing quietly.

"Got some good news for you," he said. "Maybe you
already know about it."

She turned around, placing a kiss on the corner of his
mouth. "What?" she asked, caught up in the moment.

He gave a low growl as she pressed the front of her
body against him. "Easy," he warned, pulling her even
closer.

Suddenly the rest of the world seemed very far away.
Tess had missed him desperately during the long week.
Now she was in his arms again, feeling the strength of
his muscles. Resting her head on his shoulder, she
whispered, "What's the good news, Major Ramsey?"

"I've been chosen to fly in the first team."

Her heart skipped a beat. She stood very still,
digesting the news.

"Honey?"

"What? Oh, I think that's wonderful," she answered
faintly, unable to muster the necessary enthusiasm.

Shep held her at arm's length, appraising her face.
He noted a shadow of fear in her blue eyes and recalled
how terrified Tess had looked as he'd disembarked from
the van after the emergency landing. And now, she
looked the same way—her face was drained of color,
eyes wide, lips parted in surprise. He gave her a small
shake. "Why are you frightened, Tess?" he asked
gently. A warm smile pulled at his mouth. "Come on,
what is it?"

Tess pulled away, turning and walking to the bathroom. Shakily she put away the antiseptic cream in the
medicine cabinet. Shep was going to be the first to fly
the B-1. The first. The last? Fear clawed in her throat as
Tess stared at herself in the mirror. Swallowing against

tears, she walked back to the bar where he had remained sitting. How handsome he looked. He had taken off his uniform coat; his light blue shirt was open at the collar, minus the dark blue tie. He looked more relaxed tonight than he had ever before.

"I—" she stumbled, pushing a stray strand of hair from her temple. "To be honest, I'm scared, Shep," she blurted out, giving him a wary look. He probably expected her to be ecstatic about the appointment. After all, she had worked her tail off educating the public about the B-1 and understood what it meant to the future of avionics. And with education, fear always dissolved. But not this time. Because this time she was frightened for the man she loved.

Shep stood, bringing her back into his arms, holding her in silence for a long moment. He could feel her heart beating wildly in her breast and embraced her tightly. "Why are you scared?" he wanted to know.

Tess shut her eyes tightly, burying her head against his chest. His heartbeat was so solid, so steady. Did Shep ever get upset or lose control? Only in matters that concerned her did he become emotional. Tess remembered the night they had argued heatedly at his house. Tears began to run down her cheeks and she raised her hand, trying to brush them away. "It's nothing," she whispered tightly. "Just my overactive imagination. I—I guess that in-flight emergency last Sunday has made me jumpy."

Shep laughed gently, placing a kiss on her silken hair. "In that case, I'll accept your worry as a sign that you care," he said. "Believe me, honey, I'll be very careful." He gave her a quick kiss. "After all, I have you to come home to." He offered her a smile of encouragement. "Let's discuss this after dinner, okay? Come on, I'll help you in the kitchen. I make a pretty mean salad when I put my mind to it."

Tess rallied, blotting the tears away. Her heart had

wrung in anguish when he had said "care." Was that all
they shared? A feeling of caring for one another? She
knew the answer. It was much much more than that.
She loved him. "Okay," she agreed, trying to gather
her scattered thoughts. "I think I can scrounge up a few
steaks."

He gave her a final squeeze, releasing her from his
arms. "Why don't you get into your jeans and get
comfortable?"

"What about you?" she asked.

He glanced down at the uniform he was wearing.
"Well, it's either this or my birthday suit. I'll make this
uniform as comfortable as possible." He unbuttoned
the cuffs, rolling them up on his strong forearms.

Tess managed a small smile. "I was just thinking that
you might get your clothes dirty working in the kitch-
en."

"Oh. Then the sight of an Air Force uniform doesn't
bother you?" he teased.

"Never did."

"It's a good thing," he growled, heading toward the
kitchen, which was airy and filled with hanging plants.

She changed into a pair of jeans, a scoop-necked
pink T-shirt and socks. Padding quietly into the kitch-
en, Tess halted at the entrance, a smile playing at the
corners of her full lips. Shep had all the necessary
vegetables neatly arranged in a row on the draining
board in front of him. Then he began chopping away
methodically. She admired his skill with the knife, the
sureness of his quick, clean motions. Folding her arms
across her breast, Tess leaned against the entrance.

"Maybe you missed your calling."

Shep glanced over his shoulder. "Oh?"

"You look so professional at what you're doing, I'm
tempted to just stand back and let you fix dinner."

"Why don't you?" His gray eyes warmed as he
turned and admired her relaxed form. "Take the night

off. How about if I pour us a glass of wine and you sit at the bar while I do the work?"

"Sounds good to me," Tess said, walking to the cabinet and taking down two crystal goblets. "Ever broil a steak?"

Shep came over with the wine after uncorking it. "A few times. Trust me?" he asked.

"With my life," she murmured, suddenly serious.

He placed the bottle on the draining board, handing her the glass filled with a delicate rosé wine. Their fingers touched as she took the glass. Before he released it, he leaned over and kissed her lips. His mouth parted her lips, telling her of his need for her. Finally, after a heady few seconds, Tess drew away. Her blue eyes were wide with gold flecks of stirring passion. She walked to the bar, making herself comfortable on one of the padded stools. He stood there, hands on his hips, an amused smile lingering on his strong mouth.

"Kissing you is like having dessert," he said.

She colored prettily beneath his approving gaze. "But my stomach is still starving."

He feigned hurt, returning to the task of making the salad. "That's not a very romantic statement from an Irish princess."

Tess sipped the wine. "Whereas you, Major Ramsey, are proving to be an incurable romantic."

"Comes with the territory, didn't you know?"

"Hmm, I thought as much. That's why the American public sees you all as romantic catches. Test pilots are men who fly on the edge of danger. What woman wouldn't like to have a romantic hero like that drop into her arms?"

Shep shrugged. "I'd rather have a romantic heroine drop into my arms." He walked over to Tess, placing the salad on the bar.

"You're looking at the wrong person then," she laughed, blushing beneath his intense appraisal.

"No, I'm not. Look at what you've done in the past year since Cy's death. You kept your job as assistant against heavy odds and proved your mettle under fire. Furthermore," he murmured, reaching out and placing his finger beneath her chin, "you've matured into a very lovely woman. I'm proud of you, Tess. Proud of the way you're handling everything despite the emotional catch up you've had to play. That takes real courage, Princess."

Tess swallowed hard. The caress of his finger beneath her jaw was feather-light. Her heart pulsed strongly within her breast. "I don't feel very much like a heroine," she managed quietly.

Shep allowed his hand to drop, and he stood there, mirth dancing in his gray eyes. "Now you know how test pilots feel. We don't see ourselves as heroes either. We just do a job. Just like you've been doing your job. And very well, I might add."

Tess lingered over her glass of wine as he prepared the steaks. Afterward, at the dining room table, she decided to broach the subject of Derek Barton.

"What happened between you and Barton?" she asked quietly.

Shep grimaced. "He tried to question my credentials in front of everyone. Then he turned on you." He put the goblet down in front of him, his brow furrowed. "I didn't mind the personal insult to me. But when he started on you, and you weren't there to defend yourself, I had to speak out. Fred came to your aid also, I might add."

She raised her brows. "Fred did?"

"Yes. You're beginning to have people on your side in management."

"Finally," she groused, forcing a tight smile. Tilting her head, she gazed over at him. "You didn't get into a fight in the boardroom, did you?"

"No. Luckily," he mused. "Can you see it now? I'd

lose my flight status on the B-1 program for sure if that had happened."

"What makes you think he won't make waves anyway, Shep?"

He ran his finger lightly around the rim of his glass. "He might try, but there weren't any witnesses to the incident. It's his word against mine. Besides, all I did was bloody his mouth and probably loosen a few teeth. Too bad I didn't break his damn jaw. That would have shut him up for a while."

She nodded. "That would have stopped him from gossiping at least," she agreed. "What was the outcome?"

He shrugged, getting to his feet and clearing the dishes from the table. Tess followed him to the kitchen, helping him wash the utensils. "The outcome is the same, honey. We've got an enemy on our hands. He knows that I'll be watching his ball bearings. And he's also aware that you're going to continue to check the specs on them through your laboratories to make sure they meet requirements."

Tess took a towel from the drawer and began drying the dishes as he washed them. "Barton and his company are a strong argument for not taking the low bid," she remarked.

"You've been testing his product. How does it stand up?"

"He's meeting the minimum spec, Shep. Technically, there's nothing wrong with that because our engineers have built in safety factors far above the tolerances that are needed. It's just that Barton will cheat if you don't keep an eye on him constantly. I don't like having to distrust a contractor like that."

"There's no honor with his type," he agreed.

Tess prepared a light dessert of strawberry crepes later. They lingered over coffee in the living room. Shep placed his cup and saucer on the coffee table.

"Come on over here, we've got some talking to do," he urged, holding out his hand.

She left the overstuffed chair she was sitting in and walked up to him. It was natural to fold her body next to his on the couch, to rest in the protection of his arms. Tess nuzzled his neck, closing her eyes, content. The meal had been excellent. But more important, the company had been perfect. She hadn't recognized the extent of her loneliness since Cy's passing. Placing her arms around Shep's torso, she gave a small sigh.

Shep leaned over, watching her. "I owe you an apology," he began quietly.

Tess raised her thick lashes, meeting his lambent gray eyes. "Why?"

"We haven't really gotten a chance to talk about what happened up at Edwards." He gently placed her head against his shoulder, his hand resting on her hair. "Something important happened up there, you know. And between the in-flight emergency and your having to get back to work, we didn't have the time to discuss it."

Her heart began a slow pound. "A lot has happened in a short period of time," she agreed, her voice barely above a whisper.

"Yes," he answered tentatively. "First things first, though. I should have let you explain why you were at my home, Tess. I was so damn mired in my own self-pity that seeing you was a hell of a shock."

"I know. But I didn't have any other options at the time, Shep."

He squeezed her. "I realize that now, honey. I'm sorry I came roaring in throwing accusations. Instead of running, you turned to answer on all accounts. That took courage. Putting myself in your place, I don't know if I could have done it. You must have known that I would be upset."

She placed a small kiss on his jaw. "Upset, angry,

and confused," she agreed. "But I had to come, Shep. I was beside myself all Sunday. Between those damn phone calls from reporters I tried your number so many times. I felt like I was trapped in circumstances beyond my control." She gave him a rueful smile. "I don't like things totally out of my control," she admitted.

"Makes two of us," he answered, smiling. His expression became tender as he gazed into her upturned face. "But something more important happened last weekend. Something I had been wanting to tell you for the longest time, Tess."

She was pulled into the web of his simmering desire. Tess shivered inwardly, wildly aware of his body against her own. "I wasn't ready before," she said. "I had to put so many things into perspective, Shep."

"I understand that," he whispered, leaning down, capturing her parted lips. His mouth moved with ease, testing, teasing, and finally eliciting a deep passion in return. Gradually he pulled away, studying her wordlessly. The music in the background softened the sound of their rapid heartbeats. He saw a shadow of worry deep in her sapphire eyes. Gently he cradled her chin in his hand. "What are you frightened of?" he inquired.

"It will sound silly."

"Try me."

"You'll probably laugh your head off."

Shep shook his head. "I'll never laugh at anything you find scary, Tess. Now what is it?"

She took a deep breath, leaning back against his warm, hard body. "I worry about your flying the B-1 the first time."

"It's a well-designed plane, honey. Nothing will go wrong. Or, if it does, we'll handle it."

"Typical test pilot philosophy."

He smiled, enjoying the play of emotions across her readable face. "Yes, but my attitude is based on experience, Tess. I've been testing aircraft for three years now. And before that, I accrued thousands of hours in fighters and bombers. I've got an awful lot of experience in handling and effectively dealing with emergency situations aboard any sort of aircraft."

She searched his serious face. "You love flying, don't you?"

He inclined his head forward. "I live for it, honey." That was only partially true, he realized. As much as he loved flying, he loved Tess even more. He wanted to blurt out all of his feelings to her. But he wasn't sure that this was the right moment. He wasn't sure about anything when it came to Tess, he realized in an agony of indecision.

"Is that why you joined the Air Force?" she asked, interrupting his thoughts.

"Yes," he answered shortly, deciding the time for revelations was past.

"You won't be a test pilot forever. I know they move you on to other commands after five years or so."

He pursed his lips. "I know," he answered slowly. "And that's bothered me. I've thought about leaving the Air Force and joining an aeronautical company as a civilian test pilot at that time."

Tess felt a cloak of dread beginning to suffocate her. Suddenly, she was feeling trapped for no explicable reason. Her throat closed with tears as she again saw Shep's crippled plane flying through the sky on only one engine. The fear was too real, too strangling. "Why couldn't you feel you were contributing just as much from behind a desk, Shep? That way, you wouldn't have to leave the Air Force. You have enough time to retire in another twelve years or so. You don't want to throw that away, do you?"

He gave her a strange, quizzical look. "Honey, I've found my niche in life," he began earnestly. "Flying is my life. I know it's hard for you to understand, but I can't wait to sit in the cockpit of a plane again."

Her heart was aching painfully. Her blue eyes showed her hurt and confusion. "And—and you wouldn't give that up for anything?"

Shep cocked his head. "Give up my livelihood? That would be like my asking you to give up your career."

Pain twisted in her chest, and she forced herself out of his arms and to her feet. She looked down at him. "If—if I thought my career was going to interfere with other parts of my life, I would give it up."

"Wait a minute," he said, rising. Gripping her arms he forced Tess to look up at him. "Where is all this leading? You're asking a bunch of hypothetical questions, and I don't see the reason behind them, Tess. No one is asking you to give up your job. I certainly haven't. Nor would I. I feel like you're casting about for something. What is it, honey?"

Tess steadied her uneven breathing. Just the nearness of his male body sent her into a state of yearning she had never believed possible. Shep affected her so deeply, yet he had never said he loved her. Never said that he wanted anything more than a casual affair. Why should she feel so hurt that he didn't understand the thrust of her questioning? She loved him desperately. She didn't want to lose him. She had little experience with close relationships. What was happening? Was this the beginning of the end? Maybe she was inventing a dream of what might have been with Shep. . . . She stepped out of his grasp.

"It's late," she heard herself say, "and I'm very tired, Shep. Thank you for a lovely dinner."

Shep stood there, analyzing her vulnerable face. He heard the pain in her voice, saw it in the azure intensity of her eyes. A sense of helplessness overcame him, and he dropped his hands from his hips. "Yeah, I guess it is late," he mumbled, rolling down the cuffs of his shirt.

As he buttoned up the dark blue jacket and put the flight cap on his head, he remained silent. His gray eyes were dark as he opened the door. "Look," he began, "we've both had a long and trying day. Let me call you sometime this weekend."

"If you want."

Shep leaned down, placing a kiss on her unmoving lips. Lips that had been warm and yielding minutes before. He quelled the frustration he was feeling. As he drew away he murmured, "That's something I want very much, Tess. Good night."

Chapter 14

TESS HAD DRIVEN UP TO PALMDALE WITH DAN WILLIAMS.
During the past week, as the date of the rollout drew
near, she had become less talkative. Inwardly she
remained in a state of anguish over her parting with
Shep. He *had* called her that weekend, but they hadn't
seen each other since. Occasionally, Dan would ask
what was wrong. Tess would murmur "nothing" and
force herself to work until she forgot momentarily
about Shep—about how much she loved him.

Parking near the ramp area, Tess saw the huge crowd
that had gathered for the rollout. Getting out of the
car, she walked at Dan's shoulder, trying to control the
painful beat of her heart. Soon she would see Shep
once again. Could she handle the confrontation? Her
head said yes. Her heart simply wrenched with newfound pain.

Tess saw the Air Force contingent up ahead and
anxiously searched through the sea of faces and silver
braid for Shep. Several test pilots were milling around
the outer perimeter of ranking military officers looking
ill at ease with all the pomp and circumstance. Just as
she reached the first step of the platform, a hand closed
about her arm. Tess turned.

Shep smiled down at her. It was a cool smile. He said only, "Come with me." His fingers tightened slightly as he led her away from the crowd. Tess glanced up at him. He was wearing an olive green flight suit that had been adorned with all the official patches of the first B-1 test team. A blue flight cap sat at an angle on his head, his hair a dark contrast to the uniform and his bronzed skin. A shiver of dread went through her as Tess felt his eyes deliberately settle on her. He opened a small door leading to the main hangar, guiding her inside. Once there, he shut it, allowing his hands to rest easily on his slim hips.

It was silent within the hangar. She glanced around, staring at the gleaming white B-1 standing there. She was torn between Shep's grim expression and the intrinsic beauty of the bomber that rested thirty feet away from them. Her heart pounded strongly. Finding nothing to say on a personal level, she motioned toward the plane.

"It's beautiful."

Shep nodded. "Yes, it is."

Taking a steadying breath, Tess looked up at him. Words were useless as she met his gray eyes. A shudder ran through her.

"Why have you avoided me this week, Tess?"

She opened her mouth and then closed it, feeling close to tears. "I—"

Shep placed his hand on her shoulder. "As soon as this rollout ceremony is completed, I want to talk with you." His voice hardened slightly. "And I don't care if it takes the rest of the day, Tess. Somehow, we got off track last Friday. I feel like a wedge has been driven between us and I don't understand why."

The uncertainty in his husky voice released a backlog of tears. Tess reached up, shakily brushing them from her cheeks. "All right," she murmured brokenly.

He rested his other hand on her shoulder, studying her darkly. "Tess, I've been wracking my brain twenty-five hours a day trying to figure out your reactions." His fingers tightened against her flesh. "I don't know what I said to make you act so distant." Frustration became evident in his tone. "We've gone through so much together." His face lost the look of hardness as he searched her eyes. "Dammit," he breathed thickly, "come here."

Her breath lodged in her throat as Shep pulled her into his arms, against the hard planes of his masculine body. Tess gave a small cry, throwing her arms around his neck, tilting her face upward to meet his descending mouth. It was a kiss that took her breath away. His mouth, so strong and yet gentle, forced her lips apart, coaxing her to take part in the celebration of their love for one another. Her brain screamed that it wasn't love. Her heart spiraled upward on a crest of joy that left her weak with need of further contact with Shep in every way. Finally he withdrew.

"Come on," he urged, "let's get back. Meet me over here afterward."

She nodded mutely, leaning heavily against his body for momentary support. The hunger in his eyes, the protective stance he had taken with her sent a new surge of hope through her heart. She loved him. Tess knew it more than ever. But Shep had never said those precious three words. Why? Why? Gripping her purse tightly, Tess followed him out the door into the brilliant sunlight.

The usual line of speakers came up to the microphone to comment on the momentous occasion. Tess noticed distractedly that Senator Diane Browning was present along with several other congressmen to see the B-1 rolled out of the hangar. At least a hundred reporters were jammed in to interview the important personages after the speeches were made. And the test pilots who were to fly the B-1 were among those questioned after the speech making was finished. The blinding lights of television cameras, the popping of flashbulbs and the shouted questions from the eager press all added to the confusion.

Tess could not tear her gaze from Shep's composed features as he and the other two Rockwell men fielded the barrage of questions. Because he was the only Air Force pilot among them, Shep stood out. The dark blue flight cap with the gold oak leaf denoting his rank rested on his head. She stood back, admiring the group. Each man had that same intense look about him. Were they all eagles in human form, she wondered? The head Rockwell test pilot, Dave Faulkner, was an ex–Air Force pilot. Would Shep follow in Dave's footsteps? Being a test pilot in the military was a prestigious step upward in the ranking system. Only the best military pilots were chosen for the test pilot school. Many of those men went on to become high-ranking officers and sometimes generals. Tess smiled to herself. Shep didn't care about being a general. All he wanted to do was fly.

Finally Shep excused himself and walked through the thinning crowd toward her. Tess saw the grim determination in his eyes and wondered what had put it there. She had gone over to Dan earlier, explaining that she was taking the rest of the day off. If Dan was surprised, he didn't show it. He had said only, "You deserve it. I'll see you tomorrow morning."

Shep reached out, gripping her elbow, guiding her toward the hangar where all the official military and civilian cars were parked. "It's past lunch," he murmured, opening the door to his car for her. "Are you hungry?"

She nodded. "Yes, I am."

He gave her a small smile. "Good. We'll go over to my place and grab a bite to eat."

The coolness of the air conditioning in the car was a sharp contrast to the dry heat of the desert. Tess sat back, thankful for it. Shep occasionally glanced over at her as he drove them the twelve miles from Palmdale to Lancaster, but neither of them spoke.

At his house Shep showed her into the kitchen. "I'm going to change into some civilian clothes," he explained, walking down the carpeted hall. "I'll be back in a moment."

Tess nervously chewed on her lower lip, seating herself at the kitchen table. Shep emerged ten minutes later in a pair of well-worn jeans and a short-sleeved beige shirt. It set off the darkness of his tan and the raw umber color of his hair.

"Stay seated," he said. Moving to the refrigerator, he drew out a bottle of wine, uncorking it. As he poured her a half a glass of the pale pink rosé he said, "You look tense."

Tess placed her purse on the table and fingered the stem of the cool glass. "I am. Why do I have this feeling of apprehension?"

He rested his body against the counter, lazily swirling the contents of his glass. A gentle smile tugged at the corners of his mouth. "Because we're going to clear the air," he answered. "But let's get some food first."

Half an hour later Shep laid out two salads of baby shrimp, raw vegetables, and sliced avocados. Over the meal he began the discussion she had been dreading.

"You didn't seem as enthusiastic as the other Rockwell people about the B-1 being rolled out," he noted.

"No? What was I supposed to do? Turn somersaults?"

"Well, if my memory serves me correctly, I think I remember that your eyes used to light up whenever you mentioned the bomber. Now all I see is apathy. What happened? Has the responsibility they've piled on you made you less enthusiastic?"

"No . . . not exactly," she murmured, pushing her salad away. She took another sip of wine. It was the last of her second glass and the alcohol was beginning to tell.

Sensing her reticence, he tried a different approach. "I don't know about you, Tess," he began softly, "but I thought our relationship was finally coming around after we spent the night together here." He rested his arms on his well-muscled thighs, clasping his hands together. "I thought you had let go of your grief and your loss of Cy." He shrugged. "Maybe, and more important, I was sure you'd gotten rid of that damn guilt you've carried with you since the first time I kissed you." He searched her vulnerable face, frowning slightly. "Loving you was—is—a dream come true, honey." He reached out, capturing her hand, squeezing it gently. "Ever since the first time I saw you, I had to know you, Tess. It was a hell of a lot more than just physical need too. But I'm not sure you knew that. I saw in you exactly what I needed in a woman, and I was content to wait until you had lived through your grief." His frown deepened. "And I thought we'd finally made a breakthrough last week."

Tess stood, unable to bear his closeness one second longer. His voice was balm to her aching heart, soothing her tortured, fearful soul. His touch was electric, teasing and tantalizing. But she needed more; she needed his love. She walked a few feet away from him and then turned, meeting his gaze fully. "What do you want from me, Shep?" she asked, her voice tremulous.

"You," he answered simply.

Tess's lips parted, her eyes glistening with unshed tears. "You had me," she retorted.

"What are you talking about?" he asked, rising.

She curled her fists at her sides, her throat aching with hurt. "Isn't that what you wanted?"

"I wanted all of you, Tess. Not just in bed, for God's sake. Is that what you thought all along? That I wanted a roll in the sack and that was it?"

Her lower lip trembled, and she raised her chin stubbornly. "I don't know *what* to think about your actions, Shep."

His eyes narrowed. "I told you before, Tess, I was interested in you from the first night I saw you. I made a mistake in kissing you there on the balcony. I've tried to rectify that mistake by giving you the time you needed to recover from Cy's death. I've tried not to push you too far too fast."

"Oh, God, Shep!" she cried, tears streaking down her cheeks. "I'm not like a lot of other women. I don't know how to play the normal games people play. I don't know what you want from me. I feel so terribly unsure when I'm around you!" She turned away, burying her face in her hands. "I don't want to play games with you," she sobbed. "And I don't want some stupid, casual affair. I can't take it!"

His mouth thinned and he quietly approached her. In one gentle motion, he turned her around. Her lashes were wet with tears. He felt his heart wrench deep in his chest. He cradled her chin in his hand. "I never wanted a casual affair, Tess," he said quietly. "Is that what you thought? That all I wanted was an affair with you?"

She nodded miserably, longing to fall into his arms. The urge to tell him of her love was overwhelming. She took a deep, unsteady breath, searching his tender expression. "What *do* you want from me?"

He whispered her name and pulled her against him. She released a small sob, burying her head against his shoulder. His arms were strong and loving as they embraced her. Her tears wet the material of his shirt, making a darkened patch. The solid warmth of his chest, the steady beat of his heart began to soothe away some of her unnamed fears.

"Honey," he murmured huskily, "I love you. I think I've loved you from the first time I met you, though I didn't know how much until I spent that day driving around by myself. What I feel for you goes much deeper than I'll ever be able to tell you." He leaned over, caressing her parted lips. "I was so damn stupid. Why didn't I tell you this before? I thought you knew. . . ."

Tess blinked, her heart thundering wildly in her breast. "I—I didn't know," she began lamely.

She smiled, gripping her tightly to him, loving the feel of her pliant, supple body against him. "God, woman, I've loved you forever. I need you, Tess."

She responded instinctively, reaching upward, her lips meeting his strong mouth. A low groan vibrated within his body as he pressed hungrily against her searching, tremulous lips. Fire ignited deep within her body as she wrapped her arms around his neck, drawing closer. In one fluid motion Shep lifted her off the floor. Tess rested languidly against him, content with his nearness as he carried her to the bedroom. "This time," she heard him say, his voice vibrating with desire, "I'm going to show you just how much I do love you, Tess. This time we've got no deadlines to make. No duty to answer."

Her heart was filled with intense longing for him as Shep gently laid her upon the bed. The sunlight streamed through the pale green drapes, giving the room a soft pastel color. It was as if they were out in the Sierras once again, beneath the huge flowing branches of the sequoias. He sat down beside her, purposefully unbuttoning the front of her plum-colored dress. Each touch of his fingers ignited new fires of hunger. Somewhere in her mind she recalled the fervor of their first loving. This time, it would be slower . . . even more exciting. The folds of the dress fell away from her body as he lingered above her, his gaze sweeping across her with tenderness. She relished the passion she saw in the depths of his eyes. Tess's lips parted as he lightly ran his fingers down the lace and silk camisole, brushing the curves of one breast. A small, sharp gasp broke from her lips as he teased the hardening nipple that thrust provocatively upward against the silken fabric.

The sunlight cast soft shadows on the planes and curves of her body as Shep slowly removed each piece of clothing. Finally she lay beneath his gaze, completely naked, but not embarrassed by the adoration that burned in his eyes. As Shep leaned over, she reached upward, sliding her arms around his neck, drawing him down upon her. A throbbing hunger had her returning his fiery kiss with equal fervor.

Her lashes moved upward, revealing azure eyes golden with unspoken love. Moving her fingertips beneath the material of his shirt, she reveled in the expanse of wiry hair across his chest. To her delight he was just as sensitive to her touch as she was to his. Within minutes he was naked, pulling her against his straining, hardened body. A small gasp of pleasure broke from her lips as he brought her hips against him, making her aware of his arousal. Shep placed small kisses on her eyes, nose, and finally her mouth. Drunk with desire, driven by the passion he had released with his masterful touch, she arched upward, begging him to complete the union.

Shep slid his fingers through the thick cascade of her silken hair, wrapping it around his fist, pulling her head back against his other arm. Her breathing was fast and shallow, her body trembling with need of him. Resting above her momentarily, he caressed her cheek, looking deeply into her widened eyes. "Know that I love you," he whispered huskily. "More than life. You are my life. . . ." He leaned down, pressing his mouth against her pliant, waiting lips. As he lifted his head, he saw tears on either side of her face. His heart contracted and he felt an overwhelming desire to protect her.

She reached up, her fingertips touching his strong jaw. "I love you," she whispered, her voice tender with passion. He groaned, closing his eyes tightly, bringing her against him, burying his head in the silken tresses of her hair. Moments melted into one another like lava pouring from a volcano of molten desire. She felt his hand on her thigh, stroking the tender flesh. The weight of his knee forcing her thighs apart brought new urgency to her aching, ready body. Closing her eyes, she moved upward to meet him. A cry of pleasure broke from her lips and she clung to him. Slowly, slowly he brought her into rhythm with himself—a rhythm so primeval, so delicious that she climbed to heights of euphoria never before experienced. An explosion rocked her inwardly, bringing such incredible pleasure that she could only utter a small cry of joy.

Slowly Tess opened her eyes. She was aware of her cheek resting against the damp hair of his chest, of the slow pounding of his heart beneath her ear. Her hair lay like a silken coverlet on his chest, her arm limp across his flat, hard stomach. She felt drugged with euphoria. The slant of the sun's rays seemed different. Had she slept? Or had time rushed by unnoticed during that incredible sensation of climax with Shep? Tess didn't know; she was content to languish within the protection of his arms, her five senses more alive than ever before. She tasted the salt of his body against her lips, breathed in the male scent of him, felt the tickling sensation of his hair beneath her cheek and the rise and fall of his chest. Some instinct told her he was sleeping, and she closed her eyes, needing nothing more but the closeness he offered.

Chapter 15

THE SECOND TIME SHE AWOKE, TESS WAS AWARE OF Shep's hand tracing the outline of her cheek and jaw. Her eyes lifted, meeting his tender gray gaze. He gave her a small smile, one corner of his mouth lifting upward. The sunlight no longer filtered through the room, meaning it was late in the afternoon. The melodic call of a bird in a nearby tree mingled with the far-off sound of a jet taking off in the distance. Tess stirred languidly, pressing herself against Shep, burying her head against his shoulder.

"I love you, Irish princess," he whispered, placing a small kiss on her forehead.

"It sounds so good to hear that," she admitted softly, reaching out and stroking his broad, well-muscled shoulder.

"God, I should have told you that a long time ago," he murmured, a frown beginning to form on his brow. He sat up, resting his back against the headboard. He pulled Tess into his arms so that she rested against his body. "But I was afraid of moving too fast." He looked down at her, searching her face. "I was walking a tightrope with you, Tess. If I told you too soon, before you got over your guilt about Cy's death, it might have destroyed everything." He shook his head. "As it was, I damn near told you too late. You thought all I wanted was an affair."

She nodded mutely. Her dark auburn hair spilled across her shoulder and down below her breast. His nearness was intoxicating. "It wasn't your fault, Shep," she murmured, her voice sultry with the passion they had shared. "And you were right: If you had told me that three months ago, I probably would have retreated from you."

He smiled, placing a kiss on her cheek and holding her tightly within his arms. "We won't let anything come between us again, will we, honey?"

At his words a new fear jolted through her. The emergency aboard the T-38 smashed into her mind, and Tess wrestled with the dread. There was already something between them. Hesitantly Tess lifted her lashes, staring up into his gray eyes. She could lose him at any time.

Logic clashed with emotion. She had worked almost two years on the blueprints of the B-1. She had seen positive test results indicating it would fly without a doubt. But it didn't matter. That was all computer analysis, tests in wind tunnels with wooden models. None of it meant anything to her aching heart. Tess tried to withdraw from the fear that was rapidly destroying her happiness. She forced herself to remember she was in Shep's arms now. Concentrating on his arms about her, she wearily rested her head on his shoulder, a small sigh escaping from her lips.

Shep sensed her quandary. "Honey, what is it?" he asked.

"Nothing," she murmured in a small voice.

A wry smile pulled at his mouth. "You know, part of loving someone is telling them all your worries and fears," he reminded her gently. "I saw worry in your eyes, Tess. Want to discuss it?"

"You'll think I'm crazy," she said defensively.

He released a sigh. "How do you know? You're making that judgment before I even get a chance to defend myself."

He was right, she decided. "It will sound so inane and unbelievable that—"

Shep laughed softly. "My Irish princess, what am I going to do with you?" He moved her out of his arms and sat up. "Come on, let's take a shower and then we'll talk. Okay?"

Her eyes widened. "A shower?"

He grinned boyishly, standing and holding out his hand to her. "Sure."

"Together?"

Amusement danced in his gray eyes. "Is there any other way?" he drawled, gripping her hand.

A spiraling sense of happiness chased the dread away for the moment as Tess leaned against his warm, hard body. "Well—" she got out, "I've never taken a shower with anyone before."

Shep maintained an even expression for her sake as he slowly led her toward the bathroom. "I see. I think you'll enjoy it."

The steam rose and billowed within the roomy shower, curling the tendrils of hair at her temples. Tess stood beneath the warm water, giving herself up to Shep's knowing hands. He slid the soap over her body, his touch tantalizing. She had never realized how arousing a shower could be. He brought her against him, his strong fingers gliding down the length of her curved back.

"You have a beautiful back," he whispered, nuzzling her ear with delicious slowness. He drew his hands upward over her long torso feeling each of her ribs, caressing her taut breasts. She gasped softly, pressing herself more demandingly to him.

A smile curved his lips. More than ever Shep loved

her guileless reactions. At first, she had been nervous.
Even if she hadn't told him, he would have known this
was a new experience for her. He wondered what kind
of marriage Cy Hamilton had had with Tess. Shep made
himself a promise: He would show Tess all the different
ways a man could express love for a woman. He would
take her up to the Sierras and show her how beautiful
lovemaking could be out in the wild. He would swim in
a cool mountain lake with her. He would . . .

He uttered a low growl, allowing his hands to slide
over her firm, responsive flesh. He felt the hardening
peaks of her nipples pressing insistently against his
chest and he smiled to himself. Lifting her chin, Shep
moved his mouth against her lips, parting them gently.
Her mouth was honey. She was a beautiful rose unfolding beneath his care. Wrapping his arms about her, he
embraced her tightly, deepening the kiss.

Fire uncoiled from the glowing embers within her
body as the touch of his mouth teased her throbbing
lips. The warm water streamed across her body in
cascading rivulets, creating new, arousing sensations.
A low gasp escaped from her as his hand slid sugges-
tively down her body, stroking her inner thigh. Clouds
of steam billowed upward. The strength of his mouth
against her flesh drove her mad with desire for him
once again. A low moan of need rose in her throat as
his mouth seared her hungry lips. She felt Shep's arms
tighten around her body, lifting her up against him.
Her fingers sank deeply into his shoulders, a moan of
pleasure escaping from her lips as she took him inside
her. Molten fire spread through her body, building in
intensity. Moist heat surrounded and enveloped them
as a hot fire burned brightly, achingly within her. A
shudder coursed through her and she rested wearily
against Shep, fulfilled once again.

Tess stood within Shep's embrace as he gently towel-
dried her, occasionally leaning down to kiss her lips

in silent adoration. Finally, he helped her into his robe, tying the sash about her slender waist. There was a smile in his eyes as he caressed her upturned face. The full impact of his love was now evident in his every movement. Tess waited until he put on his jeans and zipped them up before throwing her arms around his shoulders. "I love you," she whispered, a quiver in her voice. "I never knew how much until—"

"Sshhh," he whispered against her lips. "I see it in your eyes, honey. Come on, I'm starved. How about you?" A crooked smile played across his strong, virile mouth as he studied her.

Tess returned the smile, keeping her arm around his naked torso. Shep looked even more masculine in only a pair of jeans, his broad chest covered with the dark mat of hair. "Me too," she agreed.

Tess reclined on the carpeted living room floor, picking idly at a variety of fruit on a plate which sat on the coffee table. Shep leaned back, moving his arm behind Tess's shoulders and drawing her near. The quietness that now invaded the house was lulling, healing. He had cut up fresh chunks of pineapple, bananas, dates, and papaya for them. Tess had rummaged around in the refrigerator and found some raspberry yogurt to make a dip for the fruit. Now they sat next to one another, sharing the sweet fruit and tart yogurt.

She remained within his arms, content to feel the heat of his body next to her own. Was it possible to tell Shep she had never shared so much with anyone? Simple acts such as a shower together? Or feeding one another slices of juicy fruit in the gathering dusk of the evening? For the first time Tess realized that her marriage to Cy had been lacking in many areas. It wasn't Cy's fault or her own. It was a difference not only in philosophy and life-style, but in the men who loved her. She glanced at Shep's relaxed face. He looked years younger, the lines erased from around his mouth and brow. There was a glimmer of joy deep within his gray eyes. Tess was seeing him completely at ease for the first time and it pleased her immensely.

"You've given me so many firsts," she said.

He roused himself, barely opening one eye. "Test pilots are always breaking new ground. Doing new things," he drawled.

Tess laughed, giving him a playful jab in the ribs. "That has nothing to do with being a test pilot! You really use your career to explain all your deeds or misdeeds, don't you?"

He laughed with her, nodding his head. "Yup, I do."

"Still, Shep," she said, her voice becoming soft, "you've shown me so much . . . in such a short period of time."

Shep took her into his arms. "And there's so much more for us to share, Tess," he murmured against her ear, kissing her. "Now," he said, his breath moist against her cheek, "want to tell me what caused that worry in your eyes earlier?" He gave her a reassuring squeeze. "And I promise I won't think you're crazy or silly."

Tess turned in his arms, her voice low, almost inaudible. "When you had the problem with the T-38, I almost died, Shep. During that emergency I realized just how much I loved you." Her eyes grew soft and misty as she met his tender gaze. "I—I didn't know at that time if you loved me. I didn't know what to do with my emotions. I didn't know how to tell you what I felt. And when you kidded me about your being picked to fly the B-1, my stomach just knotted. For some reason the fear of losing you the way I had lost Cy devastated me to such an extent that I just withdrew from you."

The pain was evident in her voice. "I should have told you earlier that I loved you," he apologized quietly. "I saw how upset you were when I landed. I should have realized then."

The silence deepened. "Are you still afraid of losing me in an airplane crash?" he asked.

Tess closed her eyes, burying her head against his shoulder. "Yes. God, I've just found you, Shep. I—I couldn't cope with losing you too—"

"Honey, I'm not going to be torn away from you like Cy was," he reassured her, his voice husky with conviction.

Tess bit down on her lower lip to stop it from trembling. "My head knows that, but my heart doesn't!" she cried. "I can't believe it, Shep! I work with those blueprints day in and day out. I know how that plane works just like you do. But when I think about you climbing up that twelve-foot ladder into the cockpit of the B-1, I just get shaky with fear. I've cried so much about it the last week since you were assigned to the first team."

He frowned, his nostrils flaring with unspoken frustration. Absently he stroked her unbound hair, trying to soothe away her very real fear. Finally an idea surfaced. He dislodged Tess, pulling her to her feet. "Come on," he urged, "let's get dressed. There's someplace we need to go."

She gave him a startled look. "What are you talking about?"

Shep leaned down, dropping a kiss on her lips. "Trust me, Irish princess. I think what we're going to do will help put your fears to rest." He gave her a pat on the rear. "Come on."

Shep drove them into Edwards Air Force Base just as night was beginning to overtake the day. He was inexplicably buoyant as he pulled up to the hangar which housed the B-1. Helping Tess out of the car, Shep guided her through a small side door. Most of the hangar was swathed in darkness, but there were a few

lights on in one corner, chasing the shadows away.
Their footsteps echoed in the silence. A few technicians
ambled around, lunch pails in their hands as they made
their way toward the exits.

He halted at one of the many offices along the
southern wall of the hangar. "Bill?" he called, sticking
his head inside.

"Yeah? Hi, Shep. What the hell are you doing here?
We're about ready to wrap it up. These twelve-hour
days are getting pretty long."

Shep smiled, bringing Tess inside the cramped office.
"Got a favor to ask of you. Bill, this is Tess Hamilton,
an executive from Rockwell."

Bill, a balding man of fifty, rose and offered his hand.
"Ms. Hamilton. A pleasure."

"Call me Tess," she said, releasing his hand.

"Roger," he teased, his broad face breaking into a
genuine grin. He cocked one eyebrow at Shep. "What's
the favor?"

Shep gestured toward the door. "I want to take Tess
up in the simulator. Would you take the panel so we
can run a simulated test flight? She needs to get the feel
of the bomber."

Bill looked a bit surprised and then shrugged. "Sure,
why not? But this will cost you, Major," he warned, a
gleam in his dark eyes.

Shep returned the grin. "Anything you want."

Bill, who was a bit on the portly side, squeezed
between the wall and his desk. He rolled up his white
shirt-sleeves on the way out, moving quickly across the
concrete floor of the hangar. "Okay, I want a ride in
that bomber you're going to fly."

Shep laughed. "You and everybody else! I may not
be able to promise that. We can negotiate my payment
later."

"Damn, what I'd give to fly in that baby. She's a
purty thing, isn't she?"

Shep glanced down at Tess. "Most people think so," he said, a glint in his eye.

Tess's curiosity overcame her initial apprehension as they covered the distance between the office and a small control booth which sat across the floor. Shep pointed out a huge mechanical apparatus which sat on steel legs thirty feet above the hangar floor.

"This is our B-1 simulator, Tess. Bill is one of the people who sits in the control booth and feeds in the computerized cards which are then played into the circuitry of the simulated B-1 cabin. This is where we've been getting our training on how to use the equipment aboard the real bomber."

"We're going up there?" she asked.

"Yes, ma'am. Figured a 'flight' in the B-1 would help dispel some of that fear you have."

His argument made sense. Without another word Tess climbed aboard the platform which held the small control booth. Bill flipped a switch and slowly the entire ensemble rose upward toward the simulator, which was suspended on long steel legs. Shep kept his arm around Tess as they rose upward.

"We train in here to get the feel of the plane without ever leaving the ground. It lessens the potential of damaging the real bomber. The cockpit of this simulator is an exact replica of the B-1 we'll be flying. The days of just strapping into a prototype and taking your chances are over. Nowadays, trainers and simulators help the test pilots to gather valuable experience before they ever take an aircraft up. We also work the kinks out of the different systems aboard the simulator so that changes can be made in the actual plane before it's flown." He smiled down at her, looking handsome in his Air Force uniform. The platform gave a small jerk and then halted.

"Okay, Shep, she's all yours. What kind of card do you want?"

"Nothing fancy. No emergency procedures. I just want to give Tess an idea of takeoff, landing and flyability."

"Roger. I got just the card. Get situated and give me a call when you're ready." He smiled over at Tess. "Enjoy the flight."

Tess gave Bill a sickly smile, following Shep out on the narrow catwalk to the simulator. He opened the rear hatch door and stepped inside, helping her aboard.

It was the first time she had ever been in a fully constructed B-1 cockpit. The silence was awesome as she carefully made her way forward. "Stay there for a second," he ordered, going to the front. Within moments, cabin lights appeared. He gave her an encouraging smile. "Come on, you take the right seat. You'll be my copilot for this flight."

Tess hesitantly settled into the seat. Before her was a panel of gauges and dials that would mystify anyone not acquainted with airplane instrumentation. Shep settled in, patiently helping her strap into the seat, bringing the nylon harness up and around each of her shoulders and then snapping it closed on the belt that crossed her lap. He pointed toward a lightweight microphone and headset.

"Just slip it over your right ear," he instructed, flipping on several sets of switches. The entire instrument panel lit up with a greenish hue. Shep strapped in, adjusting his mike. Giving her a quick smile, he switched on the radio frequency to the control room.

"Wiry nine-six to Control. How do you read?"

Tess listened as Shep and Bill conversed. Her initial fear eroded as she watched Shep deftly go through a series of checks with the control room. It struck her that Shep was right at home in the futuristic cockpit, totally at ease.

She watched as more dials and gauges jumped to life before her. Between her front legs rested the control stick. Unlike other bombers, which had a yoke fashioned into what looked like half of a car's steering wheel, the B-1 had a stick like fighter aircraft possessed. There was a screen approximately six inches square in front of each pilot's position. The screen, using television and infrared detection, could "see" far out beyond the cockpit area. It would show the height and outline of the terrain miles ahead of the actual position to the B-1. Furthermore, it would show air speed and elevation of the aircraft itself. She watched as Shep's right hand settled over the four throttles between the seats. He eased them forward a few inches, intently watching the fuel gauges and the other instruments which would tell him if each engine was functioning properly during the test before the actual "takeoff."

The cockpit was a living being now. The waving, pulsating needles seemed to gauge the life of the plane. Tess became involved in watching them, forgetting her fear. Shep winked at her.

"Ready for takeoff?" he asked, taking a grip on the control stick.

She smiled hesitantly, caught up in the excitement. "Roger."

"Okay, place your right hand on the stick," he instructed.

Tess gave him a horrified look.

"Go on," he urged, grinning. "You won't make us crash. After all, we're suspended on steel supports. We aren't going anywhere."

She gave him a distrustful look, edging her hand on to the stick. Slowly, she wrapped her clammy fingers around the column.

"Good," he praised. "Okay, from here on out, this will be the exact sequence we'll be following when we fly the B-1 for the first time. You'll feel the actual movement, hear the sounds and experience the takeoff." He pointed out the window of the cockpit. "And if you look out there, you'll see what looks like a huge movie screen depicting the main runway at Palmdale."

He had no sooner spoken than a full color picture completely filled the window area of the simulator. Tess gasped, overwhelmed by the ingenuity of the engineers.

"Listen closely and keep your hand on the stick," he ordered. Moving the mike closer, he called in. "Wiry nine-six to Control, ready for takeoff."

"Roger, Wiry nine-six," Bill came back. "Visibility unlimited, winds five knots north-northwest. You are cleared for takeoff."

A strange sensation enveloped Tess in the next few seconds. She *felt* the vibration, heard the rumble of the four engines as she watched Shep slowly move all throttles forward to their assigned position. Her mouth grew dry as they seemed to be rolling forward, gathering speed, the dry white desert sand along the runway slipping by in a blur. The engine noise increased, the cockpit vibrated even more and the gauges shot upward, indicating the manifold pressure on the engines. Shep called out several distances and Bill answered.

"Rotating now," Shep reported, pulling back on the stick.

Suddenly, they were airborne! Tess saw Shep gently pulling back on the stick, the bomber's nose thrusting skyward, leaving the runway far below them in a matter of seconds. She stared over at Shep, realizing the intensity of his concentration upon a myriad of tasks that demanded his attention. No longer was he an ordinary man. Now he was a pilot flying, listening to his plane, analyzing gauge readings, talking to the control tower. Was this how he had looked during that emergency in the T-38? The view screen flashed on and Tess watched in amazement as the terrain indicator showed them at fifteen hundred feet and at an airspeed of two hundred knots.

Shep pressed a button on the stick to permit cabin communication with her. "We'll do a couple of bump and go's in the landing pattern. I'll be taking a ninety-degree turn to the left here in a moment, so don't get frightened when you feel the shift," he warned.

Within seconds he moved the stick to the left after pressing the left rudder with his foot. Instantly the B-1 simulator responded and Tess felt the entire cabin tilt to the left. Her fingers tightened around her stick until Shep leveled the bomber back out onto an even keel. He looked over at her, smiling.

"See? Not so bad, right?"

She gave a nod of her head. "This is amazing," she confided. The entire experience left her amazed. After "landing" the B-1 simulator, Shep unstrapped and leaned back, smiling. "Well, you look a little more relaxed now. What did you think?"

Tess gave a small laugh, shaking her head as she unsnapped the complicated harness. "It was an incredible experience!"

He pursed his lips, his eyes gazing at the panel. "We've been able to simulate all calculated emergencies that might develop with the bomber during flight, Tess. I've spent hundreds of hours in this simulator just like everyone else. Our reflexes are so well-developed that we just don't worry about something going wrong on the first flight of the bomber." His eyes narrowed on her. "Can you see why I'm not worried about it? Training takes the bugs out of our reflexes. All of us have complete confidence in our knowledge of the aircraft. Even you look relieved by this half-hour flight."

She took a deep breath, exhaling slowly. Her blue eyes grew warm with love as she looked at him. "You're right," she answered softly, "a little education has helped take some of my fear away."

"Are you going to let that worry run your life, then?" he asked.

She gave a slight shrug. "I'll always worry about you testing planes, Shep. This has helped, though."

He rose, stretching his lean frame. "I figured it would. Come on, I think it's time we drove you back to L.A. Did you drive up with Dan or by yourself?"

Tess stood. "No, I drove up with Dan."

"Good, I'll have the pleasure of driving you back, then."

After thanking Bill for his part in the simulation, they ambled out of the hangar. The stars hung large and bright overhead. Shep put his arm around Tess's shoulder, drawing her near. He leaned down, his breath warm against her face. "I love you, lady," he whispered.

Tess gave him a hug, resting her head on his shoulder. "You are something else, Major Ramsey," she murmured. "And I'm so glad you love me."

He laughed softly, opening the car door. "Tell me that when you see me climbing aboard the B-1 for that first test flight."

She met his laughter-filled eyes gravely. "I've got three months to put my fear of loss in perspective before that flight," she answered. "And I'll do it. With your help."

Shep leaned over, kissing her lips tenderly. "Maybe a few more flights in the simulator will help." And then he grimaced. "My only worry is Barton and the damn bearings his company is manufacturing."

"Don't worry," she answered grimly, "I'm watching the progress on that like a hawk."

Chapter 16

DECEMBER 21, 1974

"WELL, THAT SHOULD DO IT," CHARLIE STARLING FROM Rockwell concluded. His bloodshot gaze traveled around the long rectangular table. The test pilots in their one-piece flight suits stood out from the design and aeronautical engineers who were present. Other crucial people from various contractors and subcontractors stared blankly, saying nothing. The silence was almost explosive as Charlie closed the B-1 flight manual of operation on the lectern in front of him. They had spent the better part of the morning at Palmdale going over the last-minute details before the first scheduled flight of the B-1 on the twenty-second of December.

Charlie's gaze settled back on the pilots. "I'll see you men at 0430 tomorrow morning here at Ops. We'll see what the meteorologist is saying about those winds." He grimaced. "Hope like hell they subside. If they get above twenty knots, we'll scrub the mission and wait a day."

Shep groaned to himself. He closed his small notebook, unzipped the right thigh pocket of his flight suit and slid it into the opening. The last thirty days of his life had suddenly been compressed, it seemed, into

211

seven days. His mouth thinned as he thought about the
Christmas gift he still hadn't picked up for Tess. As a
matter of fact he hadn't done any Christmas shopping.
The first flight of the B-1 was scheduled for tomorrow,
but as Shep studied the wind flow charts from the
meteorology office, his instincts told him it would be
postponed. Releasing a sigh, he stood up as the mixed
assemblage of crew chiefs, engineers, and military
people rose.

His excitement over finally getting to fly the B-1 had
been increasing for the past month. Where had time
gone? It seemed that as he and Tess had surmounted
the obstacles of the past year, his life had gone into
overdrive. Tom Cunningham fell into step with him as
they went down the long hall.

"Well, buddy, you ready?"

"You'd better believe it."

"When's Tess coming up? She won't miss this, will
she?"

Shep managed a wry grin, pulling the flight cap from
his pocket and settling it on his head. They left Ops,
walking out into the windy, cold desert day. "Yeah,
she'll be up later this afternoon. Apparently she's
having another go-around with one of the subs who is
manufacturing some pretty shoddy bearings for the
bomber."

Tom glanced at him. "Barton, by any chance?"

"How'd you guess? Come on, I'll buy you lunch over
at the O club at Edwards."

After a long lunch, they remained sitting over their
coffee. Tom bluntly broke the pleasant silence.

"Is Tess still afraid you're going to crash and burn?"

Shep wrinkled his brow. "I've put a lot of her fears to
rest by taking her up in the simulator on three different
occasions. The last time I had Bill produce an in-flight
emergency so that she could see how we deal with
problems."

"And?"

He pursed his lips. "I think it took away some of the dramatics for her."

"What kind of an emergency did Bill duplicate for you?"

"The one where the port bomb-bay door is torn off during flight."

Tom grinned. "That's a pretty hairy one. Did she faint?"

"No. Tess stuck in there like a trooper. I was proud of her. She's coming to grips with her emotions, Tom. I love her even more for the fact that she's trying to overcome the fear."

Tom's brown eyes twinkled. "It's called maturing, my boy. And she has come a long way in the past year. When I first saw her that night at the party, she looked more like a lost little girl than a woman."

Shep recalled that night, the feelings that had coursed through him, and the need that had burned inside of him like a bright flame. "Yes," he murmured, "she's one incredible woman now."

"And you say she's going to tangle with Barton today? That ought to be a real test of her composure." He grinned. "Glad it's her and not me. I'd punch the guy out like you did."

"Believe me," Shep answered fervently, "it was a pleasure."

"Easy, son," Tom drawled in a teasing tone. "The pilots can't go around beating up subs."

Shep shrugged, finishing off his cup of coffee. "When I talked to Tess yesterday, she didn't say why she was calling Barton in. I know she's been following the lab testing reports on his bearings, but I don't know what will happen."

Tom rose, smiling. "That lady has moxie. And quit looking so worried. She'll handle Barton. Just like she handles you."

Shep laughed, pulling out money to pay for lunch. "The lady has a way with me," he agreed, a feeling of warmth surging through his chest. He had tried to curb his excitement at seeing her again. Over the last three months their relationship had cemented beautifully. The last barrier between them was her fear of his dying in a plane crash. Shep loved her for being brave and trying to come to grips with her fear.

As he paid the cashier, his brow drew into a frown. He was worried for her at this moment. She was supposed to meet with Barton shortly after lunch. He wanted to be there to protect her, but another part knew she could handle it. Still, it was going to be the first time she had actually come face-to-face with Barton since his gossip had ruined her life for over a year.

Tess swallowed against the constriction in her throat. She waited nervously as the hands of the clock slowly ticked toward one thirty. Fingering the neat pile of lab reports at her left hand, she shored up her determination. Dan had already approved of her plan. All that was needed was to implement it. How many sleepless nights had she spent thinking about Barton? Pushing a stray strand of hair off her shoulder she looked up, hearing Barton's voice in the outer office. Grimly Tess settled into the chair a little more deeply, awaiting the confrontation. It had been a long time in coming.

Derek Barton stepped through the door. His dark pin-striped suit only emphasized the man's weasellike black eyes and ebony hair. There seemed to be a perpetual snarl on his lips. Or was it the fact that one corner of his almost lipless mouth turned upward, giving him that appearance? Tess marshaled her thoughts, her objectives. A cool, businesslike smile came to her lips.

"Sit down, Mr. Barton," she invited, motioning him toward the leather chair near her desk.

Derek smiled back. It was a meaningless smile. "Thank you, Ms. Hamilton. Or do you still go by Mrs.?" he inquired in a tone laced with sarcasm.

Tess stood up, moving around the desk and across the room to shut the office door. She didn't want anyone else to hear what would be said. Hesitating briefly, after she had insured their privacy, she walked back and sat down at her desk. The fear she had felt before was rapidly being replaced by a growing sense of anger. A sense of great calm came over her, and she folded her hands in front of her.

"It's your choice, Mr. Barton," she returned.

He gave her a brief smile, bowing his head momentarily. "Tell me, to what do I owe to this personal conference with design engineering?"

Tess moved the lab reports in front of her, lifting the first page, which was filled with numbers. "I'll get right to the point, Mr. Barton. It has come to my attention via our lab that the bearings your company is producing for the B-1 bomber are again not up to specs. We've repeatedly warned you about the quality of the product you're putting out for us. We've got a fifty-four-million-dollar plane that could be seriously damaged by defects in your fifty-dollar bearings." Her eyes narrowed. "Let me put it more simply. For want of a shoe the horse was lost."

Barton's black eyes became pinpoints of anger as he stood. "Are you implying that—"

Tess handed him the reports. "See for yourself, Mr. Barton. None of the bearings you've manufactured have withstood stress tests by our labs."

Barton's lips thinned into a single line. He took the reports, sitting back down and perusing the results.

Tess fought to keep her personal feelings out of the

confrontation. It would do no good to accuse him of spreading stories about her and Shep. There was a powerful urge to drop innuendos as Barton had. Instead Tess stilled her own anger.

"I can bring you a set of *our* lab reports and refute this evidence," he said, throwing the papers back on her desk.

"I believe if you'll check, your contract clearly states that the engineering agent's test lab results will be used in questions of specification performance. Mr. Williams, our legal staff, and myself are more than convinced that you are not honoring the contract you've signed with us, Mr. Barton." She shrugged. "Consequently I am informing you that we will no longer need your services on the B-1 project and that your contract with us is terminated. Our written notice of termination is being sent to your corporate offices."

Barton gasped, his face draining of color. It took a few seconds before he recovered from the shock. "Why you—"

Tess stood quickly, her voice cutting. "Let's not drop into a personal battle of words, Mr. Barton." She pointed at the reports. "You've been given ample warning. We've documented all our correspondence with you over the past year. And never once have you addressed our concern with the specs on the bearings."

His face turned purple. "You won't cancel that contract," he snarled, walking menacingly up to her desk. "I know the real reason for your antagonism to me," he breathed. He jabbed his finger at her. "You're doing this because I caught you and that damn Air Force test pilot having an affair! But you're not going to railroad me out of seventy million dollars because I caught you in the act, honey. You may be Williams's assistant . . . you may think you wield power, but just wait. I've got a battery of attorneys that will make a laughing stock out of these damn figures. I've worked on more than one job where numbers were altered in favor of the buyer. You aren't going to pull the wool over my eyes. I don't give a damn what your reasons are."

Tess leaned against the desk, both hands flat on the surface. "Now, you look here, Mr. Barton. My decision has nothing to do with personal feelings. You were repeatedly warned that your bearings were short on titanium. In fact four of your deliveries were rejected outright and had to be replaced with bearings meeting the specifications." Tess straightened her shoulders, head held high, eyes blazing. "I'm not going to have that bomber in jeopardy for a lousy bearing that won't withstand maximum stress tests. We're talking about men's lives! You may not care, but we do."

Barton strode angrily toward the door and then turned. "You care about that plane because your boyfriend is going to be flying it first time out!" he hurled back savagely. "So don't go crying humanity to me when your interests are strictly selfish!" He took a long, unsteady breath, his nostrils flaring. "You won't get away with this," he snarled. "You can expect to hear from my attorneys today. Nobody can cancel a contract with me without a court battle. And, honey, when I get done dragging your personal reasons for this vendetta into the courtroom, you'll wish you'd never heard my name. I'll smear you publicly. Rockwell will fire you just to prevent further embarrassment to the company." He grinned confidently. "I hope Williams knows the story behind your reasons for trying to take this job away from me. It won't work, *Mrs.* Hamilton."

Tess walked around the desk, her body ramrod straight with anger. She approached Barton, halting only a few feet from him. "Rest assured, Mr. Barton, my boss knows everything. And if you make libelous accusations against me or anyone else, I will personally slap you and your company with a lawsuit. Our lab

reports stand. As of today, the bearings your company
has made are being replaced in the B-1. You're out of
the game, Mr. Barton. So pick up your marbles and
we'll see you in court.''

Shep slowly walked around the glistening white B-1
bomber, checking out all the external surfaces of the
plane one last time. It was nearly seven o'clock in the
evening, and darkness was falling rapidly. Only a few
last-minute details were being attended to by the
ground crew for tomorrow morning's flight. He halted
at the nose, gazing admiringly up at the cockpit.

A sense of excitement surged through him. Despite
the many man-hours spent poring over computer
printout sheets, flight curves, and wind tunnel projec-
tions, in the end it all came down to a pilot's hand on
the stick lifting the bomber off the runway. Reluctantly
Shep turned away, heading toward the side entrance.
Tess would be arriving shortly, and he wanted to be
home in Lancaster in time to greet her.

"Shep?"

He jerked his head up, eyes momentarily widening as
he saw Tess at the hangar door. Instantly he noted her
drawn features. "What's wrong?" he asked automatically, quickening his stride and closing the distance
between them.

Tess gave him a tired smile, welcoming his arms as
they slid around her waist. Reaching up, she kissed
him. He gave her a worried look, saying little as they
stood together. "Nothing is wrong. Well, no, I should
rephrase that—not everything is right."

"Barton?" he guessed grimly, leading her out into
the dusk. The briskness of the wind hadn't died down
during the day, and it didn't look good for the flight
tomorrow morning.

"Yes."

"He put up a fight?"

Tess nodded. "Do me a favor. I need a drink. How about if we go over to the O Club before going home?"

"Hop in," he invited, opening the car door.

Over a Bloody Mary, Tess told Shep of the confrontation. He sat there, listening. Finally, he took a sip of his scotch and took her hand. "He's bluffing, honey. There's no way Barton's going to drag himself or his company into court to save his contract. He's mixing apples with oranges, and no court worth its money is going to allow him to do that."

Tess squeezed his hands, remembering their strength when he made love to her. She recalled the sensitiveness of his fingers as he held the control stick, guiding the B-1 simulator through emergency situations. They were hands she loved, and Tess traced the outline of them absently with her fingers.

"Maybe I'm just overreacting," she admitted tiredly.

"Hey," Shep whispered, forcing her chin up to meet his warm gray eyes, "I'm damn proud of you, Tess. You handled your end of the confrontation like a pro. He didn't." A derisive smile pulled at his mouth. "And I certainly didn't handle him like a pro," he chuckled. "You're growing in leaps and bounds, lady."

"Look," he said quietly, "I've got to be back here at 0430 tomorrow morning in preparation for that flight. Let's go home, have a light dinner, and go to bed."

Tess agreed. A proper period of rest before flight was mandatory. "Crew rest" allowed pilot and crew eight hours of sleep before any flight. But for tomorrow, there was an even more important reason to get a good night's sleep. It wasn't just an ordinary flight.

Fear gnawed at Tess. But excitement and anticipation drowned it as she looked at Shep. He had been the right pilot to pick for this first flight. He possessed a

keen, analytical mind and incredible reflexes. And
something more . . . an uncanny sixth sense that surfaced when he was in that simulator. It made Tess feel
confident that he could handle the B-1 no matter what
problem might arise.

"You're right," she agreed. "Let's go home."

Chapter 17

Night fell rapidly across the Mojave Desert. The winds continued to fan the chilly landscape, pushing tumbleweeds silently through the darkness. Tess lay in Shep's arms, eyes wide, listening to the wind singing through the trees that surrounded the western edge of the house. She ran her fingers across his damp chest in a loving gesture, satiated by the tenderness of their loving. She felt his mouth against her hair.

"You're thinking so loud I can hear you," he said, his breath warm against her forehead and cheek.

Tess tried to block out the fear that now clamored to be recognized. They had just made the most beautiful love she had ever experienced. Would it be the last time? Tomorrow morning at eight A.M. he was due to lift the B-1 off the runway at Palmdale. She closed her eyes, burying her face into his shoulder, wanting, needing the solace he always gave her in moments of quiet anguish. Shep rose up on one elbow, tucking her protectively beside him.

Only the fullness of the moon cast a pale light through the curtains, giving the room a thin, transparent wash. Tess surveyed his shadowed features as he met her eyes. How strong and confident he appeared, she thought. There was no doubt, no fear about tomorrow morning's flight in his eyes. No, there was nothing but concern for her in his face. Her heart wrenched, and she slid her arm around his neck, pressing her body close to him. "I love you so much," she whispered, her voice muffled against his chest.

"Ahh," he murmured, holding her tightly, "my Irish princess is frightened." Shep released her, giving her a sound kiss on her lips. "It'll be a piece of cake," he assured her. "You wait and see."

Tess roused herself, lifting her head, meeting his warm gray eyes. "If I could, I'd hold back the morrow," she said.

"You won't have to, honey," he returned gently, caressing her cheek. "The morrow holds a whole new era for us. A very exciting one."

She managed a small smile. "It will definitely be exciting."

His features became more sober. "Do you still want to be out there with all the reporters, congressional people, and interested onlookers?"

Tess remained silent in contemplation. How could she stand waiting at his home until the flight was completed? What if something happened during take-off or during the flight? How would she know? But standing there watching the B-1 trundle down the runway and lift off was going to be just as agonizing. Tess tried to shove away the horrible nightmares that had plagued her every time she slept. They had been vivid, colorful nightmares filled with the sound of the B-1's jet engines. It had been the screech and whine of the engines that had awakened her each time as she saw the bomber nosing downward in an uncontrolled dive toward the bone-colored desert floor. She always awoke screaming in her own bed, her cries echoing through the empty house.

It had happened five nights in a row. And each time,

she shakily pulled the robe over her damp, trembling body and got up. She would sit in the darkness of the kitchen at the table, her hands cupping a mug filled with hot tea. Now her eyes glistened as she gazed up into Shep's handsome face. "No, I'll be there," she whispered tightly, her throat closing with tears.

Shep gave her a tender smile, watching her closely. "I love you for your courage, Tess," he said quietly. "It's common to have doubts, even nightmares, before a major flight like this."

She shakily brushed a stray tear away from her cheek. "I've had them every night," she sobbed.

Shep groaned, rocking her back and forth in his arms. "Oh, honey," he crooned, "it'll be okay. Nothing's going to happen to me." He gave a rueful laugh. "Hell, I have to come back off that flight because I have to pick up my Christmas gift for you."

Tess managed to laugh with him over the ridiculous statement. "You haven't done your Christmas shopping yet?"

He shook his head. "Let's put it this way—I wait until the last minute every year."

Tess gave him a long embrace. "I don't care about gifts," she whispered fiercely against his shoulder. "You're all I want. All I'll ever need, Shep."

"Well," he drawled, humor tinging his voice, "one way or another I'm going to get that gift. Even if I have to fly that bomber over Lancaster to pick it up."

Tess giggled. "I can see it all now. Don't you think the residents of Lancaster would be mildly shocked to see you come swooping down Sierra Highway?"

He grinned, placing a kiss on her eyes, nose, and finally her waiting mouth. "That's my lady," he encouraged huskily, touching her lips with his strong, calloused finger. "Come on," he urged, drawing her near, "let's get some sleep. We've got a busy day ahead of us tomorrow."

Tess settled down beside him, her body fitting perfectly against his own. His mere presence overwhelmed her fears, and soon, her lashes dropped against her tearstained cheeks and she slept deeply throughout the remainder of the night.

"The mission's been scrubbed," Shep said unhappily, halting at her side. His mouth was set into a thin line. Reporters, at least a hundred of them, milled around the door which led to the briefing room. The spokesman for the flight, Charlie Starling, handled the shouts, calls, and questions. Shep moved Tess off to one side, trying to look inconspicuous in his olive green flight suit.

"Why?" she asked, remaining close to his side as another swell of reporters surged toward them.

"Winds were too strong at the higher altitudes where we were going to fly the bomber," he answered grimly, watching the reporters advance. He gave her a quick squeeze on the arm. "I'm going to try to get free in a few moments. Meet me over at the restaurant. I'll buy you breakfast."

Tess sat with a cup of coffee in hand at a table in the corner of the dining room. People milled in and out of the doors. Since the mission had been cancelled for the day, newspaper reporters and television crews from around the world were descending on the establishment after reporting the disappointing news to their offices. It had been almost an hour since she had left Shep's side. Tess knew he had to speak with the reporters; it was another part of his job as a test pilot. But he didn't like it. He wasn't a public relations person—he was a pilot.

She slowly moved the cup around in her hands, staring at the dark contents. She had been given a one-day reprieve . . . Her heart wrenched in new anguish, the knots in her stomach finally beginning to untie. Yet when she saw Shep's disappointment, Tess felt her guilt. Somehow she had to overcome this fear of losing him. She couldn't be an anchor around his neck. Flying was his whole life. How could she spoil it for him through her own fear? Taking a deep breath, she resolved to try to be more supportive during the cancellation.

"Got any of that left?" Shep asked, walking up to the table.

Tess jerked her head up at the sound of his voice. He took his flight cap off, throwing it on the table and sitting down, looking dejected. She smiled, taking the pot and pouring him a cup of coffee. "Like a stiff belt of whiskey in it?" she asked.

Shep grimaced, taking a sip of the steaming liquid. "You bet. Those damn reporters descended on me like a pack of wolves."

Tess reached out, covering his hand. "I'm sorry, Shep. I really wanted the bomber to take off today. Maybe tomorrow . . ."

He gave her a glance, his gray eyes dark and unreadable. "If those winds aloft would only dissipate."

"What would happen if you flew anyway?" she asked.

"Charlie's worried that it may put undue and unnecessary stress on the plane. We'll be flying up to ten thousand feet and the winds at around seven thousand are more than he wants us to have to cope with the first time around. He wants a smooth flight." Shep shrugged. "He's cancelling it because of political reasons, Tess. Not because the plane couldn't withstand a little buffeting here and there."

She frowned. "What do you mean?"

"You saw that gaggle of politicians that came out from D.C., didn't you?"

"Yes . . . I recognized Senator Browning."

"And you saw Stockwell?" he ground out.

"Oh, God, is he here?"

"Of course he is. And he'd love to see something, anything, go wrong with the flight. That way, he could go screaming to the American public that the B-1 is a financial disaster. The white whale, as he calls it."

"Is that what they're calling the B-1?" She hadn't been in touch with Fred over at PR lately and wasn't abreast of the latest political developments surrounding the B-1.

Shep muttered a curse. "White whale, white elephant. What does it matter?"

She felt the intensity of his frustration. "Shep, I know you're angry. And I don't blame you. All you want to do is your job, which is to fly the B-1. I know you don't agree with all the political seesawing that's going on about the bomber. These are problems that we'll just have to live with."

"Well," he said, some of the anger draining from his voice, "the mission was scrubbed today precisely because of that. Thanks to Stockwell, who would love to see us crash and burn."

The words, spoken so coldly, sent a shiver of fear arcing up her spine. "Crash and burn" he had ground out. Tess's eyes widened in silent alarm. Is that what Stockwell was really wishing? Did he really want to see the bomber crash? Her grip on Shep's hand tightened. Fighting to keep her promise to Shep, she said quietly, "That's not going to happen. I'm going to make a point of being within earshot of Stockwell to watch his disappointment when you lift that beautiful bird off the ground."

He looked over at her, his gray eyes filled with frustration. Almost instantly, his eyes grew lighter, a new tenderness gleaming in their depths. He picked up her hand, drawing it to his mouth and kissing it. "You know something, lady? I love the hell out of you."

* * *

Senator Stockwell strode triumphantly into the restaurant. A pleased look wreathed his face as he sat down with his aides and staffers. The morning had been a resounding success. He luxuriated in the fact that he had spoken to all the major networks, as well as most of the major newspaper reporters. He rubbed his hands together, grinning over at Gary Owens, his chief aide.

"Well done, Gary. I think we poked enough holes into Browning's balloons for one day. Just think, the winds aloft were too strong. Makes you wonder if that paper plane of a bomber will ever make it off the ground." He chuckled. "Or, I wonder if they'll ground that damned white whale every time the winds are a little too strong. Sure doesn't sound like much of a deterrent to war, does it?"

Owens smiled politely. "No, it doesn't, sir. But I think we got all those hungry reporters to swallow the gist of our argument."

"By God," Stockman said, "this calls for a celebration!"

Tess awoke with a jerk, quickly sitting up in bed. Pitch blackness surrounded her and she shakily wiped a thin film of perspiration off her forehead. Her breathing was shallow and rapid; as if she were frightened. The thick mass of her unbound hair spilled across her shoulders as she pulled up her knees to rest her head against them. The nightmare . . . Tess shivered outwardly. She didn't want to glance at the luminescent dials on the clock that sat beside their bed. How many hours were left until Shep might be torn from her existence? Stop it! Stop it, she reprimanded herself silently.

"Tess?"

She lifted her head, turning toward Shep. Her heart flowered with intense love. His voice was thick with sleep and tinged with concern. Tess felt the warmth of his strong, reassuring hand upon her back and reacted instinctively to his caress.

"I couldn't sleep."

Shep forced his eyes open, willing himself awake. He rolled on his side after glancing at the clock. "Come here," he urged huskily, pulling her back down into his arms. She settled against him, a puzzle piece that fit perfectly with his body.

"It's almost time to get up anyway," he said, glorying in the fullness of her lips as he kissed her.

Tess gradually broke away from his kiss. "How long?"

"Forty-five minutes." A careless grin lifted the corners of his mouth. "Why? Got something in mind?" he teased, sliding his hand behind her hip and pulling her daringly against him, letting her know that he was aroused simply by her being near him.

Tess couldn't help but smile in return. She was frightened. More frightened than at any time she could recall in her life. And yet Shep had slept well throughout the night before the test flight. It puzzled Tess but she accepted his lack of concern as a sign that all would go well when he was at the controls of the B-1, in less than seven hours.

Shep must have seen her become more sober because he rose on one arm above her, keeping her protectively close to him. "You woke with a start," he murmured, gently tracing the curve of her brow and cheek. "More bad dreams about the flight?"

Tess nodded, responding to his featherlike touch, a large part of her concern melting beneath his wandering fingers.

"That's normal. Dave Faulkner's wife never sleeps the night before a first test flight," he said. "So you see, you're one step ahead of Cathy in that department. Feel better knowing that?"

Tess nodded, pressing herself against Shep, reveling

in the feeling of his hard-planed body against the soft curves of her own. "Love me," she whispered throatily, kissing him hungrily, seeking the strength of his mouth.

Shep groaned, embracing her tightly, capturing her eager lips in a fiery, branding kiss that was meant to take her breath away. Finally he dragged his mouth from her trembling lips, staring down at her in awe. "I love you," he said huskily, "more than life. You're a part of me, Tess. A very large part," he continued softly, cupping her face, holding her blue gaze. "And I want to love you so thoroughly that we'll be one from now until forever. Whatever that means. . . ."

Tess uttered a small cry, throwing her arms around his broad, incredibly strong shoulders. Desire was woven in the tapestry of love, making the simple act of physical union a symbol of what she was experiencing in her heart. Pressing against him, she claimed his mouth. She became mindless, reacting to his adoring hands as they skimmed and tantalized each curve, valley, and secret place of her body. His mouth settled against the hard, yearning peaks of her breasts, and she uttered a cry of pleasure, arching unconsciously like a tautly strung bow against his hardened maleness.

Each touch, each sublime featherlike caress was building her need to become one with him. She trembled visibly as he moved his hand down the length of her long torso, across her abdomen, lingering momentarily on the silken triangle of hair before parting her thighs. A flame burned deep in her lower body, a fire out of control as he stroked those dark, moist recesses. She was a harp to be played, to be strung tautly, and brought to a full melodic crescendo beneath his coaxing, masterful fingers. Her breath came in short, shallow sobs. Mindlessly she gripped his shoulders, begging him to complete the union, wanting only the oneness between them that nothing could ever destroy. Within seconds she felt him thrust deeply into the welcoming confines of her eager body.

White-hot pleasure plunged deeply within her, shocking her. Slowly he brought her into rhythm with himself and she responded, a cry of joy bubbling up from her throat as the final, explosive gift was shared equally between them. She sank her head against the dark carpet of hair on his chest, her nostrils flared, drinking in great drafts of air, unable to do anything but cling weakly to him. Shep pulled her damp form against him, rolling on his side.

He could feel the pounding of her heart. A small trickle of sweat had gathered between her breasts and he leaned down, kissing it away, reveling in the heated warmth of her flesh. Nuzzling against the fullness of her breasts, he held her tightly, content as never before. At that moment he was unable to give words to his emotions, so strong were they. Only by holding, touching, kissing her could he convey those silent feelings of his heart. They had loved before dawn, a dawn that would bring many changes in their lives. Shep ran his hand down her lovely body, wanting to tell Tess that she was safe and that there was no need to worry. On this dawn they had laid a new foundation; one that would last them a lifetime. He closed his eyes, feeling a good kind of tiredness that can come only from love freely given and taken. "I love you," he whispered thickly. "Always and forever . . ."

Darkness grudgingly lifted its cloak from the Mojave Desert, a thin gray streak outlining the mountains on the distant horizon. Nothing stirred or moved out on the dry, arid earth except nocturnal feeders like rabbits and coyotes finding shelter against the coming daylight. The B-1 sat in solitary splendor out on the ramp, its loyal ground crew making final checks. There wasn't a whisper of wind on December 23, 1974. Even the tumbleweeds were motionless as the men worked in quiet unison around the aircraft. The B-1 sat like a royal sentinel facing the awesome silence of the desert.

The crew chief walked a hundred feet away from the bomber. Putting his hands on his hips, he gazed upward toward the cockpit. A gleam of satisfaction shone in his narrowed eyes as he studied the bomber. His chest filled with pride as he watched his crew finish the preparations for the test flight. Today was the day. He knew it. He could feel the tension running through his men. Glancing back at the eastern horizon, the crew chief saw the grayness of the dawn turning to pale pink behind the shadowed mountains in the distance. Nothing stirred. Nothing moved. He scratched his head, mystified. It was as if the world were now holding its breath in anticipation. Even nature seemed subdued by the incredible beauty of the bomber that sat there like a bound eagle straining to lift skyward once and for all. "Well," he muttered to himself, "you're going to get your chance today, honey." He walked back toward the bomber, issuing final instructions to his men.

All along the designated area which paralleled the runway the B-1 would roll down, television cameras were being positioned. The chilled desert air made the men work faster. News reporters from around the world chose their locations. Roll after roll of film was checked. Each reporter had two, three, or sometimes four cameras loaded with thirty-six-frame film. No reporter or television cameraman wanted to be caught without ample film in case the bomber ran into trouble. No, it was too big a story politically as well as dramatically to be caught without film or means of photographing the grisly results.

Staffers from each congressional camp brushed off the dew-laden chairs in the grandstand which faced the airstrip that the B-1 would roar down. There was a polite distance between the two camps' chairs. Microphones were being set up and tested by Rockwell people. Other members of the early morning crew made sure the red, white, and blue bunting was hung perfectly around the ceremonial box that would house the key officials from Rockwell and the Air Force. The pale wash of rose deepened in color along the horizon and the grayness that had hovered over the hushed desert began to fade gradually.

Shep finished tying the nylon laces on his black flight boots and straightened up. He shut the locker after pulling a bag which contained his helmet and oxygen mask from the top compartment. Today was the day. He knew it.

His hair was still dark and shining from the recent shower, his skin scraped free of the darkness of his beard. His body was still warm and tingling from making love to Tess an hour earlier. A new feeling of happiness lingered in him.

A slight smile touched Shep's mouth as he headed out of the locker room to the briefing room. As he walked down the long, deserted hall, the sound of his boots echoed against the tiled surface. Today he was going to take an untried plane skyward. A bomber that had never tested her wings against the currents of the wind as she knifed through the air. He would help guide her upward and be there to experience every sensation. Shep was an anomaly to other test pilots. They called the plane "it." Rarely did Shep hear them refer to the bomber as "her." He had always felt that jets were like women—sensitive, fragile, touchy, beautiful, and deadly if not handled with respect. A glimmer of excitement shone in his gray eyes as he swung around the corner and entered through a door whose sign read OFF LIMITS.

The face of every engineer, test pilot, designer, and ground crew member in the room was grim. They all sat around the table, their individual notebooks open, pencils and pens ready to scribble down last-minute notations. Voices were hushed, respectful. Charlie Starling raised his head, surveying the three men who would be riding in the B-1 within a few short hours.

"Okay, any questions?"

The three men shook their heads.

"Play it safe today," he instructed. "We got good winds aloft from the looks of the upper air charts. You get any warning lights on, you get back on the ground. I know you don't normally get panicky about a little light blinking, but this morning it's different. We don't need to have an in-flight emergency with those damn vulture politicians waiting to see us burn. Remember, keep the landing gear down and locked throughout the flight. The gear is supposed to be able to go up and down, but today is not the day to find out." He shook his head. "Can you imagine if you brought the landing gear up and then couldn't get it back down? Stockwell would be jumping up and down in the grandstands clapping his hands. Gentlemen, we don't need the B-1 to belly in on foam over at Edwards on the first flight. Get the plane up and get it down. Next time we'll raise and lower the landing gear when we don't have the eyes and ears of the world watching our every move."

Dave Faulkner, the Rockwell pilot, smiled. His blue eyes gleamed with mischief. "Don't worry, Charlie. We'll get it up and down. Won't we, guys?"

Shep and Pete nodded simultaneously.

Faulkner rose, stretching his six-foot frame. "Come on, let's get this show on the road. I, for one, have got Christmas shopping to do."

Shep stood, grinning. "Thank God I'm not the only one."

The whole room broke into subdued laughter. Shep walked around the table, picking up the preflight book which would be used in the ground check of the B-1 before they took off. He glanced over at Faulkner.

"I'll meet you over at the plane in a minute," he said.

"Fine."

Shep opened the door and found at least thirty news reporters waiting. Patiently he worked his way through the crowd, leaving them quickly behind. The halls were no longer empty, but teeming with life. Excitement thrummed through the busy corridors. He felt it in his body, in his pulse. He looked at his watch—only one and a half hours to go.

Tess turned when the door to the small room opened. She was with several other key Rockwell executives finishing off an early morning breakfast. Her lips parted, heart beating strongly as she saw Shep enter. He looked incredibly handsome in the flight suit, that devil-may-care glint in his gray eyes as he approached her. Shep greeted the other executives and then gave his attention to her. A careless smile played across his mouth as he studied her. "Got a few minutes?" he asked, taking her by the arm.

His touch was like a brand, reminding her of the exquisite love they had shared only hours earlier. "Always," she murmured, following him into another room through an adjoining door.

The room was quiet. The picture window faced east where the sun was just starting to rise. Tess stepped over to the window, pulling the opaque drapes apart.

"It's a lovely day," she said.

Shep stood behind her, his hand resting on her shoulder. "Yes, it is," he agreed quietly. His fingers tightened and he forced her to turn around. His eyes narrowed slightly as his gaze traveled to her mouth, and he felt his body tighten with desire for her once again. Finally he met her wide blue eyes.

"Listen, in a few minutes I've got to go," he began quietly, placing his arms on her shoulders. "Will you be all right here?"

Tess nodded. "I'll be fine. I promise."

"That's my lady," he whispered, leaning down and placing a light kiss on her lips. He drew back, sensing her fear and her will to master it. There was a hint of darkness deep in her eyes. He offered her an encouraging smile. "You're a pretty brave person, you know that? I love you for your courage, Tess."

Tears sprang to her eyes and her lips trembled. She was at a loss for words, her throat closed with sudden emotion. Reaching up, she caressed his cheek. "I can't think of anyone I'd rather have flying that plane right now," she whispered, her voice quivering.

He tilted his head, a question in his gray eyes.

She dashed a tear away. "It's you," she explained. "Your touch. You have a sensitivity that defies description, darling. You've given me my freedom. You've allowed me to come into my own. You'll do the same thing for the B-1 when you sit at her controls. That plane will respond to you the same way. I know she will." Tess shared a tender smile with him. "That bomber has the heart of a beautiful woman, and you have a way with women. I'm not really going to worry about you anymore. I know she'll fly for you."

He whispered her name, crushing her in his arms. "God, how I love you, Tess," he murmured brokenly, burying his head in the rich cascade of her hair.

A new feeling of love went through Tess as she lay contentedly within his hard embrace. It was as though she had just made another major breakthrough in understanding him and his undying love of flying. Suddenly, that bomber sitting out there on the ramp was a living creature made of rare metals, pulsing electrical circuitry, her engines the throbbing heart of her sleek body. Somehow, Tess felt a kinship with the bomber. And she suspected that Shep shared her feeling that it was almost a living being. It was difficult to describe how she felt, but inwardly she knew that Shep understood exactly what she was saying.

Finally he released her, holding her at arm's length. "Listen," he said huskily, "I have only one question for you, Tess. And I want the answer to it when I land at Edwards. Promise me you'll give me your answer then?"

She gave him a quizzical look, reacting to the intensity in his voice. "Why—of course. What is it?"

Shep allowed a hint of a smile to tug at the corner of his mouth. His gray eyes were dark with passion. "Will you marry me?"

Her heart leaped, beating erratically in her breast. Her lips parted, a small gasp escaping. Joy surged through her so strongly that she thought she might suffocate from happiness. His fingers tightened momentarily on her arms.

"Don't say anything right now," he went on. "Just meet me back at Edwards. When I land and get done with the post-briefing, then you can give me your answer. I love you, lady."

His head descended and his mouth covered her lips in a soul-branding kiss. A small cry escaped her throat as she threw her arms around his neck, pressing herself against him. Happiness entwined with fear. She clung to him, breathless with wonder. Slowly Shep released her, his gray eyes glittering with barely held passion. "I'll see you at Edwards," he said, and left her standing alone, torn by conflicting emotions. Would it be the last kiss he would ever leave on her throbbing lips?

Chapter 18

THE SUN ROSE, CASTING ITS LONG FINGERS ACROSS THE desert floor. Palmdale basked in the golden flame of the cold morning. Nearly a hundred thousand people waited in quiet anticipation. Last-minute checks on cameras and film were completed. The Rockwell people sat back, their faces unreadable, as the last speech was given. Tess sat next to Dan Williams, her hands clasped tightly in her lap. To her left was Senator Diane Browning and her staffers. The Senator had delivered a rousing speech for the bomber. Stockwell and his group sat to her left, looking grim. They reminded Tess of a group of jackals waiting for the wounded beast to fall and die so that they could jump on the bleeding carcass.

Tess compressed her lips which still tingled from Shep's last kiss. She saw the crew being driven out to the bomber in a jeep. The bright blue flight suits of the two Rockwell people were brilliant in the sun's blinding glow. Her heart hammered without relief in her breast as she watched the three of them descend from the vehicle. Shep was the tallest of the three. Tess wondered if this would be the last image she would have of him. The last time she would see him alive.

Shep walked to the bomber, then stepped aside,

allowing Faulkner to climb up the twelve-foot ladder which was located behind the front landing gear. He lifted his head, looking back toward the grandstand area. There were so many people in the ceremonial box that he couldn't pick out Tess. He knew she was there. Reaching out, he momentarily touched the surface of the B-1. The satin white smoothness had been warmed by the sun's rays, and it almost felt as if the bomber were pulsing with life beneath his hand. Shep gave the metal a slight pat of his hand and then ascended the ladder into the cockpit area.

There was an air of unsettled tension in the cockpit as each of the three men went about his assigned tasks. Each had gone over his own particular job hundreds of times before. Shep climbed into the right-hand position, leaving his helmet and mask on the floor behind the seat for the moment. Together, he and Faulkner began the long list of preflight checks on all the systems aboard the B-1. The sun rose skyward; the heat in the cabin became uncomfortably warm. A small trickle of sweat ran down Shep's temple. Finally the list was completed. Faulkner glanced at him.

"Ready?"

Shep grinned, reaching back and pulling his helmet out of the duffel bag. He placed the carefully made helmet on his head. "Ready, ready now," he answered.

Faulkner, who was ex–Air Force and had flown his share of missions in the B-52 SAC bombers, grinned. "Ready, ready now" was an old catch phrase used by SAC bomber crews. "Okay," he said, turning and looking at Pete Vosper, the flight engineer who sat behind them at another console, "let's go for all the marbles."

They strapped into the nylon harness, snapping the chin straps on the helmets closed against their jaws and clapping the oxygen masks across their faces. Shep lowered the dark visor to cut the sun's blinding rays. He leaned forward, flipping on another row of switches. The tension became brittle in the last few seconds before the engines were switched on.

Faulkner gave a thumbs-up to the crew chief standing beside the B-1 on the ramp. Immediately, the ground crew backed away. He looked at Shep. "Okay, let's do it."

Shep nodded, pressing the button which would start all four engines. The auxiliary power units kicked in and suddenly, the four General Electric engines roared to life. The B-1 shuddered slightly as the two nacelles took the brunt of power pulsing through the engines.

Shep smiled to himself—she felt good and steady. His hearing was tuned to the noise of the engines. It was well known that test pilots could almost psychically sense something going wrong by the most imperceptible pitch or change in engine sound. He glanced over at Faulkner.

"Sounds good."

"Yeah. Readouts look good. Okay, give tower a call and we'll get this show on the road."

"Roger."

Tess's hands tightened until her knuckles turned white as the four huge engines were fired up. The roar seemed to shake the world around her. Automatically, as if someone had orchestrated the movement, everyone in the stands stood up in silent anticipation. The bomber was only a quarter of a mile away, and the engines effectively blotted out any further conversation. A small cry went up from some as the B-1 slowly began to roll away from the ramp area. Tess's heartbeat quickened. The B-1 moved down the taxi strip like a beautiful belle at a ball. The sunlight gleamed off her skin with blinding brilliance. The long needle nose and the dark windows of the cockpit bobbed slightly as the tricycle landing gear moved over small depressions in the concrete toward the takeoff point.

Tess moved her hands to her breast, her throat growing dry as the B-1 passed majestically in front of the reviewing stands. She had the wild urge to raise her hand and wave, knowing Shep was at the window closest to them. The wings of the B-1 were in full forward sweep position for the takeoff. One of the unusual features of the bomber was its wings, which could be swept back when the plane was moving at low altitudes to maintain its flyability.

"God," someone said behind her, "that's a beautiful plane!"

"That baby was made to fly!" another said.

Tess shut her eyes tightly for a moment, praying that they were right.

"Slats down," Shep said.

"Roger." Faulkner nodded, guiding the bomber along with the rudders.

Shep leaned forward, hitting the switch. "Flaps down," he reported, leaning to the right and watching the flap on the right wing coming down. "Locked and in place."

"Roger. Left one looks good too."

Shep checked the lights that would verify that the flaps were locked in place. "Roger." He made other final checks, aware of the power pulsing through the bomber. The tension had given way to an incredible sense of excitement. The sunlight had raised the temperature inside the cockpit to an uncomfortable level. Every man was sweating, but everyone ignored it.

Faulkner kept his hand on the four throttles beneath his fingers, hitting hard left rudder. Slowly the B-1 halted and moved around in a semicircle beneath his guidance. Before them was an empty runway with a yellow center line down the middle. Faulkner aimed the nose of the B-1 straight down the line. "Okay, Shep, give tower a call. We're ready to fly this bird."

Hitting the button on the control stick, Shep made the call. All ground communications were hooked into the loudspeakers so that those in the stands would know what was taking place.

"Wiry nine-six to tower. Ready for takeoff."

"Tower to Wiry nine-six, affirmative. Winds are five knots west-southwest, visibility fifteen miles. You are cleared for takeoff. Good luck."

"Roger, Wiry nine-six. Thanks." Shep grinned and gave Faulkner a thumbs-up. "You heard the man, let's go."

Tess put her hands against her mouth as she stood listening to Shep's confident voice. Fear drenched her at the same moment a spiraling thread of hope spread through her. The stands quieted, and it seemed as if the entire earth was holding its breath in anticipation of the takeoff. The growling of the huge engines deepened. Every camera was on, all the photographers had their fingers poised over their shutter buttons, waiting.

The B-1 started forward. The engines thundered even more loudly, the air literally vibrating with the power. The bomber quickly gathered speed as she continued down the runway. Tess held her breath as the bomber flashed by the reviewing stands. At least four thousand feet of the strip had been eaten up, and the aircraft was still thundering down the expanse. Tess's heart ached. Suddenly the nose came up, lifting the nose wheel off the runway. A cheer rose from the crowd, and people screamed and yelled encouragement. Cries of happiness filled the air. The bomber was suddenly unleashed from the hold of the earth, her beautiful body launched skyward by the roaring jet engines. Sunlight glanced off her wings and nacelles.

Tears ran down Tess's cheeks as she watched the graceful bomber leap into the cerulean blue sky. People were jumping up and down with happiness. Someone

came over and hugged Tess. Everyone was cheering as
the white bomber climbed higher and higher into the
sky, the jet engine noise diminishing as more and more
distance was put between them. The landing gear
remained down and locked, but it did not diminish the
spectacle in the least.

Fear receded in Tess as she stood there with thousands of other people crying and laughing. It had taken
seven years to get the B-1 off the drawing boards and
into the air. And now all she could do was watch it fly
like a graceful gull through the blue of the sky. Dan
Williams gave her a hug; he was grinning from ear to
ear. "We did it!" he cried.

More tears fell from her eyes. Cy's life had been
devoted to that plane. He had worked unceasingly on
the bomber for six of those seven years. An ache began
in her heart, and Tess wished that he could be here to
see his brainchild fly. Joy overrode her momentary
grief. Shep was at the controls. He had taken over
where Cy had left off. Cy had believed in the durability
and design of the B-1. And so did Shep.

Tess drove back to Edwards Air Force Base with Dan
to see the landing. Thousands of other people who
wanted to see the B-1 make its first landing also made
the trek. Dan cleared a path through the anxiously
awaiting crowds to the stands where all the officials
were gathering. The B-1 was being flown in a triangular
flight pattern, climbing up to ten thousand feet and
then descending for a landing at Edwards. Tess wondered how Shep was feeling at this moment. Excitement gripped her, and she discovered a new kind of joy
entering her heart. He was where he loved to be, she
thought, gazing up at the cobalt-blue sky.

"Look! There she is!" someone shouted ecstatically
from the stands.

Tess smiled, awed by the white speck that was growing larger and larger by the second. The B-1 was a graceful white charger thundering down out of the blue corridors of the sky toward the desert surface. Tess marveled at the skill with which the pilots brought her back down to the airstrip. The nose was high, the flaps on each wing extended and down for the landing. Scores of reporters surged toward the area where the press conference would be held after the crew emerged from the bomber.

Tess remained at the edge of the open-air press conference. Dave Faulkner was the first to emerge from the bomber. A thunderous ovation began as the rest of the crew disembarked. Tess stood on tiptoe, trying to get a glimpse of Shep. He was there, walking with typical catlike grace, a grin spread from one corner of his mouth to the other. She laughed aloud, a rush of happiness surging through her. She had never seen his face glow with excitement like that before.

The three men took the small step up to the microphones. Television cameras whirred to life, flashbulbs popped, questions were thrown at them. Tess marveled at the seemingly imperturbable attitude of the three men. They had flown the B-1 for one hour and eighteen minutes at two hundred fifty miles per hour with the gear down. The leading edge wing slats and trailing edge flaps were also left down. Faulkner summed the flight up with typical matter-of-factness.

"There were only a few minor discrepancies of the kind you'd expect in the daily operation of any aircraft," he said, "but other than those, the B-1 flew exactly as indicated in our flight simulator exercises." He glanced over at Shep, grinning.

"Major Ramsey!" a reporter called. "You're the only military officer flying the B-1. How did you feel it handled?"

Shep stepped forward, becoming more serious. "There were no surprises. I felt as if I'd flown the plane before." He caught sight of Tess standing at the edge of the huge gathering. As he stepped away to allow Pete Vosper, the flight engineer, to answer the next question, he kept his eye on her. Tess looked beautifully radiant in her pale cream dress with the high neckline and long sleeves. Had it been over a year since he'd first seen her at the party? Her cheeks were flushed. He took off his dark glasses, trying to catch her attention.

Their eyes met and locked. She smiled back, forming the word "yes" on her lips, and hoping he would know what she was saying at that distance. A full smile appeared on his face and he nodded.

Tess waited impatiently outside the debriefing room at Ops two hours later. Inside, a special team of men comprised of engineers and troubleshooters from Rockwell and other companies were listening to the test pilots. It was Shep's duty to run through any unusual sights, sounds, or feelings he had experienced in the B-1. Whether or not there was actual instrument proof that something had gone wrong didn't matter. The test pilots were trained to hear, see, and feel discrepancies in any new aircraft. Gradually, the reporters drifted away and only a few diehards stayed around with Tess.

It was almost noon before Shep swung out of the door and into her path. She looked up, startled. He grinned and reached out, taking her into his arms. His mouth descended upon her lips, parting them with masterful insistence. Molten fire surged through her body. His mouth softened against her lips, tasting their honeyed sweetness. Finally he drew away, his gray eyes silvered with joy.

"Was that a 'yes' I saw out there?" he asked.

She nodded, unable to stop from smiling. "Yes."

Before she could say another word, Shep kissed her again. Several flashbulbs went off, startling her. He looked up, laughing. The reporters came forward.

"What's the occasion, Major Ramsey?" one of the men asked, hurriedly pulling out his notebook.

"The lady has just agreed to become my wife."

The reporter smiled. "Say, aren't you Mrs. Hamilton from Rockwell? The assistant to the design engineer, Dan Williams?"

Tess shared a smile with Shep, feeling safe within the crook of his arm. "Yes, I am."

"Hey, this *is* news! Did Major Ramsey just propose to you?"

She laughed. "Just before the flight."

"And naturally, you said 'yes'?"

"I did."

"No," Shep corrected, leading her away, "she's going to be saying *I do* very soon."

On the way home Tess began to relax. "How was it?" she asked, leaning back on the head rest.

Shep captured her hand. "Great."

"You looked like a little kid up there at the press conference."

"I did?"

"Yes. But only I saw it."

"Good," he said, relief evident in his voice. "Have to keep the proper image and all."

Tess laughed. "If they had seen the sparkle in your eyes, it would have been a dead giveaway."

Shep squeezed her hand gently. "Did you worry much, honey?"

"At first," she admitted hesitantly. "But after I saw her lift off, I stopped. She's so lovely, Shep."

He compressed his mouth. "She's solid, Tess. I've never flown a plane exactly like that." He looked over.

"Cy and his team did one hell of a fine job of bringing her off the blueprints and into the air. We owe him a lot. The whole country does."

She leaned over and rested her head on his shoulder. "I love you," she said softly. "More than ever, Shep."

He gave her a quick kiss on the hair. "Listen, lady, as soon as we get home and I get cleaned up, we're going Christmas shopping."

Tess smiled. "Is that an order, Major Ramsey?"

"Absolutely."

"You really don't need to get me anything, darling. I have you. I don't want anything else," she protested, meaning it.

Tess lay down on the couch while Shep took a well-earned shower and changed. The past few days had been hard on her, and sleep had been haphazard at best because of her fear for him. Eyes aching with tiredness, she let her thick lashes slowly close. The last sound Tess heard before she fell into a heavy slumber was the shower being shut off.

Shep quietly entered his home. Darkness had fallen and despite the warmth of the day, the wind was cutting through his light jacket. Whistling softly, he tiptoed from the kitchen into the darkened bedroom. When he had emerged from the shower, he'd found Tess sleeping soundly on the couch. Not having the heart to awaken her, he had gently picked her up and carried her to the bed, allowing her to sleep.

Now he turned on the small lamp which sat on the dresser opposite the large bed. Taking off his jacket, he walked over to the bed and carefully sat on the edge of it, watching Tess. A tender smile touched his mouth as he reached out, pushing stray tendrils from her forehead. Her skin was a translucent peach color, dark shadows still in evidence beneath her auburn lashes. A small frown formed on his brow as he continued to lightly stroke her satin cheek. Her skin was warm and pliant beneath his fingertips, reminding him of the incredible softness she carried within her heart. Taking a small velvet box from his shirt pocket, he set it on the bedstand.

It had been one long, exciting day for him. For Tess it had been a day of unbelievable stress. Shep glanced around the quiet room and listened to her soft breathing. They had made love here eighteen hours earlier, neither sure that he would come back from the flight. Shep leaned over, placing a kiss on her forehead. It hadn't been his turn to die. He was alive. And Tess loved him as much as he loved her. And now all he wanted to do was sleep with her at his side. Carefully he pulled the comforter from her shoulders and began to undress her.

Tess moaned, partially awakened as he slid the dress off her shoulders and removed the sleeves from her arms. Her large drowsy eyes opened and she raised her hand to protect herself from the light of the lamp. "Shep?" she whispered thickly, her voice husky with sleep.

"Everything's okay," he reassured her gently, pulling her upright and into his arms. "I'm just getting you undressed so we can go to bed."

Tess mumbled incoherently, her head resting heavily against his shoulder. Within minutes she was free of the clothing. Shep spoke in a quiet, soothing tone to her, easing her beneath the covers. Turning out the light, he shed his clothes, watching her return to the healing folds of slumber.

Sunlight cascaded into the light green bedroom. Tess stirred, instinctively nuzzling against Shep's jaw. Her arm and leg were thrown across his body, and she relished the hard warmth of his flesh against her own as she awoke. His hand lifted, lightly stroking the thick mane of her hair.

"It's about time," he said, humor tinging his low tone. "Do you realize it's almost ten o'clock?"

Tess stretched languidly, reaching up, searching for his mouth. She wasn't disappointed as he rolled over, pinning her carefully beneath his body. His mouth moved against her parting lips, eliciting a response from her. A low purr sounded in her throat as she reacted to his masterful touch, pulling him down upon her. He drew away after the heady, drugging kiss.

"Merry Christmas," he whispered, tracing the outline of her lips.

"It is, isn't it?" And then her eyes widened. "You had to go shopping!" she gasped, sitting up.

He gave her a lazy smile. "I went without you. You looked so damn tired that I didn't have the heart to wake you, Tess. I just put a comforter around you and let you sleep." He pushed himself into a sitting position. His hair was mussed, giving him a boyish look. Tess reached out, smoothing several strands off his forehead.

"I'm sorry, Shep. You've got to admit the past few days have been stressful."

"You'll get no argument out of me, lady. Do you remember me carrying you in here or undressing you?"

She looked at him out of the corner of her eye. Her blue eyes twinkled. "No. God, I must have been dead to the world," she laughed. She started to slip out of bed. Shep caught her arm.

"Where are you going?"

"I thought I'd make you some breakfast and then serve it to you in bed. Sort of a celebration for successfully flying the B-1 yesterday."

He grinned, pulling her back into his arms and kissing her soundly. "We have another reason for celebration," he murmured, taking the green velvet

box off the nightstand and placing it in her hand.
"Merry Christmas, honey."

Tess felt the smoothness of the velvet against her
palm and gave Shep an awed look. Tears gathered in
her eyes as she glanced at him and then back at the box.
Her hand trembled.

"Is—is this what you went shopping for last night?"
she asked quietly, fingering the box gently.

"Yes. Actually, I ordered it a few weeks ago. All I
had to do was find time to go pick it up." He gave her
an encouraging smile. "Go ahead, open it."

Her heart pounded in her breast as she opened the
lid. A small gasp escaped her. She had seen many
diamond rings, but none like the one she now held. It
had a rose-colored hue to its sparkling depths. "It's
lovely!" she breathed, holding it up to the light. No
matter which way she turned it, the pale pink color
gleamed from the depths of the gem.

Shep watched her with interest, a smile lingering
deep in his gray eyes. He took the ring out of the box
and picked up her left hand. "It's an engagement ring,"
he explained.

She gave a small laugh, watching as the ring slipped
easily onto her finger. "The color, though . . . it's so
unique. So beautiful! I've never seen a diamond quite
like this."

"One in a million," he said, "like you." He continued to hold her hand, watching her with a tender
expression in his face. "I noticed that you wore pink or
rose colors when you weren't at the office. And your
Irish shawl has that color running through it. There
were three things that struck me that first night I met
you, honey. First, your beautiful face, then that old-
fashioned dress you wore, and finally the Irish shawl.
You were a Victorian lady stepping into the twentieth
century in your lace and ivory. The shawl's color
enhanced your auburn hair and flushed cheeks, making

you look like an incredible creature from the past gracing that party." He stroked her head, his fingers trailing through the strands of her hair. "I want you for my wife, Tess," he said huskily, searching her tear-stained face. "Be my best friend and my partner and share my life with me."

A sob caught in her throat as Tess threw herself into his waiting arms. Shep held her in the gathering silence, their hearts beating in unison. "Whether I wanted to admit it or not, Shep," Tess murmured, "I've been yours since the first night we met. And looking back over the past year, I can see how much I've matured. I wanted you but I didn't understand my own emotions." Running her fingertips along the tightly muscled curve of his arm and shoulder she said, "I've always loved you. Always."

Shep buried his head in the rich folds of her luxuriant auburn hair, inhaling her sweet scent. "You've always been mine," he growled. "And now we have the rest of our lives to keep discovering one another." He gave her a pat on the rear, holding her at arm's length. His gray eyes were curiously bright as he gazed into her upturned face. "I love you, Irish princess, and I'm going to take the rest of my life to show you how much. Come on, I'll help you make breakfast. I'm starved."

Tess smiled brokenly, dashing away the telltale tears streaking down her cheek. "We're going to make a great team, you and I."

He helped her from the bed, holding her within his arms. "The greatest," he agreed huskily, seeking her lips and finding them. In the warm quietness of the room, the sunlight filtered through the green drapes, casting muted shadows upon the floor and bed. Somewhere outside the window a meadowlark began his melodic song, announcing the beginning of a new day, a new life.

ONE WEDDING...

FOUR LOVE STORIES

Where better to fall in love than at a resplendent June wedding?
As Nick and Diane walked down the aisle together little did they
know how their most cherished of days would set the scene for
four life-long love affairs.

AVAILABLE NOW   PRICED: £3.99

Silhouette Special Edition

COMING NEXT MONTH

WALK AWAY, JOE
Pamela Toth

Emma Davenport was just the sort of woman Joe Sutter avoided: She was sweet, sincere and pretty as a picture. Getting involved with Emma wouldn't be fair, yet something wouldn't let him walk away...

HIGH COUNTRY RANCHER
Judith Bowen

Nola Snow knew what she wanted from life—to marry a Native American man and follow the old traditions. She longed for a real family, for roots. Carson Harlow was a prospector with whom she had nothing in common—except attraction!

UNMARRIED WITH CHILDREN
Victoria Pade

Lexi Kincaid and Jess Haley were perfect for each other—they just didn't know it yet. But their five-year-old daughters did. This was one time when the children knew best.

Silhouette Special Edition

COMING NEXT MONTH

GRAND PRIZE WINNER!
Tracy Sinclair

That Special Woman!

Kelley McCormick intended to have the trip of a lifetime when she won the lottery, but even she had never envisaged that she would meet a man like Grand Duke Erich Von Graile Und Tassburg. He really was Prince Charming material.

BROOMSTICK COWBOY
Kathleen Eagle

Enchanting Amy Becker had chosen his best friend over him, so Tate Harrison had cut his losses and lit out. But now Amy was a widow, a very pregnant widow, and she needed help. Would she ever admit she needed him?

THE WAY OF A MAN
Laurie Paige

Wild River Trilogy

Dinah St. Cloud's instinct for self preservation told her to stay far away from Paul McPherson this time. He was just too handsome for his own good...